Jenny Rodwell

was born in Zim   ts, but
was brought up happily l   ⸱ Peak
District farm.

Sent to boarding school aged eleven, she stayed only long enough to get
the five O-levels needed to get into art school.

At sixteen, Jenny studied fine art at Saint Martins in London, followed by a
post-grad degree at the Royal Academy. Living in a bedsit in Earls Court,
London, the sixties suited her very well.

In a many and varied career, Jenny has worked as a barmaid, waitress,
clerk, artists' model, cleaner, picture restorer, newspaper reporter,
gardener, courier, carer, potter, art history coach, puppet maker, and
probably a few other things she can no longer remember.

On leaving art school Jenny married a journalist and had one son. They
lived in London and later in New York. She is now a grandmother.

Jenny is the author of more than twenty books on art and art history.

Her picture book illustrations for children include:
Snow White and Rose Red (Anderson Press), Fairyland (Walker Books),
and What Do You Feed Your Donkey On? (Collins).

Jenny's previous publishers include:
Michael Joseph, Harper Collins, Hamlyn, and Studio Vista.

A Word from the Author:

A few years ago, my house filling up with how-to-do-it books on painting
technique all written by me, I decided my non-fiction writing was getting
repetitive and that I would like to try my hand at fiction. I have found this
truly fascinating but more difficult than I ever imagined! I have enjoyed
every moment of writing The Ophelia Box, and fell totally in love with the
characters.

I returned to the Peak District in the early nineties and am now working
on my next novel.

Copyrights;

Text:	© Jenny Rodwell 2015
Cover & Graphics:	© W. E. Allerton 2015
'Ophelia' cover font	© Roland Huse (Rainy Wind)
Typeset & Layout:	© W. E. Allerton 2015
Font:	Garamond 12pt.

ISBN: 978-0-9930424-1-6

This first edition published 2015 by;

Cybermouse MultiMedia Ltd.,
101 Cross Lane
Sheffield S10 1WN
www.cybermouse-multimedia.com

First published by Cybermouse Books

In the design of this book, Cybermouse Multimedia Ltd. have
made every effort to avoid infringement of any established copyright.
If anyone has valid concern re any unintended infringement please contact
us first at the above address.

THE OPHELIA BOX

by

Jenny Rodwell

For

Eleanor

♀

For their excellent input and wise words, Jenny would like to thank the following:

Felicity & Phil Armstrong, Gordon Brotherston, Jarvis Cocker, Kath Dalmeny, Bryony Doran, Sarah Eldridge, Caroline Jackson, Marina Lewycka, Patricia Monahan, Alison Oldham, Judy Oldroyd, Catherine Parker, Sarah Perry, Lucia Sa, Joe Short and Maggie Wykes.

Particular thanks to Bill Allerton of Cybermouse Multimedia for all his good ideas and hard work, amazing encouragement, and for generally keeping me on track.

♂

Capricious and unpredictable, yet intricately connected like the links of a chain, the stories of Ophelia and Asa twist and turn their way through the ripples caused by three intensely dysfunctional families... some by design, some by circumstance... and others by sheer madness.

Fearing that madness will be her fate, Ophelia hides away from the future in a world of her own making, where the photograph of the dark-eyed boy is her only true friend.

Lost and uncomfortable with a life that began in great uncertainty, Asa struggles to understand himself and his genetic inheritance through a search for his missing sister, Anna.

Never entirely certain of anything around him, least of all his own motives, Asa holds on to the few things that have real meaning in his life... the face of his sister, last seen through the window of a train... a memory of his parents' shoes, and... most importantly... a lock of Ophelia's hair.

CHAPTERS

I AM...

VIKINGS

Cont'd:

AQUAPHOBIA

I AM...

♀PHELIA GUNN

♀

They called me Ophelia after a box of chocolates. I hate them. My father gave the chocolates to my mother on the day I was born, but then my mother disappeared.

We still have the chocolate box, only my grandmother keeps photographs in it now. It's not fair. The box was a present to my mother and she would have wanted me to have it.

It is not as if my grandmother is a real grandmother either. She is only my step grandmother so she has no right to put her photographs in my box.

There is a picture of a drowned woman on the lid. Her name is Ophelia and she is floating in the water with her mouth open like a dead fish. Ophelia was engaged to a prince called Hamlet but then she went mad and drowned herself before they had a chance to get married.

Everyone says I am the spitting image of the Ophelia on the box. Sometimes I get really scared that I will go mad and end up like she did.

I wish I didn't look like her because I don't want to drown. I would like to die properly of natural causes.

♀

'Ophelia, you've got green eyes,' says my stepmother. 'I never noticed before.'

'I like my green eyes.'

'Green eyes are a sign of a jealous personality.'

'People with auburn hair often have green eyes,' I tell her. 'I read it.'

'People with auburn hair often have bad tempers. Did you read that too?'

My brother lifts his blond head and stares at me with his blue eyes, and my father says,

'Ophelia, please apologise to April.'

That is my stepmother's name. April. I think it is a silly name.

I bang the door as hard as I can when I run out of the room because I know it makes April hopping mad. I run all the way down the lane to the farmhouse where my grandparents live and I get the Ophelia Box down from the sideboard.

'April's horrible,' I tell the drowned Ophelia. 'She hates me and it's all your fault.'

I put my mouth close to the box and whisper this because I don't want my grandmother to hear, but I am really careful not to touch the box. Ophelia is a cold dead thing and I don't want to feel her with my lips.

When she isn't looking I take my grandmother's scissors from the sewing basket and stab at the staring green eyes until the points of the scissors go right through the cardboard and then I scratch Ophelia's head until every bit of her auburn hair has disappeared.

'You'll go blind yourself now, and bald too I shouldn't wonder,' says my grandmother when she finds out what I have done. 'It serves you right for being a naughty girl.'

This makes me cry, but then my grandmother tells me it is not my fault I was born with auburn hair and that when I grow up I can always wear a hat. She is quite a kind person really, my grandmother.

'I'll tell you what your trouble is, Ophelia,' says my grandmother, before she sends me home to The Barn. 'You've got too much imagination. That's your trouble.'

This makes me cry all over again because I can't help having too much imagination and I can't scratch out imagination with my grandmother's scissors.

After this I am forbidden to touch the Ophelia Box again because my grandmother says it brings out the worst in me. She hides the box under her corsets in the dressing table drawer and when I find it I draw big blue eyes around the holes in Ophelia's face and I give her a lot of yellow hair.

There is a newspaper cutting in the Ophelia Box of when my father married April. I can understand every word it says and I am only six.

I am top of the class in reading and writing and my teacher says that one day I will probably be a famous writer like Enid Blyton.

Anyway, the piece of newspaper is from The Times and the date is January 20th 1946.

> The marriage took place at Saint Stephen's Church, Cairo, on January 14th. 1946 between Second Lieutenant Toby Gunn, son of Lady Effie Gunn of Kensington, and April, only daughter of Mr and Mrs Harald Siward, of Grymewyck Hall, Yorkshire. The bride

was attended by Miss Pearl Bonnet. Major Charles Manners was best man. A reception was held at Shepheard's Hotel.

I like the names. Pearl and Charles. Charles and Pearl. I like to think of them playing tennis and kissing together under a tree. When I grow up and have children that is what I am going to call them. Pearl and Charles.

The newspaper cutting is yellow now and it is beginning to crack along the crease. I am careful not to tear it when I unfold it because this piece of paper is my evidence. It is my proof that April and my father lied to each other, even on their wedding day.

There is a photograph in the box of their wedding in Cairo. April and my father with Pearl and Charles. Charles and Pearl. Charles is handsome, but not as handsome as my father.

Pearl has a round face and round eyes. She looks nice. Not like April. April looks as miserable as sin. Not that it was a proper wedding anyway because everyone was wearing army uniform, even Pearl and April.

♀

When my father married April he sent me to live with my London grandmother in Kennington but my London grandmother doesn't like babies and as soon as the war was over she sent me back.

The newspaper cutting says my London grandmother lived in Kensington, not Kennington. They are different places in London. My father says this is a misprint but April says my father is a lying bastard.

The best thing in the Ophelia Box is an old photograph taken in front of our house when it was still a barn, so it must have been taken before I came to live in Grymewyck.

The people in the picture are all leaning on hay rakes, except for my grandfather. He is the man on the tractor.

There is a boy in the photograph with dark eyes and black hair and he is squinting at the camera. I don't know who the boy is, but he makes everyone else in the photograph seem very pale.

The dark-eyed boy looks nice. I wish he was my friend but probably he is quite old by now. He might even be dead because the photograph is really faded.

I come to visit the photograph of the dark-eyed boy a lot, especially when April and my father are fighting. Sometimes we just look at each other, the dark-eyed boy and me, and sometimes we talk.

The dark-eyed boy doesn't like April either. I can tell that by the way he screws up his face when I say her name.

♀

My brother Jack is younger than me and he was born here in Grymewyck. Jack is only my half brother really and he has blond hair and blue eyes just like April.

All the Siwards have blond hair and blue eyes, even my grandfather who is really old now.

'You and I are real Siwards,' April tells Jack. 'The Siwards are descended from the Vikings.'

She strokes Jack's blond hair when she says this.

'What are Vikings?' I ask.

'My warrior lord died yesterday, his spirit passed away.
Today they'll float the funeral pyre, on longboats lit by blazing fire.'

April's a show off. She got that out of my book of children's verse and it is the worst poem in the whole book. I could write a better poem than that, and one day I will. I already know more about poetry than April does even though I am only six.

'What are Vikings?' I ask again.

'The Vikings came to Grymewyck from across the sea,' says April. 'They had blond hair and blue eyes and the men had horns.'

'They sound horrible. Am I descended from Vikings too?'

'Hardly,' says April. 'I dread to think where you came from, Ophelia. Gypsies, probably.'

April says where people come from is important. She calls it breeding, and she is a big fan of the royal family.

My brother is called John William George Edward after the kings of England but everyone calls him Jack. I just have the one name. Ophelia.

I was born in Egypt during the war but I don't remember it. After Egypt we came to Grymewyck because my father was broke. This means he didn't have any money. My Grymewyck grandmother says it is a blessing we came back because Egypt is full of foreigners and she would have been worried sick.

It is really April who doesn't like being in Grymewyck, even though she was born here. My father doesn't mind where he lives as long as he gets his Senior Service cigarettes and can go to the pub. This is what my Grymewyck grandmother says anyway.

My grandfather put a kitchen and a bathroom in the old hay barn for us, which is where we live now. It is quite like a house really, with a proper fireplace and three bedrooms, but you can still tell it was a barn. It is even called The Barn.

The trouble with a barn is that it has no proper floors or ceilings, just wooden boards. In the bedroom where Jack and I sleep we can hear everything that happens downstairs, which is usually my father and April quarrelling. If they are standing right underneath one of the gaps we can sometimes see the tops of their heads as well.

'I hope you're not thinking of going to the pub, Toby.'

'I can't stay here night after night listening to you ranting. I need friends.'

'Friends! Those yokels you drink with aren't friends. They're laughing at you. They're laughing at me too.'

April has a thing about people laughing at her and she doesn't like my father having friends in the village because she thinks they talk about her behind her back.

'April, if I have to live in this dump I need friends.'

'And do you know why you have to live in this dump? It's because you are too useless to live anywhere else. You are useless. Useless. Useless.'

This is what April always calls my father when they argue and she always grins a horrible grin when she says it.

'April, please don't start. The children will hear.'

'The children! I'm rotting away in this dump because of those children. You are so bloody useless.'

April never just says things when they argue, she shouts them. My father hates this so he gets his own back by saying nasty things himself, very quietly, which makes my stepmother shout even louder.

'Control yourself. You're sounding like the common little peasant's daughter you are.'

'I'll have you know that my family have Viking blood in their veins.'

'Your family are peasants.'

'How dare you!'

This is another of April's favourites…

'How dare you! My parents have put a roof over your head, which is more than your own mother did. Lady Gunn my foot! Lady Muck more like.'

My father gets really angry when April says nasty things about his mother and his eyes go all small and scary.

'My family had ambition, which is more than can be said for your family. The Siwards have been rolling rocks around this God forsaken hillside for a thousand years and it's what they'll still be doing in a thousand years time.'

Sometimes April attacks my father with her fists. When she does this he grabs her by the wrists and throws her onto the sofa, and then he goes to the pub.

♀

I like it much better at my grandparents' house and when April and my father are fighting really badly this is where I go.

'They're at it again,' I tell my grandparents, 'I think they're going to kill each other this time.'

'Have you had anything to eat today, child?' asks my aunt May.

May is April's sister and she is much nicer than April. She is a spinster, which means she hasn't found a husband yet, and she lives in the farmhouse with my grandparents. May always gives me and Jack food when we go there because April doesn't cook.

'April says it's not her job to look after me because I'm somebody else's bastard,' I say, 'April says she wishes I had never been born.'

'April needs her backside tanning,' says May, 'She's not fit to be looking after children, and that's the fact of the matter.'

♀

The best thing about Grymewyck is helping Percy Hammer in the hay field. Percy has worked for my grandfather since he left school and he shears the sheep and mends the stone walls, and he helps to milk my grandfather's nine cows. Nine cows seem like a lot to me but Percy says it is not, not compared with some farms.

My grandfather is horrid to Percy and says: 'Look sharp!' and 'Stir yourself!' He never says thank you. May laughs at Percy and calls him a daft ha'p'orth and April calls him an uncouth creature.

Once my father borrowed half a crown from Percy for his cigarettes and there was a big row about it. My grandfather paid back the half crown and told Percy not to lend my father any more money.

May really likes Percy. She says that when God created angels he was just practising before he made Percy Hammer. This is a funny thing for May to say because Percy isn't a bit like an angel to look at. He is tall and bony with big teeth and thick hair that looks like hay, but he laughs a lot and he listens.

Jack and I trail around after Percy for hours just telling him things while he listens. Perhaps that is what proper angels do. They listen.

When I tell Percy about April wanting to kill me he stops sweeping the yard and scratches his head.

'Get away with you,' he says, 'You're having me on.'

'April says that if she put a pillow over my head while I was asleep nobody would be any the wiser.'

'If April says anything like that again, you go straight to your grandfather,' says Percy, 'It's no good it coming from me. They think nothing of me.'

It is true what he says. No one thinks anything of Percy.

Percy's mother has knitted him a green jumper but my grandmother won't allow him in the house when he is wearing it because green is her unlucky colour so Percy has to eat his sandwiches in the yard.

♀

I really like being at the farmhouse with my grandparents but usually April comes and spoils it. We know it is her even before she comes into the room because she always slams the front door and then we hear her stamping up the passage.

'Mother, have you seen Toby?'

This happens all the time. April is horrible to my father when he is with her but when he isn't with her she thinks he has run away.

'Did you give Toby any money, mother?'

My grandmother hangs her head.

'I lent him half a crown for his cigarettes.'

'We'll not see that again,' says my grandfather and spits into the fire.

But we all know it is not really the cigarette money April cares about.

'Did you give him any more than that, mother?

April thinks my father has borrowed money to run away.

Poor daddy. She hates him because he hasn't got any money but she doesn't want him to have any in case he uses it to escape.

If he did run away I wouldn't blame him a bit.

♀

April has forbidden me to talk about my real mother, but when April isn't there I talk about Maisie all the time.

'What does Maisie do?' I ask my father.

We are lying on our backs in the long grass at the bottom of the garden. He is hiding from April and I am looking up at the sky through the branches of the big sycamore tree.

'I told you what she does. Maisie's an actress and during the war she travelled all over the world and gave concerts for the soldiers.'

'Is Maisie beautiful?'

My father sighs because I have asked the same question a hundred times before.

'Your mother is a very beautiful lady.'

'Like Vera Lynn?'

'Much more beautiful than Vera Lynn.'

'Tell me what Maisie looks like?'

I ask him this all the time.

'She's got auburn hair and green eyes, just like you.'

'Is that why you gave her the box of chocolates when I was born, because she looked like the woman on the lid?'

'That's right.'

'Where is Maisie now?'

This is the question my father never answers.

'That's enough,' he says, and looks round nervously. 'This conversation must be our little secret, Ophelia. We don't want to upset April. She does try to be a good stepmother to you.'

I want to know everything there is to know about my real mother, but I can see my father is getting cross so I try to forget about Maisie by counting the leaves on the tree. I concentrate so hard the leaves start to go fuzzy at the edges and melt into the sky so all I am left with is an empty white space.

It would be good if I could magic other things away as easily. If only I could make April disappear just by looking at her. And it would be really, really good if I could make Maisie come back.

I stare hard at the white space without blinking and try to hold on to it for as long as possible, but then it vanishes and I am looking up into the tree branches again. My father sighs and reaches for his cigarettes, groping around for them in the grass without bothering to turn over.

He and April have had another fight and it was a really bad one this time. April scratched my father's face and there is blood all over his collar. They were fighting about Maisie. April called my mother a common tart, and my father said it takes one to know one. I think April is just jealous.

Sometimes April and my father argue about my other grandmother in London. My London grandmother has no home now and my father wants her to come and live with us at The Barn, but April says over her dead body.

One day soon my father will be rich. He will be very rich and very soon, but first he needs to find some capital. I don't exactly know what capital is.

My father is going to leave Grymewyck but this is our secret and I am not allowed to tell April. He is going to take me with him and we will be going any day now. Perhaps tomorrow. My father says we will probably go to London and I ask him if we can go and live with Maisie but he just sighs.

'Try to forget about Maisie.' he says.

Then I ask if we can stay with Charles and Pearl and he sighs again and blows a little smoke ring. He says he hasn't heard from Charlie Manners for ages, not since they were in the army together, and he has no idea what happened to Pearl Bonnet.

A precious pearl with a heart of gold, that is what my father calls Pearl Bonnet. And he tells me something else. Pearl Bonnet is rich.

My father says he will get in touch with Pearl very soon, perhaps tomorrow, and then he runs out of cigarettes and sends me to the village shop to buy some more. He must have borrowed another half crown from my grandmother because he tells me to go the long way round through the boggy field so as not to be seen from the farmhouse.

'Can I have a liquorice bootlace?'

'It must be our little secret,' he says with a crooked little smile

…ASA CHEN

I don't remember my parents, but I would recognise their shoes anywhere, even now. My mother's were dark grey suede, like moles, and my father's shoes were so hard and shiny I could see my face in the polished black leather.

I remember Yakob's shabby shoes, with broken laces and a loose sole. Yakob. I know the name but I cannot remember the man. It was a long time ago and I was only three years old at the time.

We were under the table, myself and my sister Anna. The tablecloth touched the floor all round so it was quite dark, and everything was quiet except for the scraping of knives and forks above us. Someone was calling.

'Kuckuck! Kuckuck!'

Anna raised her finger to her mouth. 'Shh.' They were looking for us.

My sister shuffled across the parquet on her bottom and stroked our mother's foot. Nothing happened, so she did it again, and this time the grey suede shoe slithered sideways towards my father's shiny black shoe and pressed against it.

Anna bit her knuckles to stifle her laughter, and then her laughing stopped.

Someone was banging on the front door. Cutlery clattered onto plates, our mother screamed, and the shoes all withdrew in an instant. A window shattered and splinters of glass spun across the dining room floor. Anna sat silently sucking blood from her thumb and I closed my eyes.

When I opened my eyes our hiding place was full of light. There was a black boot a few inches away from my hand and when I looked up I saw the upside down face of a soldier. He was holding the tablecloth in one hand and a chicken leg in the other.

That is pretty much all I remember of Vienna, that and the day the letter arrived. My mother wept when she read the letter and cried out for my father, but my father and Yakob had gone away. A man with a long beard and a black hat came to see my mother and he read the letter too.

'Anna will be safer in England,' said the man with the beard. 'There will be another opportunity for the boy.'

'I wish my husband was here. He would know what to do.'

'You may never see your husband again,' said the man. 'It is your children you must think about now.'

'If they can't take both my children then it is my son who should be saved. It is more important for a boy.'

♂

My mother must have got her way, because it was me they sent to England, not Anna.

My sister was wearing a red knitted hat the day I left. She

flattened her nose against the window of the railway carriage and licked the glass with her tongue, and then she wriggled to be put down. Inside the compartment a woman in a green uniform gave me a peppermint and when I looked again Anna had gone.

I stared out of the window all day and most of the night, looking through the patch where Anna's tongue had licked off the soot, and I listened to the soldiers marching up and down the corridor. I could see their reflections in the glass.

It was still dark when the train stopped and the soldiers jumped off. I watched the sparks as their boots hit the ground and when the train started to move again I turned away from the window and closed my eyes for the first time.

Asa Cohen. Distinguishing features: none.

A displaced person. A nobody. That was me. They were wrong about me having no distinguishing features though, whatever it said on my identity card, because I have a very distinguished nose.

Lots of Jews have big noses, or so my Finchley family was always telling me. Of course the family in Finchley was not my real family and neither were they Jewish, so they knew nothing at all about me or my nose.

I like my nose a lot now but it was different when I was little. Children are cruel, and the pupils of Marigold Street Church of England School where I was sent aged four and a bit were no exception.

'Run Asa, run Asa. Run! Run! Run!
Hitler will get you with his gun! Gun! Gun!'

Ignore them,' said Mr Manners, my Finchley father. 'God had his reasons for giving you the nose he did. Trust in God. God is always right.'

But God was not right about my nose. So far as my nose

was concerned, God had blundered. At the age of four and a bit I knew I couldn't rely on God.

'You have a very nice nose,' said Mrs Manners, my Finchley mother. 'And when you grow up you can always grow a moustache to disguise it.'

In the meantime I wrapped my scarf around my face and hid in the outside lavatories until it was time to go home.

'Run Asa, run Asa. Run! Run! Run!'

Run? I would have run like the wind if only I could have got past my tormentors and known which way to run. I would have run all the way back to Vienna and my sister Anna because I missed Anna a lot.

That is how things were until I met my new brother, Charlie Manners. After Charlie came home on his first leave I didn't miss Anna quite so much, and after a while I didn't miss her at all.

One day Charlie came to meet me from school. He was in his soldier's uniform, the full kit, and my tormentors were there as usual.

'Run Asa. Run Asa. Run! Run! Run!'

Charlie unbuckled his big soldier's belt and leapt over the school railings twirling the belt above his head.

'Leave my brother alone,' he roared, and my tormentors fled.

Charlie marched out of the playground and I fell into step behind him. One, two. One, two.

'I'm not really your brother, am I?'

'You are now,' called Charlie, over his shoulder. 'Next time we'll teach those brats a lesson they won't forget.'

As things turned out there was to be no next time because

that night Marigold Street was bombed and the school took a direct hit, so perhaps God wasn't such a fool after all.

Sometimes he actually got things right.

♂

I was being sent to a place called Grymewyck. It was written in big letters on the label round my neck. Grymewyck. I didn't like the sound of it. They were sending me to stay with a couple called Dr and Mrs Brown, and I didn't like the sound of them either.

Charlie in his soldier's uniform cried when the train pulled out of the station, but I was too miserable even to cry. I was worried that I would never see my Finchley brother again and I was even more worried that I was about to wet my pants.

♂

Frogs are the reason I have now returned to Grymewyck. Frogs and Dr Ben Brown. Uncle Ben, who is not really my uncle at all, still lives here, and behind the hay barn there is a boggy field that was once alive with frogs.

I am seventeen now, and the lane to the old barn seems narrower than it used to be, and the barn itself is smaller than I remember but then, I was small myself at the time.

Once upon a time something happened to me here, on this very spot. I haven't thought about it for years, but being here again brings it all back.

It was a hot summer... hay making time... and a woman was taking a photograph. The woman was so beautiful I thought she must be a princess.

'Say cheese!'

All the hay makers smiled but I was so busy gazing at the princess that my smile came too late. Afterwards, when the hay makers were eating their sandwiches, the princess ignored me and I knew she was angry because I had spoiled the photograph.

I huddled beside her in the shade of the haystack, hungry and miserable, until she relented and gave me a piece of her sandwich, but the sandwich tasted bad and I spat it out into the grass.

'Where ever did they find you?' she said. 'Have you never seen a ham sandwich before?'

Everyone laughed, except for one of the men.

'That's ham from our own pig,' he said.

'Where I come from, people don't eat pigs.' I told him.

The man had long blond hair too, but he had a rough sunburned face, like leather. He picked my spat-out sandwich out of the grass and gave it back to me.

'Where I come from people don't waste food,' he said, 'Eat it.'

♂

When I get closer I see the hay barn is no longer a barn but a house, with a stone chimney stack and a little porch with a white painted door. The door opens and a woman comes out. I pull my bike behind the hedge and duck out of sight.

'Ophelia!'

The woman's voice is angry and shrill. She stamps her foot and goes back inside banging the door behind her.

♂

In the Grymewyck village shop a little girl is asking for twenty Senior Service.

Children remember faces, especially faces they don't like, and I recognised the woman behind the counter straight away, although she of course does not know me. I was six when I was here before.

The girl has chapped knees and auburn hair bunched up in old-fashioned ringlets, and she has to stand on tiptoe to push her half crown piece across the counter. The woman gives her the cigarettes but the child makes no move to go.

'Well?' snaps the woman.

The child asks for a liquorice bootlace but so quietly the woman doesn't hear.

'Cat got your tongue?'

'A liquorice bootlace, please.'

'Does your grandmother know what you're spending her money on?'

'Yes,' whispers the child.

'Little liar. Be off with you.'

The child turns and bumps into my legs. She tries to wriggle past but I stay put in front of the door.

'One liquorice bootlace, please,' I say to the woman.

She ignores me so I say it again.

The woman slams the liquorice bootlace on the counter and I hand the bootlace to the child who grabs it and bolts.

'You shouldn't encourage her,' says the woman, 'Ophelia indeed! Did you ever hear such a name?'

The woman glares as I pay for the bootlace and I leave without making my own purchase.

I feel her eyes on my back as I pedal across the village square and head up the lane in the direction of the old hay barn. There is no sign of the little girl.

The Frog Man

♀

Probably the man was going to kidnap me. Liquorice bootlaces cost a penny each so he wasted his money and it serves him right.

I am on my way home through the boggy field and feeling really pleased with myself for not getting kidnapped when someone snatches the bootlace out of my hand from behind. I don't dare look back in case it is him so I just run as hard as I can, but then my foot gets stuck in the mud, and that is when I see the sheep with my bootlace hanging out of its mouth.

The sheep comes towards me with a funny look in its eyes so I pull my foot out of the mud and climb over the wall as fast as I can. I roll down the bank on the other side and when I stop rolling there is the man, waiting for me.

He is sitting with his legs stretched out in front of him and he is drawing something in a sketchbook. I get ready to run again but the man laughs.

'You won't get far,' he says. 'You've lost a sandal.'

I look down at my feet and one of my sandals is missing, and then I really am frightened.

'She'll kill me for sure now.'

The man stands up and looks over the wall.

'They're only sheep. Sheep won't kill you.'

I tell him it is my stepmother who wants to kill me, not the sheep, and the man frowns.

'It was an accident,' he says. 'You didn't do it on purpose.'

He climbs over the wall to fetch my sandal and while he is gone I have a look at his sketchbook. It is a drawing of the The Barn with the hills behind, and it is really good.

When the man comes back he sits down next to me and shows me his jam jar of dead frogs. Probably he is trying to scare me but I am not scared of dead frogs so he is wasting his time.

'Why are you collecting dead frogs?'

'I'm going to be a doctor. I need to know about frogs.'

I offer to help him catch more frogs, but only if he promises not to kill them.

'I'd much rather talk to you,' he says. 'What would you like to talk about?'

I tell the man about my real mother, Maisie, who is lost, and I tell him about Maisie being a famous actress. I whisper this in case April is listening on the other side of the wall and then I ask the man if he ever lost anyone.

'I once had a sister,' he says. 'I lost her, in a way.'

This makes me like the man a bit better, but I don't feel sorry for him because losing a sister isn't half so bad as losing a mother. If I lost Jack I wouldn't mind a bit, but perhaps the man's sister is nicer than Jack. Probably she is.

'I hope you find your sister.'

'I hope not, but that's a secret.'

'I have a secret too. Promise not to tell?'

'Cross my heart and hope to die.'

I tell the man about the dark-eyed boy and he doesn't laugh, not once.

'Your secret friend sounds nice. Perhaps one day I'll meet him.'

He doesn't get it, about the dark-eyed boy being a photograph, I mean, and probably he is not really interested anyway because he goes back to his drawing. Actually, I am a bit disappointed in the man.

'Where do you live?' I ask.

'I live in a place called Finchley. It's in London.'

London!

'Maisie lives in London too. Could you find her for me?'

The man looks sad.

'London's a big place. I'll look out for your mother though. How will I recognise Maisie when I see her?'

I tell him that is easy because Maisie has green eyes and auburn hair like me, and that she wears evening dresses even during the day.

The man nods and then he says something really weird.

'Give me some of your hair.'

'Why?'

'Because it will help me to find Maisie. I will recognise her by the colour of her hair.'

It makes sense, and it shows he is really serious about looking for my mother. I let the man cut off a whole ringlet of my hair with his penknife and he puts it between the pages of his book.

He packs up his things and promises to write straight away if he sees Maisie, but then I remember April.

'You mustn't write to me. She'll kill me if she finds out I'm looking for Maisie.'

'Then you must write to me.'

He prints his address in big letters on a page of his sketchbook and tears out the page for me, and it is then I see he has a camera round his neck.

'You could take a photograph of me,' I say. 'Then you could give it to Maisie when you find her.'

'Only if you promise to smile,' he says. 'I would love to see you smile.'

♀

April and my father are quarrelling when I get back to The Barn but when they see me they stop shouting at each other and shout at me instead.

'Where the hell have you been?' says April. 'Have you been with those village children again?'

'Answer April when she speaks to you,' says my father.

He is always in a bad mood when he hasn't had a cigarette. I hold the packet behind my back so April can't see it and my father shuffles around and takes the cigarettes from my hands, and then he slips out through the open door and leaves me on my own with April.

'Look at me when I'm talking to you,' she says, 'Have you been with those village children?'

April is smiling her horrible smile, which isn't a real smile at all. It is when her lips stretch into a horrible grin and she can't help it. It just happens.

'Yes.'

She slaps my face, but I don't care. April doesn't know about my new friend. I am going to call him the Frog Man.

♀

April is ill again and she is making Percy drive her to the

doctor. The illness is in her head and it was always the same with April, even when she was a little girl. That is what my grandmother says, anyway.

Then Jack says he needs to see the doctor because he is ill too, but this is only because he wants to go with April. My father watches from the window until the car has disappeared down the lane and then he tells me to pack some things quickly because we are going to London right away.

We walk to the station through the boggy field so as not to be seen from the farmhouse. April won't know until she and Jack get back from the doctor's and finds us gone. By then there won't be another train out of Grymewyck so she won't be able to follow us. This is what my father says, anyway.

I have brought my lucky rubber rabbit called Snickersneeze and my Mother Goose book, but not the dark-eyed boy. I wasn't allowed to go to the farmhouse before we left in case my grandparents tried to stop us going, so I had to leave the dark-eyed boy behind. I haven't even said goodbye to him.

The London train is late and it is getting dark. I am quite cold standing here on the platform because it is starting to rain and I haven't brought my coat.

'Chin up, old girl,' says my father. 'We're going to stay with aunty Pearl, and aunty Pearl's got a present for you.'

I don't care tuppence about aunty Pearl. As soon as I get to London I am going to look for Maisie. I am going to go to every single house until I find her.

Car headlights sweep round the station yard and April appears on the platform, and I know that is the end of my hopes of finding Maisie.

April runs along the platform screaming. She hammers at my father's chest with her fists until my father grabs her arms, and then she kicks his shins, and then they are on the ground, rolling over and over in the wet, fighting.

My basket gets knocked over during the fight and the pages of Mother Goose blow across the platform.

Snickersneeze is lying face down in a puddle. I am just going to pick him up when the stationmaster comes and tries to push me into his wooden hut but I do not budge.

'Your Ma and Pa's having a little argument,' he says. 'You just come inside with me where it's nice and warm.'

'He was taking her to live with that bitch!' screams April.

She climbs on top of my father and punches his face, and the blood runs down the side of his nose. And then the London train arrives and the light from the train windows makes the blood on my father's nose look all black and shiny.

The people who get off the train walk round my father and April but they tread all over Snickersneeze, and the people who are still on the train press their faces against the windows to get a better look.

When the London train has gone, April gets up and brushes the mud from her coat. I rescue Snickersneeze and my father collects all the pages of Mother Goose, which are ruined anyway because they are all torn and muddy.

My father takes my hand and we follow April out to the station yard where Percy Hammer is waiting in my grandfather's car.

♀

Not long after this my father leaves Grymewyck for good, but he goes without me. He leaves on his own, and he goes to live with Pearl Bonnet.

With my father gone, April stops having tantrums. She stops doing anything at all, even getting out of bed, and our teacher comes to see why we aren't in class.

After that, May comes to The Barn each morning to get

Jack and me up and dressed, and then she takes us down to the farmhouse and cooks breakfast. Usually we have fried eggs on fried bread but sometimes we have porridge.

♀

One day when Jack and I get home from school we find April in the porch with her suitcase and she is waiting for the village taxi.

She looks beautiful, like a model in a magazine, and she is wearing her camel coat and high heels and she keeps checking her seams to see if they are straight.

'Guess what!' says April. 'I'm going to find your father and when I find him I'm going to bring him home.'

'Can I come? I want to come!' cries Jack.

He jumps up and down in front of her to make her notice him, but she waves him away.

'No, darling, you must stay here and look after Ophelia. Besides, whatever would your father think if he came home to The Barn and found everyone gone?'

♀

My grandfather is pulling off his boots in front of the fire when Jack and me run into the farmhouse to tell him April has gone to London. He stares at the boot he is holding for what seems like ages then he throws it at the wall.

That night May walks back to The Barn with us and sleeps in April's bed. The next day she is waiting for us when we get home from school and tells us she will stay and look after us for as long as we need her.

It is nice living at The Barn with May because we have real meals and we sit at the table to eat them, but after a few weeks April comes back. Percy has to meet her at the station in my grandfather's car and she doesn't look nearly so smart as when she left.

My stepmother is thinner now and there is something weird about her eyes. They look empty, as if she doesn't see things. And she doesn't listen either.

'Did you find daddy?' asks Jack, as soon as she walks in.

'Where are my slippers? Has May been wearing my slippers?'

'I said have you found daddy?'

'Daddy? Yes, of course I found him, darling. He told me to tell you he doesn't want any more to do with you. And that whore he's living with doesn't want anything to do with you either.'

My Father's Whore

♀

April is going back to London to fetch my father home, and she wants me to go with her.

'He won't come back,' I tell her. 'I wouldn't if I was him.'

'He'll come back if you ask him to,' says April. 'I want you to tell your father how much you miss him.'

I can see what she is up to and I don't want to go to London with her because I have just sent a letter to the Frog Man. Maisie could turn up any day now and she will be really disappointed if I am not here, but April makes me go to London with her just the same.

My stepmother is wearing her white linen dress and her gold locket with my father's picture inside, so I know she means business.

She doesn't say a word on the train except to tell everyone

in the compartment that my father is living with a whore. The other passengers all turn to look at me and I go red and look out of the window.

It is not my fault, I want to tell them. Blame her, not me. She is horrible. I hate her.

Actually, I am quite looking forward to seeing my father's whore. And I am really excited about seeing my father again.

♀

The houses in the street where Pearl lives are tall and joined together so you can't see the sky unless you look up. The sky in London is quite high but I am not interested in the sky because I am looking at the houses.

London houses are really pretty, and they are painted pink, cream or white, like junket. I hope Pearl's house is a pink one because a pink house would be best for a whore.

The pretty houses run out and the next house is small and set back from the street. It is an ugly little house built from yellow brick and it has no pillars or steps like the pretty houses, just a concrete path.

April opens the gate of the ugly house and strides up the concrete path to the front door, and the first thing I see is my father's face at the little upstairs window. He doesn't see me because he is looking up at the ceiling and sucking a pencil, which means he is on the lavatory doing a crossword. This is what he used to do when he lived at The Barn and wanted to get away from April.

When my father sees us he shouts down to Pearl not to answer the door but April walks straight in without knocking and by the time my father comes downstairs buttoning up his trousers we are already in the hall. April runs to my father and throws her arms around his neck.

'I've come to take you home,' she says. 'The children are

pining for you.'

Somewhere a wireless is playing All Things Bright and Beautiful and then Pearl herself comes out of the kitchen wearing an apron embroidered with cross-stitch teapots.

'Would you like a sherry?' asks Pearl. 'Or is it too early?'

If I was a whore I would drink sherry whenever I wanted to, whatever time it was. And I wouldn't wear an apron either, especially not one with teapots on it.

Actually, I am a bit disappointed with Pearl. She is not a bit like she was in the wedding photograph and April doesn't even bother to look at her.

'Toby, you can't possibly stay with this woman,' says April. 'She'll bore you to death.'

My father smiles at me. It is his lopsided smile, which means he is embarrassed.

'How are you, Ophelia?'

'She's not eating,' says April before I can speak. 'Ophelia hasn't eaten a thing since you left home.'

Pearl is looking at herself in the hall mirror and trying to fluff up her straight hair.

'April, dear, why don't you and Toby go through to the sitting room? Ophelia and I could go out for a little walk.'

April goes right up to Pearl and stands in front of her so their noses are almost touching and she hisses like a snake.

'Whore!' she says. 'You've stolen my husband and now you want my daughter too.'

'You have no right to speak to Pearl like that, April,' says my father. 'This is Pearl's house and I think you ought to leave.'

I am really proud of my father. It is brave of him to say this, even if he doesn't say it very loudly.

'It's all right, Toby,' says Pearl. 'I'm sure April doesn't mean it.'

'Of course I mean it, you barren bitch!'

April shouts so loudly that Pearl jumps backwards into the kitchen and pulls me in after her, and then shuts the door and turns the wireless up as loud as it will go, probably to drown April's swearing. I expect Pearl thinks I am not used to swearing.

Pearl screams when we hear the sound of breaking glass, but I am used to this too so it doesn't bother me at all. The front door slams and the house shakes as if we were in an earthquake, and then April puts her head through the open kitchen window and grins at Pearl.

'Adulteress! Whore! I'll drag you through every court in the land for this, Pearl Bonnet. I'll make you sorry you ever met the bastard.'

My stepmother's head disappears and my father comes into the kitchen with blood on his lip and holding a broken picture frame.

'It's that lovely photograph of you with Princess Margaret,' he tells Pearl. 'I can't think why April took against it.'

He puts the pieces on the table and fits them together, but not very well. Pearl sniffs and wipes her eyes with a corner of the teapot apron.

'I'll mend it, my love,' says my father. 'I'll make it as good as new.'

'Let's have a sherry,' says Pearl. 'We all deserve a little drink.'

I tell her I am not allowed sherry and she looks surprised.

'What would you like instead?' she says.

'I'd like to go home, please,' I whisper. 'April forgot to take me.'

At home my grandmother will be feeding the hens and it is time for my visit to the dark-eyed boy.

'You can stay here with us,' says my father. 'Pearl will take you to see the statue of Peter Pan.'

Pearl claps her hands.

'What fun!' she cries. 'I've always wanted a daughter.'

'It's not forever,' I tell her. 'It's only until April remembers where she left me.'

It is really nice to see my father but I don't want to stay here, not forever.

Pearl's eyeballs look as if they are floating in water even though she isn't crying, and my father is smiling his crooked smile even though he is not looking at me.

'This is your home now, Ophelia,' he says. 'April doesn't want you.'

Golden Dreams

The letter from Ophelia is addressed to the Frog Man and it was posted without a stamp. I take it to my room and unfold a coloured pencil drawing of a woman with vermilion hair and pea green eyes. She is wearing a long yellow dress and her eyes extend beyond the outline of her face. Underneath the drawing are the words:

This Is Wot Masie Will Lok Like

Maisie, when I find her, will be a grown up version of Ophelia, with hair like Ophelia's and the same beautiful green eyes.

I will recognise Maisie immediately because of her hair, and I have a specimen of that hair. Or rather I have a specimen of Ophelia's hair.

The auburn ringlet is on the locker beside my bed. I am looking at it now and feeling bad because I got it under false pretences. I would really like to find Maisie, though. She sounds cool.

♂

I go to the pictures, thinking Maisie might be in the film. I am meant to be revising so I don't tell Mr and Mrs Manners where I am going. In any case, my Finchley parents don't approve of films.

They don't approve of magazines either, but on the way home from the cinema I go into a newsagent's shop, just in case Maisie has given up acting and become a model. I buy a calendar because the photograph on the front catches my eye.

The woman in the photograph is naked and lying on crumpled red velvet. She has blonde hair so it probably isn't Maisie, unless of course Maisie has dyed her hair. The calendar is called Golden Dreams 1952.

♂

Shit. My absence must have been noticed because when I get back Charlie's car is parked in the drive. My Finchley parents always send for Charlie when they don't know how to deal with me. I can hear them arguing even before I get to the front door.

There is an argument every time Charlie comes to the house these days because Charlie and his wife are getting divorced and his parents don't approve of divorce.

What God has joined together, let no man put asunder. This is what Mr and Mrs Manners think about divorce.

I roll up the Golden Dreams calendar and push it into my inside pocket.

'I've been talking to mum and dad,' says Charlie when I go in. 'You're eighteen this summer and I want you to come and live with me at Courtfield Mansions. Would you like that?'

Would I not! Courtfield Mansions is the flat in Fulham where Charlie lives and it is the coolest flat in the world.

'Now?'

'When you are eighteen you may do as you please,' says Mr Manners. 'Until then you are my responsibility.'

'You're suffocating Asa like you suffocated me,' says Charlie. 'Let him come now. I'll make sure he does his revision.'

'God guided Asa to our home,' says Mrs Manners. 'As long as he is with us it is our Christian duty to watch over him.'

'I'd rather live with Charlie,' I say.

'Go to your room, Asa,' says Mr Manners. 'We'll discuss this later.'

In my room I unroll my Golden Dreams calendar and lie on the bed staring at the woman. She looks lonely on her red velvet and I wish I was there with her, just so I could take care of her.

Downstairs, Charlie is still shouting at his parents. I can't make out what he is saying but I hope he is pointing out that it wasn't God who guided me here. Hitler is the reason I have ended up in bloody Finchley. It had nothing to do with God.

Charlie puts his head round my bedroom door and pounces on the calendar.

'Marilyn Monroe,' he laughs. 'Nice boobs.'

'Will they let me come?'

Charlie shakes his head.

'Afraid not. I'll collect you on your eighteenth birthday, and I'll be here before breakfast.'

'That's weeks away.'

'You've got exams coming up so you'll be busy. Until then, try to avoid any more arguments. It only makes things worse for you.'

He tosses the calendar onto the bed and laughs.

'At least you won't be lonely. Not with Marilyn to keep you company.'

When Charlie has gone I lock my bedroom door and get out my paint box, and I cover Marilyn Monroe's blond hair with a mass of ringlets. Red, to match the crumpled velvet she is lying on.

♂

Mr and Mrs Manners know about the Golden Dreams calendar. I tied a piece of cotton to my locker handle and stuck the other end to the shelf inside. When I got home from school the other night I found the cotton dangling loose.

They have found my diary too but that doesn't matter because I write it in Latin. I am taking Latin because I need it to get into medical school but it comes in handy at home too.

'*Deus est stultus!*'

God is stupid. It makes me feel better to say it out loud.

'Don't show off, Asa. We know you're clever. You don't have to prove yourself to us.

'*Odio vobis!*'

I don't really hate Mr Manners, but it is embarrassing having them know about my sex life. At least they didn't confiscate the calendar. I need my Golden Dreams more than ever now. They are the one good thing about life in Finchley. Roll on my eighteenth birthday.

♂

I have only two memories of life before Finchley. One is shoes under a table, and I can remember these in detail, even now.

The other memory is a face pressed against a window pane. It is the face of a child, but the face is distorted by the glass. The child is wearing a red hat and has straight black hair like mine so this must be the face of my sister, Anna.

Her face haunts me day and night, but especially at night. I try hard to blot it from my mind but Anna always comes back when I don't want her and when I am least expecting her. Memories are like that, I find. They creep up on you like ghosts.

There are other ghosts from Vienna but these are mainly smells. Vanilla is one of my smell ghosts, or something very like it, and chocolate cake. And the smell of antiseptic is sometimes so strong it catches in my nostrils and makes me sneeze.

Mrs Manners insists on taking me to the doctor, not because of the sneezing but because she hears me talking to the ghosts. In my presence, but as if I wasn't there, she tells the doctor that I am a loner and I spend too much time daydreaming in my room.

The doctor tells Mrs Manners that I am at a difficult age and will grow out of it. Adolescence, he calls it, and it is all to do with hormones.

I have tried hard to forget about the family I left behind in Vienna but it is not easy, not while Mr and Mrs Manners consider it their Christian duty to keep my real family alive in my thoughts.

Every evening after supper Mr Manners says a prayer for my mother and father, though even he now agrees my parents are probably dead. After that he says a special prayer for dear little Anna.

Mr Manners thinks Anna might be alive and he has never given up looking for her. This worries me because a living Anna could be even more of a problem than a dead Anna. For a start, what would I say to her after all this time?

After the war Mr Manners went to Vienna looking for my

family. He even went to the house where I used to live, but the people there had never heard of the Cohen family. He told me this quite recently. I knew nothing about it at the time.

Meanwhile, my little sister is with me more than ever. She never leaves me alone, not for a minute, but she is at her most persistent when I am trying to get to sleep. I have tried putting my head under the pillow but this doesn't help because Anna is inside my head and she is driving me mad.

'Go away,' I tell her. 'You're dead and I'm tired.'

I have a suspicion that Anna is angry because I am alive and she is not, and this is why she torments me the way she does. She has a point, I suppose. It does seem a bit unfair.

Happy birthday to me! I am now of age and leaving Finchley this very day. I have been up since dawn, waiting on the front step with my bags, but Charlie doesn't arrive until after midday.

'You promised you'd be here before breakfast.'

'I haven't had my breakfast yet.'

The first thing I do is show him my new passport.

Britannis Civis. Passport No. D1765342

A nobody no longer.

'Try smiling some time,' says Charlie when he sees the photograph. 'It doesn't hurt once you get used to it.'

Charlie himself smiles most of the time. He is a very smiley sort of man.

'Don't leave home on an empty stomach,' begs Mrs Manners. 'At least have some toast before you go.'

Mr Manners looks sad and I wish now I hadn't got up quite so early because it seems ungrateful. I mean, I've lived in this house with Mr and Mrs Manners for fourteen years so another few hours wouldn't have made much difference.

'Did you remember to take everything from your locker, dear?'

Incredibly, Mrs Manners is laughing.

Mr Manners shakes my hand and gives me a brown paper package. The handshake is feeble, and he looks frail.

It is strange, but I never noticed until now that my Finchley father is an old man.

'Venit et visitabo nobis,' says Mr Manners.

Come and visit us! Shit. He might have told me he knew Latin. I grab the package and run to get into the car beside Charlie.

♂

Charlie opens a bottle of champagne the moment we arrive at his flat and the first sip goes straight to my head. I wish now I had eaten the toast when Mrs Manners offered, but the champagne is in my honour so I have to finish it.

My brother is still laughing at my passport photograph.

'You're a free man,' he says. 'You can go anywhere in the world with this. Where will you go first?'

I am so pleased to be in Fulham that I haven't really thought of going any further, but to the much-travelled Charlie this will sound childish, so I lie.

'America, probably.'

'Not Vienna?'

I shake my head. Definitely not Vienna. I want to forget everything to do with Vienna, especially Anna. Hopefully my sister is still in Finchley where I left her, and with any luck she won't be able to find her own way across London.

Charlie hands me back my passport.

'Go and look for your sister,' he says. 'Dead or alive, she won't let you go until you do.'

And that is when the phone rings.

'Don't scowl,' says Charlie, going into the hall to answer it. 'It might be someone you actually like.'

'It's probably just Sue.'

Sue is Charlie's ex-wife, and she and Charlie talk all the time on the telephone. Sometimes I wonder why Sue ever left because their phone bills must be massive, and none of the women I have seen Charlie with since they separated have been a patch on Sue.

My brother comes back looking puzzled.

'Not Sue?'

'April Siward.'

'Your latest?'

Charlie goes out with loads of women now Sue has gone. This April Siward, whoever she is, is one of many.

'I haven't seen April in years.'

'What did she want?'

Charlie frowns.

'That is a very good question.'

'Is she pretty?'

He points to one of the framed photographs on his book shelf.

'That was April on her wedding day. She married a friend of mine in Cairo but she seems to have gone back to her maiden name. I was their best man.'

It is a picture of a wedding group in which everyone, including the bride, is in army uniform. April Siward is a stunning, long-legged blonde with huge eyes and a wide smile.

In the photograph my brother is smiling broadly. The groom is smiling too, but it is a rakish, lop-sided little smile that makes him look like a spiv. Not nearly classy enough for a woman like April Siward.

Standing beside April is another woman, not so pretty. The woman has her hand on the bride's arm but she appears to be looking at the groom.

'I bet this April's got nice boobs,' I say.

This is the champagne talking. Charlie talks about boobs all the time, but when I say it I sound ridiculous. Luckily, Charlie is engrossed in the photograph and not listening.

'April had a dark side,' he says. 'Not like her friend Pearl Bonnet, the other woman in the photograph. Now there was a nice woman. Remind me to ask April what happened to Pearl.'

'April's coming here?'

Charlie replaces the picture on the sideboard.

'You are about to meet her.'

Panic and champagne rise together in my throat. I jump up, stuffing my passport into my pocket, the sudden movement making me feel sick.

'I'll leave you to it. I don't want to play gooseberry on my first day.'

Charlie pushes me back in my chair.

'You'll do no such thing,' he says. 'I might need a chaperone. Anyway, I thought you wanted to see April's boobs.'

♂

April Siward is cool, but her boobs are disappointingly small and pointed. They look as if they might be hard to the touch, although I have an urge to touch them just the same.

Her face is something else. You don't see faces like April Siward's in Finchley, not even on calendars.

She is wearing a simple white linen dress and a gold locket, and as she steps into the hall she gives Charlie a dazzling smile. When she catches sight of me the smile fades.

'You're as lovely as ever,' says Charlie. 'You haven't changed at all.'

Charlie likes pretty women and for some reason they seem

to like him. Now I come to think of it this is probably why he and Sue are getting divorced. I should have thought of that before.

'Darling Charlie,' says April. 'You haven't changed either, not one teeny weeny bit.'

My brother has actually changed quite a lot since April's wedding day. His thick sandy hair is now flecked with grey, and he has a little paunch that wasn't there when the photograph was taken. April, however, seems not to notice these changes and I feel a little pang of jealousy as she stands on tiptoe and kisses my brother on the lips.

'I'll go to my room,' I say.

'You most certainly will not,' says Charlie. 'Not on your birthday.'

'A birthday!' cries April, not looking at me. 'How exciting. We should celebrate.'

'And so we shall,' says Charlie. 'You must join us for dinner, April.'

April turns to me and smiles briefly.

'Are you sure I won't be in the way?'

Feral is the word that comes to mind as I return the brief smile. Stunning as she is, there is something about April Siward that reminds me of a stray cat.

'How old are you?' she asks.

'Eighteen.'

'I bet you've broken a few hearts.'

I hate being talked down to.

♂

The restaurant is all gilt mirrors and pink lampshades, not the sort of place I had hoped for on my birthday, but April is delighted. The owner greets my brother by name, which delights her even more, and leads us to an alcove table with high-backed seats and pink velvet cushions. April immediately slides onto the cushion beside Charlie.

'Champagne!' cries Charlie, and the champagne arrives as if by magic.

Beneath the table April's knees are squashed against mine. I move my legs to give her more room, but our knees are still touching. This time I do not bother to move away.

Charlie proposes a toast. He drinks to me, the birthday boy, and to April, his long lost friend, and then he orders dinner.

'I hope you approve,' he says. 'I've chosen my wife's favourite wine. Sue liked it so much I started importing it.'

I should have mentioned this. Charlie is a wine merchant, which is another thing Mr and Mrs Manners don't approve of, and this is why Charlie never runs out of champagne.

Under the table April's kneecaps grow tense.

'Your wife?' she says. 'I thought you were divorced.'

April has done her homework and Charlie must surely have noticed.

'My ex-wife,' he says.

The kneecaps relax and April is all smiles once more. Charlie winks at me and I relax too. My brother is a compulsive flirt but he is nobody's fool.

April sees the wink. She puts an elbow on the table to exclude me from further conversation and turns her attention to Charlie. She does not, however, stop playing footsie with me under the table.

'It's been far too long, my dear,' says Charlie. 'Why have you been hiding yourself away?'

April gulps and dabs her eyes with a corner of the pink napkin.

'My marriage didn't work out. I wasn't going to burden you with it, but now I've told you anyway.'

Charlie takes her hand.

'That's what friends are for,' he says. 'You can share your burden with us.'

And share her burden April does, for many minutes, and when she has finished Charlie lifts her hand to his lips and kisses it.

'Why would Toby want another woman when he could have you? He must be out of his mind.'

'I'm so lonely,' says April, smiling through her tears. 'I have no children, you see. No family to comfort me.'

Charlie bows his head, sharing her sorrow and glancing at his watch at the same time.

'I would have loved a brother or sister. You are so lucky to have Asa.'

At least she has remembered my name.

'It's getting late,' says Charlie. 'Where are you staying, my dear?'

April is expecting to stay the night with Charlie. Even I can see that.

'With friends. But they won't be waiting up for me.'

'They'll be concerned about you just the same. Friends always are, but don't worry. Asa and I will make sure you get home safe and sound.'

Outside, my brother hails a taxi and opens the door for April, who fumbles in her handbag looking for money. She is clearly reluctant to get in but Charlie takes her firmly by the elbow, helps her inside and closes the door on her.

As the taxi pulls away and disappears into the darkness I am left with the eerie sensation that April Siward hasn't really left at all. I find myself looking around to make sure she has really gone.

Before I get into bed I unpack a few clothes and hang them in the wardrobe. This rambling mansion flat with its high ceilings and big echoing rooms is my new home, and I am staking my claim. It is as different from Finchley as anything I could have imagined or hoped for.

Mr Manners' package is on my bedside table and I wish it were not because I know what it contains. The brown paper parcel contains my sister Anna, or at least as much information about her as Mr Manners has been able to dig out.

It crosses my mind that Anna herself might be in there too, that she has somehow smuggled herself into Charlie's flat by hiding in the package. I switch the light off quickly and in the kitchen I hear Charlie uncorking another bottle of champagne.

Kidnapped

♀

As it happens I only stay at Pearl's house for one night, because April comes for me early the next morning and she looks terrible. She looks as if she had slept on the street because her white dress is all creased and dirty and there are ladders in her stockings.

Perhaps she really did sleep in the street. I hope so. It serves her right.

April stamps her foot and demands to talk to my father, but my father has locked himself in the lavatory and is refusing to come down. I am sitting on Pearl's knee and Pearl is reading out loud to me.

'Daddy loves Pearl, not you,' I say. 'I love Pearl too.'

My father has promised to take me home to Grymewyck if I am nice to Pearl but I have to stay here for one whole week.

After that I can go home if I still want to. My father has crossed his heart and hoped to die so I know he means it.

April stamps her foot again.

'Ophelia is not a baby. She is quite capable of reading for herself.'

I put my arms around Pearl's neck and stick my tongue out at April.

'Get your coat, Ophelia,' says April. 'You are coming with me.'

I snuggle closer to Pearl, which makes April even more cross.

'I'll count to ten,' she snaps. 'If you're not ready by then I'm going home without you.'

Home! Nobody said anything about going home. Pearl is stroking my hair but I push her hand away.

'Are we going back to Grymewyck?'

'Where on earth do you think we're going? Timbuktu?'

I scramble off Pearl's knee and run to April.

♀

April walks really slowly on the way to the underground station and I know she is doing it on purpose because she can see I am in a hurry to get home. I don't want to miss Maisie, who could turn up in Grymewyck at any time, and I know the dark-eyed boy will be wondering where I am.

I even hold April's hand to make her go faster. I don't notice the painted houses any more, but April notices and she wants to talk about them.

'Isn't it pretty?' she says, stopping in front of a pink house with black and white tiled steps. 'What a pity the whore's house is so ugly.'

'I like Pearl's house better,' I say, although I don't really like Pearl's house at all. 'It was built on a bomb site. Pearl told me. She chose it specially.'

If I can make April angry she might walk faster and then we will get to Grymewyck sooner.

'Pearl's ever so rich,' I tell April. 'She's so rich she works without being paid.'

'I can well believe it.'

April smiles the smile that is not a real smile and walks slower than ever.

'Pearl knows Princess Margaret,' I say. 'They're really good friends.'

April stops dead and looks down at me.

'How do you know that?' she says and squeezes my hand so hard the bones grind together.

'She went to Buckingham Palace to see her. Princess Margaret wanted to thank Pearl for all the work she does without being paid.'

April walks quickly after that, so quickly I find it hard to keep up with her.

♀

We collect our suitcase from the left luggage room and April heads for the station exit, which I know is the wrong way because the platforms are in the opposite direction. I run to catch up with her and pull on her arm

'Where are we going?'

'Home.'

'The train to Grymewyck goes from over there.'

'We're not going to Grymewyck,' says April, slapping my hand off her arm. 'You are going to live with me in London until your father comes to his senses.'

♀

Hooray! Vermin is here. She is walking up and down on the window sill and blinking at me through the glass.

I jump up from my camp bed and open the window very carefully so as not to scare her off and I push a piece of cold fried egg out onto the ledge. Vermin waits until I have closed the window and then she picks up the egg and flies away.

April says pigeons are vermin and carry disease so I can't feed Vermin when April is here. That is why I called her Vermin. I think it's a pretty name.

Vermin's feathers are purple and green and she has red legs and sad red eyes. She is nothing like the pigeons at home. My real home in Grymewyck, I mean. Not here.

This is not my real home. This is a room at the top of a very tall house and it costs £2/5s/6d. a week, which April says is daylight robbery. There is a sign on the front door. No Students, No Blacks and No Irish. In the hall there is another sign that says No Visitors.

I had to drag our suitcase all the way up to the top of the house when we arrived and then I had to go all the way down again to get a shilling for the electric meter from the housekeeper. That was twenty-eight and half days ago.

April is a waitress now. She works in the snack bar on the corner of our street and sometimes I go there and she gives me sausage or fried egg on toast. If the man who owns the snack bar is around she pretends not to know me so I just go home and she brings the food back when she finishes work and we heat it up in the Baby Belling.

In the evenings we sit in front of the electric fire and April reads magazines or tries on clothes, but I just sit. April has the chair and I sit on the bed.

When it gets dark April puts on her headscarf and dark glasses and goes out for a walk. Sometimes when she can't sleep she goes out in the middle of the night too. Izolde, the Polish dressmaker from across the landing, has given April some of her sleeping tablets, but April says they are next to useless.

I am still looking for Maisie. London is really big, much bigger than I ever thought it would be, but I am not going to give up. I am looking for the Frog Man too. He lives in a place called Finchley but he probably comes to Earls Court quite a lot.

Every day after April goes to work I go to the underground station at the end of our street and stand at the top of the stairs where I can see the people as they get off the trains. It will be easy to spot Maisie because of her hair, and I will see the Frog Man straight away because he will be taller than anyone else.

Probably I will find the Frog Man first because he lives in London. I can still remember his address so I am now thinking it might be better to write to him.

Maisie could be anywhere. Probably she has gone to Hollywood.

♀

There is a telephone on the ground floor of the house where we live and April goes down every evening to ring my father. Everyone in the house can hear her screaming at him, even me on the top floor.

I really miss the dark-eyed boy. He would understand how I am feeling now because he is in the same situation. The dark-eyed boy is trapped in the Ophelia Box and I am trapped in this horrible room.

I miss my grandparents too of course, and May and Percy. Sometimes I even miss Jack, but not that often. Most of all I miss the dark-eyed boy because he is the only one who listens.

April has forbidden me to talk about Grymewyck and when I tell her I want to go home she just smiles her horrible smile. She smiles a lot now and sometimes the smile gets out of hand and her whole face stretches into a weird shape. It takes ages for it to go back to normal.

I hate the food April brings home because it is always soggy with someone else's tomato ketchup. April eats hardly anything and her face is getting all hollow and pointed, like a witch. She won't buy food from the shops though because she says this is a waste of money.

April says she would rather spend her wages on clothes.

♀

On Saturdays we go shopping for clothes for April. She looks for bargains and she is very fussy. Usually we go to the bargain basement in one of the big stores and she spends ages choosing remnants of satin and printed poplin, and silk and velvet, and then she gives them to Izolde, who lays them out on the floor of her room.

April tells Izolde she wants clothes like the ones she sees in her magazines. She wants bat-wing blouses, hour glass jackets and pencil slim skirts, and she wants Peter Pan collars, bolero sleeves and boat necklines.

'Eet is not possible,' Izolde tells her. 'Eet is not enough material 'ere for what you want.'

'But you're so clever, Izolde,' says April. 'I know you can do it.'

Izolde works late into the night, joining bits of material and matching patterns, and she almost always manages to make what April wants.

One day April sees a black and silver cocktail dress in the window of a second-hand dress shop. The label says Dior and the price tag says six guineas. Six pounds and six shillings is more than her week's wages. April tries on the dress, which fits perfectly. She puts down a half crown deposit and asks the owner to keep the dress for her until the end of the week.

The weekend after this, April buys a coat from the same shop. She tells me it is made from real silk taffeta and it has a dark velvet collar, which is fashionable. The coat is embroidered all over with little pearls and the price is a guinea a week for three weeks.

Sometimes April takes things without paying. She says she doesn't, but I know she does because I have seen her do it. I am not stupid.

She steals from the big department stores and she takes little things that match her new clothes. Gloves and scarves and make-up, stuff like that. When we get back to our room she lays everything out on the bed and anything that is not exactly right she gives to Izolde.

One day, just when she is about to slip a spray of artificial cherries into her bag, a man puts his hand on April's shoulder.

'Excuse me, madam. Would you mind coming with me? Unless, of course, you prefer to be arrested here in front of your daughter.'

April swings round and pushes her bag hard into the man's chest. The man loses his balance and April grabs my wrist and together we run out of the store and jump on a passing bus. She is angry about the spray of cherries, which she chose specially to match her new hourglass-style tweed jacket.

One day, when April's wardrobe is full of new clothes, she goes down to the telephone on the ground floor and tells the operator to connect her to Fulham 2620.

Dr Ben Brown

Uncle Ben thinks I am in Grymewyck because of a girl, which in a way I am. I have come back because I want to see Ophelia again.

It bothers me that I never found Ophelia's mother, Maisie, but it was a bad time for me. In my addled teenage brain, Maisie and Marilyn Monroe had become as one. I was in love with them both. Hormones. That is what the doctor said at the time.

I am over Marilyn Monroe now and feeling a bit foolish about the whole thing, but I would still like to keep my promise and find Maisie. That is what I want to tell Ophelia.

There have been two real life girls since Marilyn. One works in the university library and the other I met at one of Charlie's parties. Uncle Ben wants to know about both of them.

'Are they Jewish?'

'I don't know,' I tell him. 'How would I tell?'

'Are they called Miriam or Ruth?'

♂

I should say something about my uncle, who is the reason I came to Grymewyck in the first place. Uncle Ben is an old school friend of Mr Manners and not my real uncle at all. When the school in Marigold Street was bombed I was sent here to Grymewyck to stay with Uncle Ben and his wife.

I hardly remember Mrs Brown, who died not long after the war, but I still visit Uncle Ben. He lives alone now and I am the nearest he has to family so he likes it when I call him uncle.

'Try to speak a little German with the child,' Mr Manners had written to his friend all those years ago. 'I don't want Asa to forget his own language before he goes home to Vienna.'

We had spoken German together a few times, but only in the house and only when there was nobody around to hear us. Uncle Ben had felt awkward speaking his own language, and so had I.

♂

'I thought as much,' says Uncle Ben when I ask him if he knows anyone called Ophelia. 'I knew it wasn't your old uncle you'd come to see.'

'She's not a girlfriend, uncle Ben. Ophelia is a little girl of about six or seven.'

'It's an unusual sort of name. I don't think it's Jewish.'

My uncle knows all about unusual names. Once upon a time his own name was Ephraim Benjamin Braun but he changed this to Ben Brown before the war and by the time he arrived in Grymewyck that is who he was. Doctor Ben Brown.

After the war my uncle had tried to go back to his real name but it was too late. The villagers didn't want a foreign doctor with a name that sounded like a jellied pig's head. They wanted Ben Brown. He has been retired for many years now but here in Grymewyck my uncle is still known only as Doctor Brown.

♂

In the lane leading to the hay barn I almost collide with a small fair haired boy on a tricycle, who comes round the corner at top speed and skids to a halt a few inches from my front wheel.

'I'm looking for Ophelia,' I say. 'Do you know where she is?'

'Ophelia's gone.'

'When will she back?'

'Dunno.'

'Do you know where she went?'

'London.'

'Wait,' I say, as the boy is about to pedal away. 'Did she go with her stepmother, the lady she used to live with?'

The boy scowls and nods and then he turns his tricycle around and pedals back in the direction of the barn. I wait until he disappears around the bend and follow him.

A woman is hanging out washing on the line but it is not the angry blonde I saw on my last visit. This woman is plump with mouse-coloured hair and she is smiling to herself.

I watch for a while as she pegs the clothes in a neat row and, from where I am standing, I fancy I hear her humming..

♂

Mr Manners, Charlie's father, had suffered from angina for years and had told nobody, not even Mrs Manners. His death was sudden, leaving us all in a state of shock.

April Siward's phone call comes a day after the funeral.

'It's April Siward,' whispers Charlie, his hand over the mouthpiece. 'What shall I say?'

'Tell her to get lost.'

I am annoyed when I hear Charlie inviting her over, but I know I have been poor company for my brother, who is feeling guilty about his father's death.

There had been yet another argument the evening before Mr Manners died and Charlie is blaming himself for the final attack. Nothing I say makes any difference.

'Your father had *angina pectoris*,' I tell him. 'Loosely translated, it means 'a strangling feeling in the chest'. It could have happened at any time.'

'You don't know that,' says Charlie. 'You've only been at medical school a few weeks. You're not a doctor yet.'

Sue would know how to cheer him up, but Sue is on holiday and I have not been able to contact her.

Charlie pours himself another whisky and hands me the bottle. I decline this recognition of my coming of age because I am not in the mood and because I don't want to end up in the same state as Charlie. My brother is very drunk.

'Dad always liked you better than me,' he says. 'He was proud of you. Dad would have done anything for you.'

'You know that's not true.'

We both know it is perfectly true. Mr Manners had always been proud of me, and he had been especially proud when I got into medical school. I am feeling more than a little guilty about Mr Manners myself.

'All that Quaker nonsense,' says Charlie. 'Dad never tried to impose any of that mumbo jumbo on you.'

'I'm a Jew. I was off the hook.'

The doorbell rings.

'There's April,' I say, getting up. 'I'll be in my room if you need me.'

This sounds grown up and I am rather pleased with myself.

April Siward arrives in cream linen slacks and a tan suede jacket with snakeskin trims. The jacket is draped carelessly around her shoulders and her hair is tied back gypsy-style in a silk scarf. April has obviously spent some time achieving this casual effect.

She is clearly irritated when she sees me but cheers up when I tell her I am on my way to my room. Charlie suggests a walk and she does not hide her delight when I say I have work to do.

Charlie goes for a walk with April and returns late, alone but in high spirits.

'Where's April?'

'Gone home. She's playing hard to get.'

'Christ, Charlie. You must be desperate.'

'April understands loneliness. She's an only child too.'

The following night April turns up again and suggests jazz on Eel Pie Island, and the night after that she takes Charlie to more jazz at a pub she knows in the Old Brompton Road. She turns up in a different outfit each night and the glint of triumph in her eyes is brighter every time I see her.

Mrs Manners telephones each evening as always and before long she asks to speak to Charlie.

'He's working late,' I lie. 'I'll tell him you rang.'

Charlie never returns his mother's calls.

'Why so happy?' I ask, when he gets in late.

'I'm in love,' says Charlie. 'I'm not just happy, I'm euphoric.'

I reach for my dictionary;

Euphoria: an exaggerated feeling of happiness that is not necessarily well founded.

April arrives early for her Friday night date with Charlie, who is still at work. I let her in, show her into the sitting room and leave her alone. A few moments later I hear the clip-clop of her high heels on the hall parquet and she puts her head round my bedroom door.

'So this is your den. How cosy.'

She comes in, uninvited, and stretches herself out on my bed. I take no notice and carry on with my work.

'I've come to keep you company,' she says. 'Just pretend I'm not here.'

April hums and thumbs her way through my Grey's Anatomy, which she has helped herself to from the book shelf, and when my phone rings she takes the call without asking. It is Charlie to say he has been delayed.

'Charlie says you're to take care of me until he gets back,' says April, leaning back on my pillow. 'What would you like to do?'

She kicks off her shoes and rubs the back of my chair with her stockinged toes. I close my book, stand up and take my jacket from the back of the door.

'You can do whatever you like. I'm going out.'

'Anywhere exciting?'

'I promised Charlie's mother I would go through Mr Manners' papers with her. It seems Charlie has more important things to do.'

Finding Maisie

♀

April has gone out in her newest jacket, the one with the snakes' tails hanging from the collar. She looks a bit like a snake herself now she is so thin. The jacket suits her down to the ground.

It took her ages to get ready so I suppose she has gone to see the man at Fulham 2620. He is welcome to her, whoever he is. Perhaps she will stop pestering my father now. April still telephones my father every evening and she always tells him I cry all night because I am pining for him so much.

The Frog Man didn't come, even after I wrote to him. Perhaps he didn't get my letter, or perhaps he has gone away to be a doctor.

Vermin's gone away too. I don't know where she went, but she doesn't come to the windowsill any more. April says

Vermin has probably been poisoned, and a good thing too.

April will be late home tonight. She might not even come back at all, so I can stay out as long as I like.

It is quite scary being here after dark and my hiding place behind the litter bin stinks of wee but I have a really good view of the station platforms.

A man who works at the station wants to know who I am waiting for and if my mother knows where I am. I tell him it is my mother I am waiting for and he goes away.

I see Maisie just when I am about to give up and go back to the bedsit. She is standing outside the station, so she can't have come by train after all.

Maisie is leaning against a lamp post and she has her back to me but I know it is her because of the hair. My mother's hair is just like mine and she is smoking a cigarette. I never thought of Maisie as a smoker but I expect she got that from my father.

My tummy goes all watery and when I stand up my legs feel so wobbly I have to sit down straight away, but I don't take my eyes off Maisie in case she disappears again. She is talking to an old man who must be a friend because he has got his arm round her waist, but then she shakes her head at the old man and he walks away.

Maisie crosses the road to talk to another man who is waiting for her in his car. The man winds down the window and she bends over to say something through the open window and then he reaches across the inside of the car and opens the door for her.

'Maisie!'

I shout her name at the top of my voice but Maisie doesn't hear because of all the hooting when I run across the road. I get to her just as she is about to close her door and then turns and sees me. Her face is rough and greasy like an orange, which is not how I thought Maisie would look.

'It's me!' I shout. 'It's Ophelia!'

I am just thinking I should probably get into the car with her when the man starts the engine and Maisie shuts the door.

I press my face against the window but my mother is not looking because the man has pushed her skirt up to her knickers and he's got his hand between her legs.

♀

April must think she is a ballerina or something because when she is not pulling stupid faces at herself in the mirror she is dancing round the room in her petticoat. She has always been different from other people, but she seems to be getting worse. Sometimes I think April might be a bit mad.

When she gets tired of twirling about she flings herself down on the bed and laughs and laughs until she almost chokes. I wish she would choke. It would be really good if April choked herself to death.

'What are you gawping at?' she says. 'You should be asleep.'

I crawl further down the camp bed and pull the blanket over my head. This is where I go now to talk to the dark-eyed boy. It doesn't matter any more that I don't have the photograph because I have learned to imagine him, but I can only do it in the dark.

Tonight I have something very important to ask the dark-eyed boy because I am thinking of running away and I am not sure how to do it. I ask him very quietly but April hears anyway and pulls the blanket off me.

She slaps my legs and says next time I talk to myself she will give me a good hiding, so perhaps I won't run away after all.

That wasn't the real Maisie I saw outside the station. It

couldn't have been because the real Maisie is beautiful and that woman wasn't beautiful. She was so horrible that I am trying not to think about her. It was probably a woman trying to look like my mother.

It is a bit boring waiting behind the litter bin all day but one of them must come soon. I wonder which one will come first.

The Frog Man might be best because he knows the way to Grymewyck and he could take me home. I don't think Maisie has ever been to Grymewyck so she might not know how to get there.

In the end it is the policeman who comes for me and he is really nice. He leans over the litter bin and says it can't be very comfortable down there so why don't I come out and talk to him properly. The man who works at the station is with him, so he must have known I was here all the time.

♀

I am on my way to Grymewyck in a police car and the policeman who is driving the car says we will be there in less than an hour. The car is really big and the leather seats are so shiny I am sliding around in the back so I keep bumping into the policewoman who is with me.

The policewoman has locked the doors in case I slide out onto the road but probably it is to stop me from running away again.

We are going really fast now and I feel a bit sick but I don't care. I can't wait to get home. I didn't tell the police about April because I thought they might take me back to the bedsit. I just told them my home was in Grymewyck, which is the truth.

I didn't tell them my name either, but they have found out from somewhere because the policewoman keeps calling me

Ophelia. She says my aunt is looking forward to seeing me, so May knows I am on my way home.

♀

May must have moved house because there is a strange woman with a teddy bear under her arm waiting for us at The Barn and a strange car parked by the gate. The policeman and the policewoman lock me in the police car and go to talk to the woman.

Probably they will try to take me back to April now, but I won't go. I lie on the back seat of the police car and scream, and I kick the door as hard as I can. The woman comes and gets in next to me and tries to hold my legs still.

'Don't kick, dear,' she says. 'You're making marks on the nice door.'

The woman tells me she is a friend even though I have never seen her before. She tells me her job is to make sure children are happy and she gives me the teddy bear, which I throw on the floor. The woman picks up the teddy bear and sits it down on her knee.

'Are you happy to be home, dear?' she says. 'You can tell teddy if you don't want to tell me.'

She makes the teddy bear nod its head and I wonder if the woman might be a bit mad because grown-ups don't usually talk to teddy bears.

'Where's May?'

'Your aunt's cooking your tea. You're having mushrooms on toast. Do you like mushrooms on toast, dear?'

The woman is definitely mad and I can't wait any longer. I scramble over her legs and run up the path and into the kitchen, and there is May with the frying pan in her hand.

'There you are at last,' says May. 'It's mushrooms on toast for tea.'

She puts the frying pan down and locks the door and we go to the window and watch the police car bumping away down the lane. Jack is playing with his dinky cars in front of the fire and doesn't look up.

The woman who likes children to be happy is standing by the gate still holding the teddy bear. She sees us at the window and waves, and she makes the teddy bear wave too, and then she gets into her car and drives away.

'Interfering busybodies,' says May. 'Why can't people learn to mind their own business?'

Runaways

After the spaciousness of Charlie's flat, everything in Finchley seems to have shrunk, including Mrs Manners herself. She is sitting alone in the dark when I arrive, but she smiles and rallies and together we go into the study where she opens Mr Manners' desk.

The first thing I see is an unopened letter addressed to The Frog Man and I open it immediately.

Help I am wating on the stashun steps plez cum

'When did this arrive?'

Mrs Manners is staring out of the window, her mind somewhere else.

'I have no idea. What is it?'

She picks up the envelope and frowns.

'The Frog Man? How very odd. That's the person the

police were looking for. They were here this afternoon. I thought it was some sort of joke.'

'What did they want?'

'Something to do with a lost child. They'd found a little girl wandering alone on Earls Court station.'

It can only have been Ophelia.

♂

By the time I get to Earls Court the station master's office is closed and the woman in the ticket booth knows nothing about a lost child. I go to the main staircase where a man in an army great coat is relieving himself against a large metal litter bin and I re-read Ophelia's note.

Help I am wating on the stashun steps plez cum

These are the only steps on the station, so this is where she must have been waiting. Waiting for me.

I run up the road to the police station where the desk officer runs his finger down a page in the incident book and makes a phone call. He replaces the receiver and tells me the little girl has been reunited with her family, and when I ask him where the girl lives he closes the book and gives me an ugly look.

'Are you a relative?'

'A friend.'

'Then you'll know where she lives, and that's where you'll find her. The little girl is safe and sound with her family.'

My poor Ophelia.

They have sent her back to her stepmother. Safe and sound she almost certainly is not.

♂

My little sister has pretty much left me alone since I came to live at Courtfield Mansions but she springs into action now. Anna is a jealous ghost and she doesn't like it when I think about Ophelia.

The familiar flattened face emerges from the darkness, hovers above my pillow and stays there. I groan and turn the other way but Anna is there waiting for me, hanging in the night like a Chinese lantern.

'Go away, Anna. I'm dog tired.'

She doesn't make a sound, but even so I know my sister is crying. She used to do this in Finchley when I wasn't paying her enough attention.

I turn on the light and my sister disappears. Anna never did like the light.

Mr Manners' parcel is still there on my bedside table and I wonder again if my sister is lurking inside the brown paper package. I get out of bed, wrap the package in my underpants and stuff it at the back of the wardrobe behind my shoes, and then I go to make myself a hot drink.

April is in the kitchen, wearing Charlie's silk dressing gown and smoking a cigarette.

'It seems we had the same idea,' she says.

She steps forward and blows her cigarette smoke into my face.

'I have news for you, baby brother. I'm moving in.'

'Does Charlie know?'

Charlie has come in and is standing behind me.

'I hope you'll be happy for us, Asa.'

Charlie dances a silly jig as he helps April out of the taxi and pays the driver. He makes several trips up the stairs with her bags and boxes and I watch from my bedroom window not offering to help.

The taxi moves off and April looks up. She sees me and waves, and the mocking little kiss she blows me before she follows Charlie into her new home is a declaration of war.

After this I work late in the university labs and spend more time than I should in the student union bar. I join the film society, take up squash, and sign up as occasional pianist for the college jazz band. All of this I do to avoid April.

♂

One evening I mistime my arrival home and meet Charlie and April on their way out.

'We were beginning to think you were avoiding us,' says Charlie. 'Come and eat with us.'

April leads us away from Charlie's usual haunts in the Earls Court Road and we head off in the opposite direction.

'Earls Court's a no go area now,' says Charlie and winks at me. 'I think April must be avoiding a secret admirer.'

♂

Our next excursion out together is April's birthday and there is no getting out of it.

'Come for my sake,' says Charlie. 'It would mean a lot to me.'

Utter bollocks, but I remind myself I am living rent free and agree.

This time we do go to the Earls Court Road because April has set her heart on a pretentious new restaurant that has just opened.

L'Elégance Parisienne has black lampshades and black walls and is so dark we can't see what we're eating, which is probably no bad thing.

'At least it's an improvement on the greasy snack bar that used to be here,' says Charlie. 'I imagine the authorities closed that down.'

April wrinkles her lovely nose at the very idea of a greasy snack bar and turns her attention to the diamond ring Charlie has given her for her birthday.

'Asa's not interested in your diamonds,' says Charlie. 'He's a million miles away.'

He is right. I am watching people going in and out of the station entrance, which is just across the road, and I am thinking about Ophelia.

♂

My brother is ecstatic. That is the wonder of the thing. Charlie is so happy that when I suggest a trip to Finchley to visit his mother he agrees straight away.

'Shall I invite April?'

I advise against it.

'It's early days,' I say. 'Let's wait and see how your mother is.'

I want to spare Mrs Manners the nightmare that is April for as long as possible, hopefully forever. Any day now Charlie must surely come to his senses and send April Siward packing.

♂

Mrs Manners puts on a brave face for Charlie's sake and finding his mother so cheerful Charlie immediately tells her there is someone he would like her to meet.

'I can't wait for you to see her. Her name's April.'

'I suppose life must go on,' smiles Mrs Manners. 'When can I meet your new friend?'

Charlie says the sooner the better as far as he is concerned and Mrs Manners smiles again.

'You will be there, won't you, Asa? I won't feel nearly so shy of Charlie's young lady if you're there too. Is she nice?'

I can think of nothing nice to say about April so I say nothing.

'Asa's just jealous,' says Charlie. 'When you meet April

you'll understand why.'

♂

The following weekend Mrs Manners waits for us by the garden gate and my heart gives a little lurch when I see her, pale and nervous in her Sunday hat and coat. Apart from daily trips to the Meeting House I know she has been nowhere since her husband's funeral.

Charlie jumps out of the car and rushes to kiss his mother. We are late of course because it has taken April two hours to get ready. She winds down her window and Mrs Manners offers April her hand.

April, in a red halter-neck sun dress and matching red lipstick, shakes the shyly proffered hand without speaking and without getting out of the car.

'You sit in the front, mother,' says Charlie. 'April won't mind going in the back.'

'Stay where you are, dear,' says Mrs Manners when April doesn't move. 'I'll be quite happy in the back with Asa.'

She climbs in next to me and I give her hand a little squeeze. Charlie rests his arm on the back of his seat and turns to his mother.

'Where would you like to go?' he says. 'It's your day.'

It is soon decided. We will go to the gardens at Wisley, a favourite place of Mr Manners when he was alive. I remember the trips to Wisley without enthusiasm but Mrs Manners is delighted.

During the journey she leans forward to ask April if she is interested in gardening but April has her window wide open and doesn't hear.

At Wisley, April develops a blister as we walk around the flowerbeds and hobbles along on her high heels complaining loudly.

'My feet are killing me. Damn these stupid shoes.'

Mrs Manners is concerned for April's feet and suggests lunch so April can sit down and take her shoes off. During lunch Mrs Manners tells April the gardens were founded by a Victorian Quaker, a distant relative of Charlie's father. April stifles a yawn and Mrs Manners tries again.

'Do your parents like gardening, dear?'

'My mother's dead and my father employs gardeners. He could never manage the estate alone.'

'I'm sorry to hear about your mother,' says Mrs Manners. 'Has your father never considered moving to somewhere smaller?'

April looks shocked.

'He would never do that. Our family has lived in the same house for centuries. We are descended from the Vikings.'

Mrs Manners falls silent, crushed, and I am furious.

The lie is preposterous. I wait for Charlie to say something but my brother is not paying attention. He is on his knees, massaging April's blistered foot and playing little piggies with her painted toes.

'Charlie, stop it,' April giggles. 'You're tickling.'

'Where exactly is your family estate?' I ask. 'I hope we'll all be invited to stay one of these days.'

April hears the sarcasm in my voice and stops giggling. She looks up at me over the top of Charlie's bent head and to my amazement I see she is blinking hard to hold back her tears.

It occurs to me for the first time that April Siward is not so much a liar as a woman who is living in a make-believe world of her own. Either she is telling the truth about her family, which I doubt, or she really believes herself to be telling the truth.

♂

It is two o'clock in the morning when I wake up and see the hall light has been left on. I get up to switch it off and find Charlie in his pyjamas standing by the front door.

'I'm waiting for April,' he says simply. 'She's gone out for a walk.'

'Does she make a habit of going out in the middle of the night?'

'She's an insomniac.'

'Is that what she told you?'

'April's not a liar.'

'You know nothing about her, Charlie. I just hope you know what you're doing.'

I have never spoken like that to Charlie before but these days I sometimes feel I have more sense than my elder brother.

♂

One evening April comes to my room, curls up like a cat on my bed and demands help. She is pregnant and she wants an abortion.

'You won't tell Charlie, will you?' she says.

'No, but you should.'

'You're a medical student, Asa. You must know people who do that sort of thing. You have to help me.'

'Not until you've talked to Charlie.'

April slams out and turns the gramophone up until someone in the flat above bangs on the ceiling and she turns it down again. A moment later she reappears at my door and looks at me slyly.

'I don't know why you're being so hoity-toity,' she says. 'I happen to know you already helped someone get an abortion.'

This is true. Last year a friend's girlfriend had fallen pregnant and come to me for advice. I had told Charlie, who had lent my friend money to pay for an abortion. Obviously Charlie has told April.

'That was different. I was helping a friend.'

'But you and I are friends.'

Friends? I look at her coldly. April Siward doesn't know the meaning of the word.

'The girl who had the operation, was she all right afterwards?'

'We sliced up a cadaver together the following week.'

'Ugh!'

April runs from the room clutching her stomach and a moment later I hear her throwing up in the bathroom.

I sigh, close my book and lean back in my chair. The time has come for me to find somewhere else to live.

♂

Charlie is sad but not surprised when I tell him I am moving out.

'You're going to live with a girlfriend, I suppose,' he sighs. 'Which one is it? I can never keep up with you.'

I tell him I will be staying with his ex-wife Sue while I look for a place on my own and Charlie frowns. He has seen little of Sue for the last two years, since the arrival of April Siward, but Sue and I have remained friends.

'This is a sudden decision,' he says. 'Has something happened?'

'Two's company, three's a crowd. You and April need your own space.'

'Can you afford a place of your own?'

I wait for Charlie to offer me money, which I have already decided to refuse. Some of my fellow medics work in the college labs for extra cash and I intend to do the same.

'I'd like to help out,' says Charlie, unexpectedly.

'Unfortunately I'm a bit strapped for funds at the moment.'

No surprise there. April must be costing him a fortune. Clearly she has not yet told him about her pregnancy and neither do I.

♂

I go to say my farewells to April and find her lying on the sitting room sofa in her outdoor coat looking ill.

'I've been shopping,' she says, blowing me a kiss. 'I'm absolutely pooped.'

I return the blown kiss and as I do so April leans over the edge of the sofa and vomits all over the carpet. Pregnancy does that to a woman, I know, but what lousy timing.

'I'll get a cloth.'

I return to find April unconscious with her head hanging over the sofa and her hair trailing in the vomit. As I lift her head her coat falls open to reveal a dark red patch on the front of her skirt that spreads quickly even as I look at it.

Charlie arrives as I am dialling 999.

'A miscarriage,' I say. 'April was pregnant.'

'A baby?'

'Fetch some cushions. We need to raise her legs.'

He does not move.

'A baby?'

Not a baby, Charlie. An abortion. In some ways my older brother is little more than a baby himself. I get the cushions myself and ram them under April's blood-soaked bottom.

My New Best Friend

♀

May has planted nasturtiums outside The Barn and I have my own bedroom now with proper curtains. It is much nicer than it was when we lived here with April but sometimes at night I hear Jack crying.

My stepmother has been gone for two years now and I don't miss her a bit. I don't even miss my father any more and I have a real friend now. Her name is Gloria.

We tell each other everything, Gloria and me, but I haven't told her about the dark-eyed boy. He is a different sort of friend and I am not sure Gloria would understand. She might even laugh.

This is my best summer ever because it is really hot, but it is not so good for Percy Hammer who helps my grandfather on the farm. The pond in the farmyard has dried up and Percy has to fill the trough from buckets every day for the cows to drink.

One day when Gloria and I are hiding from Jack in the dried-up pond we find two metal brooches, which is not at all what we were expecting to find, especially as the brooches are exactly the same.

We dig them out of the dried mud with sticks and wash them in the trough. The brooches are big and round with twisty creatures carved on the front and Gloria is really excited.

'Dragons!' she cries. 'Dragons are magic.'

Jack comes to see what all the noise is about and we show him the brooches.

'They're snakes, and snakes are unlucky,' says Jack, who does not believe in magic. 'That means something really bad is going to happen.'

We are still looking at the brooches when a big black car drives into the yard and pulls up outside the farmhouse door. A man and woman get out and I know who it is straight away. It is our father, and he has brought the whore with him.

'It's daddy!' shouts Jack, jumping up. 'I bet he's come to give back all those half crowns he borrowed.'

Jack and I often think of how many half crowns my father borrowed from my grandmother and how rich she would be now if all that money hadn't gone on Senior Service cigarettes.

Across the yard my grandmother opens the door and my father and Pearl go into the house, and the door closes behind them. We tiptoe across the yard and crouch under the open window to hear what they are saying, which is easy because my grandfather is sitting right by the window, and he sounds really angry.

'The children have a good home with May. April's not a fit mother and you can't provide for them. Why not leave Jack where he is?'

'My financial circumstances have changed,' my father says. 'It's time for Jack to go away to school. Boarding school is important for a boy.'

♀

When the black car drives away, Jack is inside it. He presses his face against the back window and sticks his tongue out at us until the car is out of sight.

'You won't leave me, will you?' says May.

She throws her red arms around my neck and tries to kiss me.

'I know you're not a Siward,' she says. 'But I've always treated you like one of our own.'

I hope May's not going to cry because I really hate it when grown-ups cry.

'Not likely,' I tell her. 'They can stuff their bloody boarding school.'

I run down to the farmhouse and as soon as my grandmother goes to feed the hens I rush upstairs to the Ophelia Box to tell the dark-eyed boy what has happened.

'They've got him,' I say, panting because I am out of breath. 'They've taken our Jack.'

The dark-eyed boy seems to understand about Jack being sent away because he looks very sad when I tell him. He knows how I feel and I think he knows how Jack feels too.

My grandfather is extra nice to me after Jack goes and gives me sixpence for helping in the dairy.

'You're a good girl,' he says. 'It's a pity it's your brother who's the Siward and not you.'

I thank him very much for the sixpence because my grandfather never gave me a sixpence before, ever.

'I'm going to do something for you,' he says. 'It's a secret between ourselves.'

I nod, thinking he is going to give me another sixpence.

'I'm going to look after you, Ophelia. I want you to be all right if anything happens to me.'

Percy is really nice too. He even takes me mole trapping in the top field where I am not usually allowed to go.

'How's the writing going?' he says.

When I grow up I am going to be a famous writer. This is a secret but I have told Percy. He thinks it is a good idea and he has promised not to tell May and my grandmother because they say books are only good for gathering dust.

May reads magazines though because there are piles of them under her bed and they are covered in dust.

'Not very well, actually. I'm stuck.'

'I'm sorry to hear that. What are you writing?'

'A book, of course.'

I am surprised at Percy for not knowing this but then I am probably the only real writer he knows.

'What's the book about?'

'It's about a beautiful lady who wears evening gowns, even in the mornings.'

'What does she do, this beautiful lady?'

'She's an actress.'

'And what does this beautiful lady look like?'

'She's got auburn hair and green eyes.'

'She sounds smashing,' says Percy. 'What's her name?'

'Pamela.'

I have changed Maisie's name to Pamela in the book, just in case April comes back one day and finds out what I am writing. I don't think she will come back though, not now, not after two whole years. No-one knows where she is or what has happened to her.

♀

When Jack comes home for the school holiday everything is different. My brother talks differently and he uses words I have never heard of. He calls April and my father Mater and Pater, and he calls me Sis. When Percy teases Jack about his posh new accent Jack calls Percy a cad and Percy laughs at him.

Jack has a friend called Thompson who lives on an island called Jersey, and another friend called Pollinger Minor who lives in a place called the Home Counties. He calls all his friends by their surnames and I ask him why, but he doesn't know. At school he is not Jack, he is not even Jack Gunn. He is just Gunn.

My brother only stays in Grymewyck for a few days and then he goes to London to spend the rest of the holiday with our father and Pearl Bonnet. Before he goes Jack tells May he would quite like to see his mother, but May doesn't know where April is. None of us know.

♀

'My mother says you haven't got a mother,' says Gloria. 'My mother says you're an orphan.'

'I have so got a mother. My mother's called Maisie.'

'Well I've never seen her.'

'That's because she's a famous actress. Most of the time she's in Hollywood.'

'Little fibber,' says Gloria. 'You're an orphan. My mother says so.'

Gloria and I are sitting on Our Rock, which is a big flat stone on the edge of the stream above the village. It is where we come when Gloria wants to talk about rude things.

'I've got a boyfriend,' says Gloria. 'I bet you haven't got a boyfriend.'

'I have so,' I tell her. 'My boyfriend lives in London and he's got a camera and he's going to be a doctor.'

'I bet he's never kissed you,' says Gloria. 'My boyfriend's kissed me.'

Gloria goes on about boys all the time these days. It gets on my nerves.

'When's your Jack coming home?'

Jack has been at boarding school for two years now and I have no idea when I will see him again. He spends some of his school holidays in Grymewyck but mostly he stays in London. I am not even sure if my brother thinks of Grymewyck as home any more.

'I don't know.'

'I think your Jack likes me.'

Gloria is always wanting to know about Jack.

'Have you ever seen Jack's thing?' she asks.

'What thing?'

'His willy, stupid. Have you ever seen Jack's willy?'

I hate it when Gloria talks like this, especially about Jack. He is my brother after all, even if he has only written one letter since he went back, and that was to ask May for ten shillings to buy tuck. Tuck is Jack's word for sweets.

I tell Gloria that Jack's willy is none of her business and she shrugs her shoulders and goes off to paddle in the stream. She wades in up to her knickers and I follow and stand on the edge with my toes in the water.

It feels revolting. I imagine myself being swept away and floating down through the village, stinking and bloated like a dead fish, so I step back quickly.

'What's the matter?' says Gloria. 'It's only water.'

'I don't want to drown.'

'Don't be so mardy. You can't drown in half an inch of water.'

Gloria and I like to watch the grammar school girls as they get off the school bus and we always laugh at their lace-up shoes. The girls from the sec mod school wear high heels and white ankle socks, and Gloria and I both want to be sec mod girls.

When I pass the eleven-plus exam and Gloria fails I go up to my room and cry.

'I don't have to go to the grammar school just because I've passed the eleven-plus,' I argue. 'Why can't I just go to the same school as Gloria?'

May says if I am not careful I will end up like Percy Hammer, not able to string two words together.

'The grammar school uniform is green,' I tell my grandmother. 'It will only bring bad luck.'

My grandmother worries about the unlucky green uniform and she worries about how much it will cost.

'After all, it's not as if Ophelia's a boy,' she says. 'If she wants to go with Gloria, why not let her?'

In the end it is Percy who convinces me.

'We can't have that brother of yours knowing more than you, can we?' says Percy. 'You go to the grammar school and show them what you're made of.'

As things turn out I see even less of Jack after I go to the grammar school. When he does come back to Grymewyck he gets bored and goes out with the village boys. Last time he drank a bottle of cider, which upset May who had to mop up Jack's sick from the porch.

'What can I do?' she says, wringing out the cloth. 'I'm not his mother, after all.'

Gloria has a net petticoat that has to be washed in sugar

and water to keep it stiff. Her mother ordered it from her catalogue, which is where she and Gloria get all their clothes.

'What does she need something like that for in Grymewyck?' says May, when I tell her about the petticoat. 'That woman needs her head examining.'

May does not approve of Gloria's parents but she asks a lot of questions about them. She wants to know if Gloria's mother cooks proper meals and what sort of things they watch on their new television set.

I tell May that Gloria's bedroom has black wallpaper with rock and roll dancers and guitars and musical notes all over it, and that Gloria has a Cindy doll and a pink transistor wireless.

'I never heard the likes,' says May.

A week before I go to the grammar school Gloria's mother offers to bleach my hair but she says I have to ask May first. May says certainly not and she has never heard the likes.

'May says that'll be fine,' I tell Gloria's mother. 'She says to say it's very kind of you.'

Gloria's mother bleaches my hair, which goes bright yellow.

'You look a million dollars,' says Gloria's mother, pleased. 'Shall I do your nails too? What about California pink?'

When my grandmother sees my hair she acts as if someone had just died, and after that she won't even look at me.

'How dare that common woman do such a thing when I expressly forbade it,' says May, her eyes red with crying. 'She's done it deliberately because you got into the grammar school and Gloria didn't.'

'Why should she have to ask you? You're not my mother.'

'I'm still responsible for you. And I don't like to see you looking like a little trollop.'

May cries every time she sees me but I don't think my hair is that bad. Actually, I quite like it.

'What's a trollop?' I ask Percy when no one else will talk to me.

'A woman who's no better than she ought to be,' says Percy.

'What does common mean?'

'Common means there's a lot of them.'

May makes me go with her to Gloria's house and she tells Gloria's mother I am not allowed to go there any more. I cry all the way home.

'You don't want me to have any friends,' I sob. 'I hate you.'

'I've nothing against Gloria's parents,' says May. 'They're just not our sort of people.'

'What are our sort of people then?'

'You are too young to understand.'

But the dark-eyed boy understands when I tell him what has happened. I can tell that by the way he looks at me, and I can tell that he is not our sort of people either.

I can't tell if he likes my yellow hair though. Probably he does.

Asa Cohen (MBCHB, DPM)

'I found your Ophelia,' says Uncle Ben. 'Her mother is a farmer's daughter from the village. I forgot to mention it earlier.'

It must be ten years since I asked my uncle about Ophelia but he is continuing the conversation as if it had taken place ten minutes ago.

My uncle's thoughts wander these days, and more often than not the people he talks about are dead, so I am amazed he remembers the conversation we once had about Ophelia.

'Maisie.' I remind him. 'Her mother's name was Maisie.'

He purses his lips.

'I don't think so. I never heard of anyone called Maisie.'

'It doesn't matter. Ophelia doesn't live in Grymewyck any more. She went to live in London when she was a child.'

'Most of them do,' sighs my uncle.

Uncle Ben gets confused these days and complains of feeling isolated in his new council bungalow, which is on a modern estate in the village of Thinge, a few miles outside Grymewyck. The people he knew in Grymewyck never visit him here.

'They've forgotten old Ben Brown,' he says. 'Just like people forgot Ephraim Braun.'

My uncle lives with his books and his past, but he is proud of me. At any rate he is proud of me when he remembers what it is I do. Psychiatry, he feels, is a Jewish tradition.

'It used to be, uncle,' I tell him. 'Things have moved on.'

'But we started it,' he says. 'Psychiatry began in Vienna.'

He likes to speak German with me but is puzzled by my English accent, and he talks about his childhood as if it was my childhood too.

'What are you doing with yourself these days?' he asks again.

I tell him again what I am doing. Being an intern in a large mental hospital for the past three years has taught me patience.

'I'm off to America,' I say. 'Just for a year. I'll be leaving in a few weeks. Until then I'm going to stay with my brother Charlie in London.'

'A man in your position should have a house of his own. You shouldn't be staying with other people.'

'I told you, uncle. My house is let.'

'How's the family?' he asks.

It is my family in Vienna he is asking about, not the Manners family. My uncle has forgotten his old school friend is dead.

♂

'Did you say you were going to America?' asks my uncle, some hours after I have told him that is what I am doing.

'New York.'

'You'll find lots of Jews in New York,' he says. 'Is that why you're going?'

'In a way.'

Uncle Ben nods happily.

'What is it you'll be doing there?'

'I'm a psychiatrist, uncle.'

'I know that, boy. I'm not senile. I asked what it is you'll be doing.'

'It's a research project. I'll be looking at the long term psychological effects of trauma.'

Uncle Ben looks doubtful and I try to explain.

'For example, the sole survivor of a car crash might suffer life-long guilt because he or she is alive and the other passengers are dead. That would be an example of a long term effect following trauma.'

I avoid mentioning the Holocaust because I know very little of my uncle's history and he never talks about his own family, but that is exactly what my job will be. I am to take part in a new project and I will be working with first and second generation Holocaust survivors.

Uncle Ben picks up his magazine and I know I have lost him, or perhaps he prefers not to hear. Or perhaps it is just that he doesn't like being patronised by me.

♂

It had been Sue's idea I should stay with Charlie while I am in London, although I have seen little of my Finchley brother during the past ten years and nothing at all of April. They are still together, though God alone knows how he has put up with her for all these years.

The last time I saw April she was haemorrhaging all over Charlie's sitting room and I am not looking forward to meeting her again.

'I'd rather stay with you, Sue?'

'I need you to talk to Charlie. I want to know what's happening at Courtfield Mansions.'

Sue and I talk on the telephone every week. It is one of her little rules.

'Why can't you talk to him yourself?'

'I don't see much of Charlie these days and when I do see him he's drunk.'

'What do you expect me to do?'

'For Christ's sake, Asa. You're the psychiatrist, not me.'

'I won't spy on my own brother.'

'Charlie's business is going downhill. Everybody says so.'

'I'm a psychiatrist, not a businessman.'

'That woman has cut him off from all his friends, including me. She won't even meet me.'

Sue means April, of course.

♂

En route from my uncle's house to the A1 I see the signpost to Grymewyck village. I am driving unusually slowly so perhaps I am looking for it.

Who am I kidding? Of course I am looking for it, and I am most certainly in no hurry to get to London and April Siward.

Leaving my car in the Stag's Head car park I walk up the lane to The Barn, which now has a mature garden and is thickly covered with roses and climbing hydrangeas. With the green hills behind and the blue sky above, the scene of my childhood nightmare is as pretty and innocent as an illustration from a children's book of fairy tales and I find myself smiling

Still smiling I open the wooden gate and walk up the garden path. I am remembering the little evacuee who was once made to eat sacred pig but is now so tall he has to stoop to get through the arched gateway.

I press my face to the porch glass and see trays of onions and apples, and a rack of boots and shoes, but the room beyond is in darkness.

♂

Returning to the Stag's Head I ask the landlord if he remembers a little girl called Ophelia who lived in Grymewyck many years ago. The landlord grunts and jerks his thumb towards a man standing a few feet away.

The man stares at me over his beer for a few seconds but says nothing. He is wearing muddy overalls and hob-nailed boots, and his stack of dusty grey-blond hair reminds me of hay.

'You knew Ophelia?' I ask.

The man wipes the foam from his mouth with the back of his hand and carries his drink to the other side of the room where he sits down with his back to me.

In Grymewyck I am still a nobody. Angry with the man, and angry with myself for being angry, I put my untouched beer down on the bar and leave.

Outside the Stags Head a school bus pulls up so close to the pub door I have to step back inside to let the children off. The last passenger to get off is a tall girl in her late teens with thick auburn hair swept back from her face and tucked into a green school beret.

I would recognise that hair anywhere. I still have some of it at home.

♂

We are having breakfast when April looks up from her magazine and tells Charlie she is thinking of having the flat redecorated.

'Does it need it?' asks Charlie, surprised. 'It doesn't seem long since it was done.'

'I have a flair for these things.'

'If it will make you happy, then of course we must have the flat redecorated.'

There is no doubting April's happiness. April is so happy she is crying and laughing at the same time. April can find no words to express how happy she is.

'Calm down,' laughs Charlie. 'You're making me dizzy.'

April hires an interior designer called Chiaroscuro, a greasy little man with a fake Mediterranean accent, who arrives each morning in time for breakfast and stays all day.

'Your wife 'as a unique talent,' he tells Charlie. 'She 'as an instinct for colour. Your wife is an artist.'

Chiaroscuro works his way through Charlie's drinks cupboard and helps himself to food from Charlie's fridge. He steals cash from Charlie's desk and one day I catch him at it and I tell Charlie.

'I'm not sure I can do much about it,' says Charlie.

'You can get rid of him, surely?'

'But April's so happy at the moment.'

'April doesn't need Chiaroscuro,' I tell him. 'It won't make a scrap of difference to April whether Chiaroscuro is here or not.'

I am right. April Siward is in a world of her own and when Charlie sacks Chiaroscuro she doesn't even notice that he has gone.

Her night time walks continue as before. Sleeping in my old room I hear the front door click open and shut as April lets herself in and out at all hours of the night. I turn over and go back to sleep, and presumably Charlie now does the same.

♂

The time has come to give Sue my promised report on life at Courtfield Mansions. We arrange to meet in the pub we used to go years ago when I was at medical school and Sue worked for a secretarial agency. She still works there, but now Sue runs the agency from a posh office in Charing Cross Road.

'Chiaroscuro indeed!' says Sue, when I tell her about the decorating project. 'Charlie must be off his head.'

'Chiaroscuro is not the problem, and neither is Charlie. The real problem is April.'

'Well I know *that*.'

'Sue, suppose I told you April can't help herself?'

'You mean she can't help being a bitch?'

'It's possible April is sick.'

'So she's a sick bitch. Do you want another drink?'

'I haven't finished this one. In fact, I haven't started it.'

Sue gets up and returns with a second glass of wine, and it is not long before she wants to know about Charlie.

'Do you want the truth?' I ask.

'I want the truth.'

'I think Charlie's happy.'

Which is more than I can say for Sue, who makes a second trip to the bar and this time returns with a bottle and corkscrew.

'Do you want to get me drunk?'

'I want to get a little drunk myself,' she says.

'You're drinking too quickly. It's bad for the liver.'

'Asa, I want to meet her.'

'No you don't. Meeting April will only make you more unhappy.'

A wasp lands in Sue's wine and she chases it around the inside of the glass with a toothpick. She is more than a little drunk already.

'Round you go, waspy,' says Sue. 'Round and round.'

'*Folie circulaire*,' I say.

I must be a little drunk myself.

'Speak English, Asa.'

'Circular insanity.'

'You're talking about April,' says Sue, alert in spite of the wine. 'Is that what's wrong with her?'

'Nowadays we call it something different. Should I tell Charlie or should I not? That is the problem.'

'What's the cause of this circular thing she's got?'

'Bile.'

'Nonsense, Asa. This is the twentieth century. We aren't living in the Dark Ages.'

'The ancient Greeks thought black bile caused melancholia and yellow bile brought on mania.'

Sue thinks about this.

'Black and yellow, like the wasp. Is it serious, this circular thing?'

'It's not always recognised. Charlie prefers to think April has a mercurial personality.'

Sue fishes the now dead wasp from her wine and lays it to rest on the edge of the ashtray.

There are rarely fewer than half a dozen people in Charlie's flat at any one time, not counting Charlie, April and myself. Most of them are waiting for April's approval of colours and fabrics and trying in vain to capture her attention even for a few seconds as she flits from room to room like an insect unable to settle. Others are simply there to drink

Charlie's wine.

April herself is exhausted but she is also exhilarated. One night I find her dancing round the newly decorated sitting room draped only in a curtain sample and after that I dare to ask Charlie if he is at all worried about April. Charlie is not.

When the work on the flat is almost complete my brother is presented with a bill so colossal he has to ask his bank for a temporary overdraft.

'We could have bought a new flat for the same price,' he tells April.

'But we don't have to, do we? Not now this one is so beautiful.'

♂

My stay at Courtfield Mansions is coming to an end and I am not sorry. Meanwhile, Sue has got four tickets for the opening night of Hamlet at the Old Vic. She tells Charlie this is a farewell treat before I leave, but I know differently. Sue is determined to meet April.

The excitement of the renovations over, April has gone back to her magazines. She flips the pages and doesn't look up.

'You know I don't like the theatre.'

Little as I relish the idea of April's company for a whole evening, I know Sue will be disappointed not to meet her.

'The royal family will be there,' I tell her.

The magazine falls to the floor.

'The royal family. Will they really?'

'They wouldn't miss Hamlet for the world.'

♂

I find Sue flattened against the wall in the crowded theatre bar holding her glass above her head to avoid spilling her drink. I rescue the glass and kiss her cheek.

'At it again, I see. You must have paid for these tickets with blood.'

'I'm a bit nervous, actually.'

'First nights are always tense.'

'You know what I mean. How's Charlie?'

'Close to bankruptcy, I imagine. The flat's cost a fortune.'

'Can't you talk sense into him?'

'Charlie doesn't listen to me.'

'I can't wait to see April.'

'You don't have to. They've just come in. That's her on the stairs.'

Charlie comes down the steps followed by April, who is wearing a white fur stole and long white gloves. She sees us and waves. The wave is regal and from the wrist, and when April smiles Sue drops her glass.

'Sue?'

'I'm so sorry,' she says. 'For a moment I thought it was the queen.'

♂

I ring Sue the next morning, closing the door so as not to be overheard by Charlie and April, who are still in bed.

'What did you think?'

'A memorable performance,' says Sue.

'I meant April, not Hamlet.'

'So did I.'

'Is she what you expected?'

'Whatever can Charlie be thinking of?'

'It's your own fault. If you two hadn't got divorced this would never have happened.'

'I don't think she'd even heard of Hamlet.'

'April wanted to meet the royal family. She thinks she's related. Sue, are you still there?'

I know what's coming next.

'Asa, why do you have to take this job in America?'

'You know why.'

'You're going to lay a ghost, I know, but I wish New York wasn't quite so far away.'

♂

The little squashed face in the red knitted hat is only a memory now. I couldn't bring it back even if I wanted to, which I most definitely do not. Anna was a jealous ghost and I know now that she was a ghost of my own creation.

I was blaming myself for my sister's death, only I was too young to understand that at the time. I felt guilty because I was alive, whereas I was sure Anna was dead.

Only when I was in my final year at medical school did I finally open the brown paper package. Mr Manners had never stopped looking for my sister, had never given up hope, and he had been right. He had been very close to finding Anna when he died, but by the time I opened the package it was five years too late for me to thank him.

Now I want to find my sister. Not the child ghost who haunted my childhood, but the real Anna. I need to find my sister because she won't leave me alone until I do.

Gloria In Trouble

♀

My brother Jack says Grymewyck is boring, and I am beginning to agree with him.

'I don't know how you stick it, being here all the time,' he says. 'Why don't you come to London and stay at Pearl's for a while?'

'When I've finished my exams, then I'll come to London.'

'Boring,' says Jack. 'I'm going to leave school as soon as I'm sixteen and then I'm going to make a load of money. Who needs exams?'

'I do. At least I need my A-levels.'

I have applied to London University to study English because my teacher says this is the best way to become a writer. She says I have a good chance of being accepted, but I don't tell Jack this because he would just laugh.

Nor do I tell him I don't want to live with my father and

Pearl Bonnet. When I go to London I intend to have a room of my own where I can write all day and all night if I feel like it, with nobody to bother me.

Grymewyck is even more boring since Percy met that man in the pub. Foreign-looking, Percy says he was, and he was asking about me.

I spotted the man as I was getting off the school bus and I think he would have spoken to me if Percy hadn't come and pushed him aside. Now I will never know who he was.

They have been watching me like hawks ever since then, and my grandmother always sends Percy to meet me off the school bus.

Gloria is having fun though. She has a boyfriend with a motorbike and she is the talk of Grymewyck, though that doesn't take much.

'That Gloria's a fast one,' says May. 'Your friend's going to get herself into trouble one of these days, you mark my words.'

'She's not really my friend, not any more.'

It is true. I hardly see Gloria now, not to speak to anyway. We sort of drifted apart after I went to the grammar school, and now she works in a coffee bar in town so I see her even less. Once she invited me in for a coffee but I felt out of place in my school uniform and never went again.

Then, out of the blue, Gloria comes up to The Barn and asks if I want to go for a walk. Gloria hates walking, she always has. I look at her tight sail-cloth skirt and high-heeled sandals and laugh.

'Did you have anywhere in mind?'

'Our Rock,' she says, and off we go.

Our Rock is where we used to go when we had secrets to tell each other, so I know this is important. When we get to Our Rock we sit down side by side and Gloria tells me she is pregnant.

'Don't look so gone out,' she says. 'These things happen.'

'Since when?'

'Since when I did it with the father, idiot.'

'Are you going to have an abortion?'

I know all about abortions from the girls at school.

'I don't want an abortion.'

'Adoption?'

'I'm going to keep the baby,' she says. 'What do you think of that?'

I can think of nothing worse than having a baby. It sounds terrifying. And what if Gloria turns out to be the sort of mother April was? That poor little baby.

'Who's the father?' I ask.

'The father's got nothing to do with it. I'm going to do this on my own.'

I think of the boy with the motor bike and the other boys who hang around the coffee bar where Gloria works and I can't imagine any of them as fathers.

'Perhaps that's wise,' I say, trying to sound wise myself. 'Have you told your parents?'

'Have you told your parents?' she mimics. 'Get lost, Ophelia. If you breathe one word about this to my parents or anyone else I will never speak to you again.'

♀

Gloria has gone missing and her mother is frantic. She comes to The Barn looking for her daughter and sits at the kitchen table smoking one cigarette after another. May opens the window and pours Gloria's mother a tumbler full of the Christmas sherry.

When Gloria's mother has gone May looks at me closely.

'I don't pretend to like the woman but I can't help feeling

sorry for her. Do you know anything about this, Ophelia?'

'I have no idea where Gloria is.'

'That's not what I asked,' says May, pushing the cork firmly back in the sherry bottle.

♀

The dark-eyed boy is much younger than me now, but I still talk to him from time to time because he still likes to know what I am up to.

'Gloria's run away,' I tell him. 'It's just you and me now.'

Probably the dark-eyed boy doesn't even know the facts of life but he listens anyway. Or perhaps he knows more than he lets on because he looks very wise when I tell him Gloria is going to have a baby.

'There's something else,' I say. 'I'm going away too, so I won't be seeing you for a while. I'm going to London next week because I've got a summer job, and after that I'll be going to the university to study English Literature.'

I don't need to tell him I am going to look for Maisie while I am there. He knows that already.

♀

Thwe wiick brown fopc jjumpps oveer th elaz dog. Every girl should learn to type. This was last thing my English teacher told me before I left Grymewyck and I am taking her advice.

The wuick nrown gox jumps over the laxy dog.

My first job is really boring, but it is only for eight weeks until the university term starts and at least I have plenty of time to practice my typing.

The quick brown fox jumps over the lazy dog. Roll on September.

Because I work during the week I can only look for Maisie in the evenings and at weekends, and because I have no idea where to look I look everywhere. I walk the streets of London looking for a woman in an evening dress with auburn hair and green eyes.

'Don't you ever get hungry?' says my room mate in the hostel where I am living. 'I never see you in the dining room.'

'I don't have time to eat. I'm looking for my mother.'

I watch other people eating though, in the pubs and restaurants where I go in search of Maisie. One night I find myself outside the snack bar where April used to work, only it is no longer a snack bar. It is now a smart restaurant called L'Elégance Parisienne.

It is getting late and I am hungry. I press my nose against the plate glass window and peer inside. The interior of the restaurant is so dark I wouldn't know whether Maisie was in there or not, but I have an urge to go in anyway. Tonight I will have my supper in L'Elégance Parisienne.

This is the first time I have ever been in a restaurant on my own and I am nervous, but at least in the dark the waitress can't see me blushing. I order omelette and salad and sit staring at a black painted wall until it arrives.

Across the road is the Earls Court underground station where once upon a time I used to wait for Maisie and the Frog Man, and now I have another idea. I will write a letter to the Frog Man.

Brooklyn,
New York

If Mr Manners' research is correct my sister came to America in 1939 at the beginning of the war, possibly on a Dutch passenger ship called the Alida.

I make enquiries and discover the Dutch shipping line no longer exists and neither does the Alida because four years into the war and four hundred miles into the Atlantic she was torpedoed and sunk by a German U-boat.

In the 1950's, the owners of the ill-fated Alida went bankrupt and the company changed hands several times before being sold to an American holiday cruise company called Lazy Leisure Cruises.

It is in the storage basement of Lazy Leisure Cruises on Manhattan's Lower East Side that I track down a rusty cabinet containing all that remains of the Alida.

I dig out details of the 1939 Rotterdam-New York crossings and thumb my way through the passenger lists, but Anna's name is not there.

And then, just as I am about to abandon the search, I find it. Dirty and crumpled at the bottom of a drawer is a cabin plan dated January 21st 1939 and my sister's name is on it.

Cohen, Anna. 7 Muhlenstrasse, 1010 Wien. Österreich.

Once upon a time this was my own address. I have it still on my identity card.

There are three other names with the same cabin number as my sister.

Klein, Lisl. Stein, Maria. Mendelssohn-Korn, Lieselotte.

I scribble the names of Anna's travelling companions in my diary and run up the stone steps, out of the chilly cellar and into the warm Manhattan sunshine.

My sister is here in America. Now all I have to do is find her.

♂

The letter I've just received is written on the back of a menu from L'Elégance Parisienne in the Earls Court Road and I think at first it must be from Charlie. But no, the letter is from Ophelia. It is addressed to the house in Finchley and has been redirected by Mrs Manners.

> We met a long time ago in Grymewyck when I was a little girl and you were collecting frogs. You wanted to be a doctor. I live in London now and I am still looking for my mother. She's called Maisie, but you probably don't remember. You have a sister. You see what a good memory I have! I'm feeling a bit low at the moment and I am looking at a black wall, so that doesn't help. Ophelia.

In ten minutes time I have an appointment at the local

Jewish community centre, and after that I am going to register at a missing persons agency where I will add my sister's name to a long, long list.

Before I go out I kiss the menu card from L'Elégance Parisienne in the Earls Court Road and prop it against my alarm clock where it will be the first thing I see when I wake up tomorrow morning.

♂

My search for Anna takes me to Moyses Opera, an agency run from a one-bedroom apartment in Brooklyn where a Russian immigrant has been tracing missing Jews since the end of the war. I try not to be excited as I run up the three flights of stairs, but even so I stumble on the top step in my haste to meet the man who has told me on the telephone that he will find my missing sister.

The door is opened by a solemn girl in school uniform who takes me into a sitting room papered with photographs of lost friends and relatives. The people in the photographs look like ghosts, and their faded sepia faces belong to another age and another country.

It is a few minutes before I notice the man sitting behind a table piled high with newspapers and files.

He places the tips of his fingers together and listens as I remind him why I am there. The man asks for my sister's name and writes it down, and then he contemplates what he has written.

'Anna,' he says at length. 'Such a beautiful name. The name means 'favour' or 'grace'. Does your sister have those virtues?'

'I haven't seen her for a quarter of a century. I wouldn't know.'

'An-na,' he says again, separating the two syllables. 'In

Hebrew it is also Hannah or Channa. But you say your sister is Anna, and you are sure about this?'

'My sister is called Anna.'

The man stares at Anna's name and strokes the paper it is written on. He must be thinking of another Anna, Hannah or Channa because he seems to have forgotten I am in the room.

'Anna,' I say again. 'My sister's name is Anna Cohen.'

The man looks up and smiles, a sweet distant smile that is focussed not on me but on the door behind me as the solemn schoolgirl comes in with coffee. She puts the cups down on the desk and says something to her father in Russian, and then she leaves the room and closes the door behind her.

'That is my daughter Miriam,' he says softly. 'Miriam, the sister of Moses.'

'My sister's name is Anna Cohen and she came to America in 1939.'

'Cohen,' repeats the man. 'Cohen the priest.'

I know of course that my Hebrew name means priest, just as I know Cohen is the most common Jewish surname in the world. Unfortunately for me.

'Is there any hope at all of finding her?'

'Cohen. Cahn. Kaplan. It is the same name, you know. In Germany you would be Kaplan. In Russia we might address you as Kahan or Kahana.'

The man lifts his head and his eyes meet mine. I recognise the look in those eyes because I have seen it many times before and when I bang my fist on the table, spilling both our coffees, the man does not even blink.

On the landing outside I meet Miriam.

'Why do you let him to do it? Has he found any of those people?'

The girl shakes her head.

'I'm very sorry,' she says. 'My father is not a well man.'

On the way home I stop at a kiosk and buy a post card of the Statue of Liberty. I address it to Ophelia at The Barn, sign it with a drawing of a frog and post it without a message because I can think of nothing cheerful to say.

I am looking at a black wall myself.

♂

The veteran I am treating stares into space looking at something I cannot see and I know I have lost him, and he has certainly lost me. He sits on the edge of his seat and waits for our session to be over. The man is in another place and I can find no way to reach him.

Anna's name expands and creeps across the page like bindweed, strangling the words I have written and making my notes unreadable. My next patient comes in, a woman who has been rich and was once famous. She survived the Holocaust but her husband and baby did not. Now the woman must wash her hands from morning to night to cleanse herself of the guilt.

The woman re-married, had another family and lived happily in New York for more than twenty years, but now her ghosts have come back to haunt her. It is the dead husband and the dead baby who live with her now.

'Why me?' she wants to know.

She talks and answers my questions, but all the time she is shaking the imagined dirt from her hands. When the woman leaves I sit back in my chair and listen. As soon as I hear the sound of a tap being turned on in the adjoining cloakroom I get up to go.

My own obsessive behaviour is giving me cause for concern.

♂

My advertisement brings replies from Austrian Jews

around the world, all of them desperate for news of their own families. I read the letters with a detachment that shocks me and know I am not a Jew looking for a lost ancestry. I am simply a young man who wants to find his sister.

It seems America is full of Cohens, and a good many of these have given names beginning with A. Thumbing through the library telephone directories I wonder where to begin. I spend my free time telephoning or visiting the surprising number of American women who happen to be called Cohen or Anna and who want to talk about it.

The Anna Cohen who writes from a northern suburb of Philadelphia was brought up in a children's home and remembers nothing of her childhood apart from a parrot called Polly. She is the right age, but I have no recollection of the parrot.

I am about to reject Anna from Philadelphia when I am struck by the woman's handwriting, which is remarkably similar to my own.

I arrive at Anna Cohen's house as she gets home from work. She is so pretty I can only stand and stare, and then I bang my forehead against her front door until it hurts because Anna Cohen is black.

She invites me in and makes coffee.

'Why?' I ask.

'I guess I wanted someone to want me as much as you wanted your sister.'

'There was no parrot?'

'I'm so sorry.'

'What's your real name?'

She looks hurt.

'I wouldn't lie about that.'

I spend the rest of the evening with my sister's namesake and that night we have sex on a water bed in a room decorated with pink hearts. The wrong Anna Cohen sleeps soundly with her head on my chest and her lovely arms wrapped around my neck. I count the stencilled hearts on her bedroom ceiling and wonder what the hell I am doing there.

♂

My year is up. I take off my white coat for the last time and look at my watch. I have heard from another Anna Cohen and I want to meet her before I return to London. Meanwhile, I have just enough time for a final visit to the Museum of Modern Art.

Art is my solace, and there is plenty of art in New York. I have failed to find my sister but in the last two years I have seen more painting and sculpture than I knew existed.

I will not miss New York, but I will miss its art.

I lie back in my seat and close my eyes. When I open them again a colourless London is rushing up to greet me. Sue, who meets me at the airport, tells me I look tired and have lost weight.

'It's good to see you, little sister-in-law.'

'Well? Are you going to tell me or not?'

'I might,' I say. 'If I had any idea what it is you're talking about.'

'The woman who answered your phone, of course. Who was she?'

'Someone I met.'

'What was she doing in your room?'

'Sleeping,' I tell her. 'And so was I. It was three o'clock in the morning. You forgot the time difference again.'

Sue is unrepentant.

'Where did you meet her?'

'In a bar.'

'What does she look like?'

I do my best to remember.

'About your height, I think. Curly hair. Plumpish. She laughs a lot.'

Sue sighs her approval.

'How long have you known her?'

I look at my watch.

'About twenty four hours.'

'Oh, Asa,' cries Sue, her voice full of disappointment. 'What terrible timing. What's her name?'

'Anna,' I reply. 'Anna Cohen.'

Jenny Rodwell

VIKINGS

Alas, Poor Yorick

My room mate at the hostel goes to bed early and I always try to slip in quietly so as not to disturb her but one night she is awake anyway.

'When did you last see your mother?' she asks.

'She went away when I was born.'

'Why?'

'She was an actress.'

'Then look in the theatres,' advises my room mate. 'That's what I'd do.'

♀

Leicester Square. London's theatre land. It seems a likely place to find an actress and my search starts with the woman selling newspapers outside the station.

She tells me about a young man who lost his wife here in a theatre queue forty years ago and still comes to Leicester Square every evening looking for her. The man is famous for it now and he has been in the newspapers.

'Will he ever find her?'

'He wouldn't recognise her if he did. The poor fellow's lost his mind now as well as his wife.'

I see him outside the first theatre I go to. The man is old with long white hair and he walks with a stick. He peers into the face of every woman in the queue and then he hobbles away shaking his head.

As I watch him disappear into the crowd I know I am not going to find Maisie in Leicester Square. It probably wasn't a very sensible idea in the first place.

♀

My office is a windowless cubby hole in the basement of the West London Chronicle and it is my job to type out handwritten letters and articles sent in by the readers. I am supposed to correct their spelling mistakes too but I don't always notice them. Roll on September.

It is Friday afternoon and I have run out of letters to type, when the editor sends for me.

'We don't pay you to do nothing, sweetie,' he says. 'Here's a little job for you.'

The editor scribbles something on a piece of paper and hands it to me.

3pm. Viking remains. TV interview. Technical college.

'You want to be a writer,' he says. 'Now's your chance.'

'What do I do?'

'They're interviewing a dead Viking,' he says. 'Go and see what he's got to say for himself.'

It is my big break.

I get on the wrong bus, and then I get on another wrong bus and by the time I get to the college the television interview is over. A van from London Rediffusion is leaving as I walk through the gates and, in front of the college, groups of people are walking away from a cordoned-off hole in the ground.

Standing in the hole is the most beautiful man I have ever seen. He is so breathtakingly beautiful that I hide behind a rhododendron bush until everyone has gone and then I go to have a closer look.

'In her green eyes did disillusion shine,' says the man. 'O haste the day when I will make her mine.'

He has curly blond hair and bright blue eyes, not at all like someone who digs up dead Vikings. The man looks more like a Viking himself.

'Did you just make that up?'

'Specially for you,' he says.

'Where are the Viking remains?'

The man holds his finger to his lips.

'Don't tell a soul, but they're in a laboratory being tested for authenticity.'

'I'm from the local paper. I'll have to wait for the laboratory results before I can write my story because I can only write what's true.'

The man smiles an angelic smile.

'I will attempt to corrupt you over a cup of coffee. Help me out of here.'

He gives me his hand and I pull him out of the hole, and then he takes me by the arm and together we go in search of a café.

As the man drinks his coffee he stares so hard at my hair I begin to feel self-conscious.

'O may I ne'er find grace, if one of her soft ringlets I

displace.'

'You didn't make that up,' I say. 'I've heard it before.'

'You look as if you'd just stepped out of a Pre-Raphaelite painting. Another doughnut?'

I tell him I have to get back to the office although I would much rather not because the editor will be furious that I have missed the television interview.

In spite of the beautiful man I feel suddenly miserable. I have been in London for weeks now and not only have I failed to find Maisie, but it seems likely I will lose my job as well.

'No, thank you,' I say. 'I don't want another doughnut.'

What I really want is to go to Grymewyck. Daniel Brandon's blond hair and blue eyes have reminded me of home.

'You can still write your story,' he says. 'Ply me with informed questions about my Viking.'

But instead of asking about the Viking I tell Daniel Brandon about Grymewyck, and how much I would like to see it again.

'Grymewyck?' he says. 'That sounds like a Viking name.'

'My stepmother would like to think so.'

He stands up and hands me my coat.

'I'll take you to your Grymewyck,' he says. 'What are we waiting for?'

'I can't just go. I'll get the sack.'

'Not if I ring your editor and tell him you've been taken ill. I'll tell him you fainted at the sight of a dead Viking.'

'I never even saw the dead Viking. He wasn't there.'

'Your editor is not to know that.'

♀

Daniel Brandon stands on Our Rock, the breeze ruffling

his golden curls. He looks magnificent, like Lawrence of Arabia or Tommy Steele. His blue eyes gaze first at the stream below and then at the sky above, and then they gaze at me.

'What an idyllic place to raise a family,' he says.

'My childhood wasn't all that idyllic.'

'Mine was, and I want my children to have the same.'

'You want babies?'

'Of course. Don't you?'

I am too taken aback to explain that I am not the maternal type and that the whole notion of having babies puts the fear of God into me. In any case, my heart is beating so loudly I doubt that he would have heard anyway, so I just smile.

'Happy?' he asks

'You brought me back to Grymewyck. How can I ever thank you?'

Daniel smiles his angel smile.

'You could write a piece about the West London Viking and the promising young curator who discovered him. I'll give you all the details.'

♀

It is obvious straight away that May adores Daniel.

'What a nice young man,' she whispers as we are leaving. 'Bring him home again soon.'

She pulls a post card from her pinafore pocket.

'I almost forgot,' she says. 'This came for you a few days ago.'

It is a picture of the Statue of Liberty and it is from the Frog Man. On the back of the card there is a drawing of a sad-looking frog sitting all alone on a water lily leaf.

♀

My piece about the West London Viking is on the front page of the West London Chronicle next to a nice photograph of Daniel, provided by Daniel himself. This is the first time my name has appeared in print and I am over the moon.

> A human skeleton discovered in a college playing field by celebrated archaeologist Daniel Brandon has been positively identified as being that of a Viking soldier. The remains are almost certainly those of a warrior from the Viking army that sailed up the River Thames in 879AD.

The editor is pleased with me and pinches my cheek.

'Not just a pretty face,' he says. 'And I mean you, sweetie. Not him.'

Daniel is waiting for me outside the office when I finish work and he wants to buy me dinner, so he must be pleased with me too.

My happiness is short-lived because the following day the editor is waiting for me when I arrive at work and he no longer looks pleased.

'A word in your shell-like, sweetie. Come with me.'

I follow him into the newsroom and he points to the national newspapers of the day that are spread fan-like on his desk so that I can see the headlines.

Alas, Poor Yorick. The Norseman Who Never Was.

All the front pages have the same photograph of a stern-looking man in a white coat holding up a skull.

'Read it,' says the editor. 'Speak up so we can all hear.'

The room goes very quiet because everyone stops typing to listen.

'Read!'

I pick up the top newspaper and read:

> The recent discovery of a Viking warrior in West London has been exposed as a student hoax. The remains have been identified as a skeleton taken from a college biology department during the summer break. A metal shield buried alongside the skeleton is now thought to be a tray stolen from the college canteen.

'Always check your sources,' says Daniel when I tell him what has happened. 'That's the first rule of journalism.'

'But you were my source.'

'No one's infallible, not even me.'

'My career is finished.'

'Nonsense. You'll be off to university in a few weeks time.'

'And what about your career? It was your mistake, not mine.'

'There's a long tradition of fakery in archaeology. Remember the Piltdown Man?'

'And now the West London Viking?'

'It might even do my reputation some good.'

I remind Daniel that I have lost my job and that if I can't find another it is back to Grymewyck for me until September. I feel more than a little resentful about this but Daniel is busy pulling the cork from a bottle of Chianti.

'Come live with me and be my love,' he says.

'You're making fun of me.'

'I will make thee beds of roses and a thousand fragrant posies.'

Daniel's smile is the smile of an angel. An angel with blond hair and blue eyes is asking me to live with him. I return the smile and Daniel raises his glass.

'To the West London Viking,' he says. 'May he rest in peace.

♀

Daniel is a family man, not a poet. It took me a while to work this out. He doesn't want to make beds of roses from a thousand fragrant posies. What Daniel wants to make is babies.

That wasn't his line either, the one about roses and posies. It was written by Marlowe and it was one of the first poems I studied after I started at the university.

We have been together nearly a year now and my lack of a proper family bothers Daniel, who wants to meet my parents and brother. Daniel says this is the normal thing to do.

'That could be difficult,' I say. 'I don't know where they are.'

'Not one of them?'

'My father lives with his mistress but I'd rather not see him. I could probably find my way back to the house but I wouldn't want to go in with you.'

It annoys me, being under pressure to have a mother, father and brother just to keep Daniel happy. I don't miss any of them except Maisie, and I have never even seen her. In fact, I have pretty much given up hope of ever seeing her.

'I didn't lose my family on purpose.'

'My sweet orphan,' says Daniel. 'I didn't mean to make you cry. You can share my family. How would you like that?'

♀

Daniel's parents live in Heliopolis, a big house on the outskirts of London, and I am to think of Heliopolis as home.

'Call me mother!' cries Mrs Brandon. 'You are as a second daughter to me.'

Her first daughter, the real one, is married with a small child.

'I'm going to be the sister you never had,' she says, and I reply with my best sisterly smile.

The Brandon's real daughter tells me when she has her period. Poppy time. She also tells me whenever she and her husband have sex. Humpy humpy.

During our sisterly chats she leaves little pauses in the conversation so I can share my secrets with her, but she is always disappointed. Sometimes I make things up just to keep her happy.

'The Brandons are a close family,' says Daniel's mother. 'We are so close that I sometimes think we are telepathic.'

I have already noticed the Brandons talk to each other on the telephone every day and am alarmed to learn they communicate in other ways as well.

Mrs Brandon tells me that when Daniel broke his arm in a school football match she knew about the accident as it happened. She felt his pain in her own arm and when the call came from the hospital Mrs Brandon was waiting by the telephone with her hat and coat on.

After this I never tell Daniel's family what I am doing in case they follow me in their thoughts. Occasionally I say I am going somewhere else entirely, just to throw them off the scent.

♀

I am watching Daniel piggybacking his sister's child round the lawn and thinking how happy he looks when Mrs Brandon comes over with her arms full of the wallflowers she has cut for us to take home.

'My son's a natural with children,' she says. 'Daniel will make the most wonderful father in the world.'

I feel faint and sway a little. The scent from the wallflowers is heavy and overpowering, or perhaps it is the jogging movement of the piggybacking that is making me feel sick.

'You look pale, Ophelia.' says Daniel's mother. 'Let me take you inside out of the sun.'

Heliopolis is airy and light, the windows large and bright, and the scent of newly-mown grass and lavender wafts in through the French window. There is nothing about this house that could possibly make me ill, but in it I feel worse than I did in the garden.

I wake up to the clink of teacups from the terrace outside and the voice of Daniel's sister.

'Perhaps she's pregnant. Wouldn't that be lovely!'

To avoid overhearing anything else I get up and go out to join them, crumpled and sticky from sleeping in my clothes. Daniel's mother offers me cake but I am still bloated from the lunch and can't face the cake. I just want to be sick.

After this I usually vomit when we visit Daniel's parents. Daniel tells me this is because I am not used to normal family life yet and that I will get over it.

'I'd really like to be normal,' I tell him. 'But suppose I don't get over it? What then?'

'It's psychosomatic, darling. Just remember, we all love you very much.'

♀

Daniel's sister asks me to look after her little girl for an afternoon and tells me not to give her any ice cream. I take the child to our local park where she asks for ice cream.

'You're not allowed. Let's go and play on the slide.'

The little girl cries and stamps her foot so I buy her an ice cream and when she has finished it she wants another.

'You'll make yourself ill. Go and play on the slide.'

She climbs the steps to the top of the slide, leans over the handrail and falls head first onto the concrete below..

My scalp freezes. My toes freeze. I freeze all over. Please, please, don't let her be dead. I rush to the child, who opens her eyes.

'Can I have an ice cream?'

'No.'

She shuts her eyes and a small crowd gathers. A woman rushes off to call an ambulance and a man pushes me aside and kneels to take the child's pulse.

'Stand back. I'm a doctor.'

'We were just on our way to buy ice cream,' I say.

The girl opens her eyes and jumps to her feet, and off we go to get another ice cream. When she has eaten it, she says she feels sick.

'Sit!'

Startled, the child sits but soon gets bored and starts rolling around on the newly mown grass. The grass clippings bring her out in a rash and she says she wants to go home. I look at my watch and see there is another half hour to go.

'Stay!'

A nurse in a blue and white gingham dress and red belt strolls past pushing a child in a pushchair and I feel sorry for her. Imagine having to do this every day! I watch the nurse until she reaches the far side of the park and as she turns the pushchair to pull it through the gate I recognise her.

The nurse is Gloria.

I shout her name at the top of my voice. Every other person in the park turns to look but Gloria doesn't hear. I jump up to run but the child grabs my ankles and brings me down on the grass with a thud that winds me. By the time I have recovered, Gloria and the pushchair have disappeared.

I go back to the park the next day and the day after that, but there is no sign of Gloria. On the following day, May telephones to say my grandfather is dead.

Grandfather Rites

♀

April arrives late and everyone turns to look as she clatters down the aisle in her stiletto heels. The vicar frowns and I try to ignore April, but even so I catch a glimpse of her black hat and piled up hair as she makes her way to the front of the church.

'Let us pray.'

I close my eyes and pray. Dear God, this is your House. Please make April trip and fall flat on her face in front of all these people.

But when I look again April is taking her place in the front pew and May and my grandmother are shuffling along to make room for her. The moment she is sitting down, April's shoulders shake and she starts to cry.

I cannot cry at funerals however hard I try and it always

takes ages for it to sink in that someone has really gone for good. In the meantime I must be careful not to ask how my grandfather's runner beans are doing, or what he wants for Christmas.

'Who's that?' whispers Daniel.

'My stepmother.'

Daniel strains to get a better look, curious to see a member of my family at last, and a moment later Jack arrives. The heavy door creaks open and clangs shut, and my brother swaggers forward to take his place beside April.

When she rests her head on his shoulder and her sobs become louder than ever, Jack looks away embarrassed.

I am amazed that April even remembers who Jack is. She hasn't seen him for years. I am still more amazed that either of them have bothered to come to the funeral, or even how they knew my grandfather was dead.

April is the first to reach the graveside. In her haste to grab a handful of soil before anyone else she stumbles and almost falls into the open grave, but the vicar catches her in time.

'Ashes to ashes, dust to dust,' sobs April.

'He should have pushed her in while he had the chance.'

The muffled voice comes from behind me. I turn and find myself looking down at the upturned face of a short fat woman in tinted spectacles and with a knitted scarf wrapped round the lower half of her face.

'Shh,' says the woman. 'Pretend you don't know me.'

'I don't know you.'

'I'm Pearl Bonnet. Your father's whore.'

'We brought nothing into this world, and it is certain we

can carry nothing out… The Lord giveth, and the Lord taketh away…'

The vicar makes the sign of the cross and the service is over. People are drifting away from the open grave but Pearl Bonnet is still there, tugging at my sleeve.

'Go away.'

'I've got a message from your father.'

I look around, wondering how to get rid of her before April sees her and makes a scene. But April is talking to Daniel, who has wasted no time in introducing himself to my family. My grandmother is leaving, helped by May and Percy, and I see my chance.

'Inside, quickly.'

In the church porch, Pearl Bonnet unwinds the scarf and removes her sunglasses. Her eyes are pink and watery, exactly as I remember them, otherwise I would not have recognised her.

'You shouldn't be here.'

'Your father's in prison. He wanted you to know.'

I have almost forgotten what my father looks like, and these day I only ever think about him when Daniel is quizzing me about my family. Even so, this news comes as a shock.

'What's he done?'

'Fraud. I don't know the details, but he needs money. We thought perhaps you could help.'

'I'm a student, Pearl. You're the one with money.'

'Not any more, dear. I invested it in your father's business.'

Pearl's watery eyes seem about to overflow.

'I lent Jack money too,' she says. 'Perhaps you could persuade him to pay it back?'

The tears are flowing freely now, so freely I feel in danger of drowning.

♀

When I get back to the farmhouse Daniel is alone in the kitchen, drinking my grandfather's whisky straight from the bottle.

'Where is everybody? What happened to April and Jack?'

Daniel looks like a man in shock. He takes another swig of whisky.

'There was the most awful row and then they left.'

May comes in and looks at me oddly.

'Where's Grandma?' I ask.

'Upstairs. She's upset.'

'We're all upset.'

'I don't know what you've got to be upset about.'

May's behaviour is so odd I feel quite nervous.

'Will someone please tell me what is going on?'

Another odd look.

'You mean you don't know?'

'I haven't a clue what you're talking about.'

'Your grandfather's left The Barn to you in his will.'

May bursts into tears and sits down, and Daniel offers me the bottle without speaking. Meeting my family seems to have affected his vocal chords.

'I hope you won't throw me out of my own home,' says May between sobs. 'It would be poor gratitude for everything I've done.'

'There must be some mistake.'

'That's exactly what April said. She's just gone off to see Dr Harvey. April wants him to testify that your grandfather was not of sound mind.'

'My grandfather was most certainly not mad.'

'Of course he wasn't,' says May. 'In any case the Will was made ten years ago. I simply don't understand.'

But I am beginning to understand.

It is ten years since Jack was sent away to boarding school. My grandfather told me then he would look after me and presumably this is what he had meant.

'April says The Barn should go to her because she's the eldest daughter,' says May. 'Jack says it should go to him because he's the boy and the blood relative. They had a terrible argument.'

'I don't want The Barn,' I say. 'Tell Grandma she can have it back.'

May sniffs and wipes her eyes with a corner of the table cloth.

'You're a good girl, Ophelia. It's a pity it's Jack who's the Siward and not you.'

Under Surveillance

I roll out of bed and onto the floor where I locate my spectacles and pull on my jeans and shoes, all without opening my eyes. After a year of hospital call-out duty in New York my reflexes are still working overtime. I grope for a light switch that is not there and then I remember where I am.

This is London. I am in my own home, and the bell that woke me is my own doorbell.

Charlie, unsteady on his feet and reeking of alcohol, is standing on the step. It is not yet light when I help him into the house, deposit him on the sofa and go to make strong coffee.

'Courtesy of your ex-wife,' I say, handing him the mug. 'Sue has kindly stocked up my kitchen cupboards. She's been keeping an eye on the place while I've been away.'

My brother slumps back against the cushions and groans.

This is clearly not the time to remind him of the virtues of his ex-wife.

'Asa, I need your help.'

It is the first time that Charlie, several years older than me, has ever asked for help, and I know straight away it is to do with April.

'You've had lots of women friends,' he says. 'Tell me what to do.'

'My track record isn't good.'

'That's only because you haven't found the right woman.'

'And you have?'

'I know you don't like April.'

His eyes wander round the room and alight on the wine rack, thoughtfully filled by Sue, but I do not oblige. Clearly, my brother has had enough to drink already.

'Charlie, why don't you just tell me what this is about?'

'April wants to leave me.'

'You're joking!'

Obviously not, but this is good news indeed. In fact, it is the best homecoming present I could have wished for.

'Her father died recently. When she got back from the funeral she moved into the spare room.'

'Grief affects people in different ways.'

'She seemed more excited than sad.'

'April always did have a mercurial personality. Were you at the funeral too?'

'She wouldn't let me go. Sometimes I wonder if April's ashamed of me. You see, her family is very wealthy.'

At what point, I wonder, did my brother lose his insight? It had happened suddenly, as if in an accident, and the accident of course was April Siward.

'Has she told you why she wants to leave?'

'She wants to fulfil her destiny.'

I see my opportunity and seize it. Leaning forward, I take Charlie's hands in mine.

'Help April to fulfil her destiny,' I say. 'Give her the independence she wants.'

Let the bitch go. That is what I really mean.

'She wants to borrow money to buy herself a flat,' says Charlie.

'That doesn't seem much of a destiny. I thought you said April was rich.'

'It's only a short-term loan until her father's estate is sorted out. Asa, I want you to do something for me.'

I am expecting Charlie to ask me for money, but not so.

'Something's troubling April,' he says. 'I want you to find out what it is.'

Drunk and tired though he is, there are tears of real pain in Charlie's eyes.

'I have to go to France,' he says. 'It's a business trip and I'm frightened April will move out while I'm away.'

'Take her with you.'

'She won't come. Talk to her, Asa. Find out what's wrong.'

'Suppose I discover something you don't want to know?'

'Until I know what is wrong I can't begin to put things right.'

There is something else Charlie is frightened of, something I hadn't fully appreciated until this moment. My brother is frightened of being alone.

And now I am frightened too. Pandora must have felt much the same way before she opened the forbidden box.

There is no point in talking to April because she will lie to me as surely as she has been lying to Charlie all these years, so I have resorted to spying.

April emerges from Courtfield Mansions just as I am about to abandon my vigil and go home. It is three o'clock in the morning, a little later than her normal witching hour, and she has dressed down for the occasion.

That any self-respecting streetwalker should go to work in a plastic mackintosh surprises me but I am not here to ask questions. I am here on Charlie's behalf to discover April's destiny.

She disappears round the corner and I turn my collar up to hide my face and run after her. April is walking quickly, despite the high heels. I hide in a doorway until she turns the next corner when I follow her again.

If I was less tired and if my quarry wasn't ruining my brother's life I could be enjoying this. I think I would have made a rather good detective

April walks and I follow until she turns into a narrow street between South Kensington and Knightsbridge. She stops abruptly. I step quickly into a doorway and hide myself behind a pillar.

I wait a few moments and when nothing happens I take a peep and see April in the middle of the road staring up at one of the houses. It is the house of a client, of this I have no doubt. I withdraw my head and wait to see what happens next.

Five minutes. Ten minutes. Twenty minutes goes by and April is still standing in the same spot, but then she turns abruptly and walks briskly back in the direction of Courtfield Mansions.

As she passes my pillar I catch a glimpse of April's face, and to my great astonishment she is grinning like a Cheshire cat.

I go to the spot where she was standing and find myself in front of an ugly yellow brick house with a concrete path leading up to the front door. Puzzled, I make a note of the address and go home to bed.

Pearls of Madness

♀

I am going mad, just like the Ophelia on the lid of the chocolate box went mad. I always knew it would happen and now it has. Hamlet drove Shakespeare's Ophelia mad and now Daniel is driving me mad.

The Ophelia on the box looks a little older than I am now so I had hoped my madness would hold off until the end of my final year, but the drowned Ophelia must have been younger than she looks. Or perhaps it's just that my madness has come prematurely.

The madness is of the counting variety. I have never heard of the counting madness before, but that is what I have got.

Counting is my way of not listening and it started because of Daniel and his family. I counted in order not to hear them. Silently, of course. They never knew when I was doing it, and they still don't.

'Do you fancy a film?' says Daniel.

One, two, three, four…

I count everything all the time now, especially words. I don't read words any more, I just count them.

It is worst with the Early English course, which is enough to drive anyone insane. I chose Early English because Daniel told me it was about Vikings.

I felt a mutual interest might give Daniel and me something to talk about, but as it turns out the Early English course has nothing to do with Vikings. It is about the Anglo-Saxons, so Daniel was wrong.

The earliest known Anglo-Saxon poem is by a man called Caedmon and it is about the Creation. It seems Caedmon was a cow hand who had never learned to read or write.

I try to imagine Percy Hammer sitting down to compose a poem after a hard day's work on the farm and can't help thinking Percy would come up with something more inspiring than Caedmon's Creation.

'Let's go to the pub,' says Daniel.

Five, six, seven, eight…

He goes to the pub alone and I pick up my book and try again. Caedmon's poem has an average of five words per line. I notice the date too. It was written in 657AD but after that business with the West London Viking I am sceptical about dates.

Daniel is in high spirits when he returns. His friend's wife is pregnant and they have been celebrating.

'Show me some affection,' he says.

'I've got a headache.'

'Can we have a baby too?'

Nine, ten, eleven, twelve…'

Daniel is still on about babies and it is making my head ache. One thousand one hundred and eight. One thousand one hundred and nine. And then the telephone rings.

'It's probably for you,' I say. 'Your sister hasn't rung this morning.'

Daniel answers and hands me the receiver. It is Pearl Bonnet and she sounds drunk. I am annoyed that she has somehow got hold of our phone number.

'Have you seen Jack?' she says straight away. 'I still haven't got my money back. Did you manage to speak to him after the funeral?'

I tell her Jack had already left by the time I got back to the farmhouse.

'My solicitor says I should stop making Jack's payments to that village girl. I want to discuss it with Jack.'

'What village girl?'

'The girl who had the baby, of course. My solicitor says Jack was a minor at the time so he shouldn't be paying maintenance at all.'

No amount of counting can help me now because I heard perfectly well what Pearl said and I know she is talking about Gloria.

My brother was fifteen when he last spent a school holiday at The Barn so it is no wonder Gloria wouldn't tell me who the father was.

'Where's this girl now?'

'I have no idea… Ophelia, I have to go.'

'Pearl, wait…'

'There's a man coming up the path. Now he's knocking at the door and… Goodbye, dear. I really must go.'

Pearls of Wisdom

A spherical, round-faced little person holding a cut glass decanter opens the door and blinks at me hard. The woman is so like a Russian doll I step back quickly, nervous of touching her in case she topples over.

'So sorry,' she says. 'I was on the telephone.'

I can think of no good reason for being here except the real reason so I tell the truth.

'My name is Asa Cohen. Do you happen to know a person called April Siward?'

The woman blinks again and I am made aware of her eyes, which look as if they are floating in their sockets.

'Are you a friend of April?'

'She's a friend of my brother, Charles Manners.'

Charlie's name has a magical effect. The woman blinks some more, gives me a watery smile and wobbles sideways to let me in.

'I hope nothing's happened to Charlie?'

She introduces herself as Pearl Bonnet and offers me a sherry, which I decline. Pearl Bonnet seems put out.

'It's a bit early for me. I haven't had breakfast yet.'

She looks surprised but indicates a chair with a wave of the decanter and I sit down.

'Charlie often talked of a brother but you don't look a bit like him.'

'Tell me about April. How well do you know her?'

'She used to be my best friend, but not any more. April thinks I stole Toby.'

The name rings a bell. I have a notion that Toby is or was a dog but then the woman hands me a photograph,

'This is Toby on his wedding day.'

It is April Siward's wedding photograph, the same one Charlie has on the sideboard in his flat, and I am remembering now that Toby is not a dog at all, but April's estranged husband.

Toby is the man with the lopsided smile, the man who abandoned April for another woman. And the other woman is, of course, Pearl Bonnet.

That this spherical little creature with eyes like bloodshot eggs could steal anyone's husband is beyond my jet-lagged imagination. As I stare at her, struggling to understand, she passes the decanter in front of my eyes, very slowly and very close to my nose.

'Are you sure you won't you change your mind?'

I change my mind because I suddenly feel in need of a drink.

Pearl Bonnet pours me a large sherry, and an even larger one for herself, and settles down on the sofa opposite to drink it.

'Where is Toby now?' I ask.

'In prison.'

The watery eyes are perilously close to overflowing.

'I'm so sorry,' I say hastily. 'But tell me about April. When did you last see her?'

'She was here at about three o'clock this morning.'

'That's an odd time to pay a visit.'

'I know. Usually she's here by two.'

It occurs to me that Pearl Bonnet is perhaps a little mad, that her brain has been affected by many years of sherry drinking. I should have recognised the signs. She reaches for the decanter yet again and I get up to go.

'I'm not mad,' she says sharply. 'April Siward comes to my house in the early hours of the morning, rain or snow. She's been doing it for years, ever since Toby came to live with me. She stands under the lamp post outside my house and looks up at our bedroom window and then she goes away laughing. She was here last night and she'll very likely be here again tonight.'

Drunk she may be, but what Pearl Bonnet says tallies exactly with what I already know. The mystery destination of April Siward's nocturnal wanderings is revealed at last.

'Why does she do it?'

'She wants Toby back, of course. April always wanted what she couldn't have. She abandoned two lovely children, you know. She just dumped them on her sister and hot-footed it to London after Toby.'

This makes no sense, so perhaps my earlier instincts had been right after all. Either that or we are not talking about the same person.

'The April I know is an only child,' I say. 'She told me so herself.'

'That's what she told Toby when they first met. It even

says so on their wedding announcement, but it's a complete fabrication.'

'The April I know has just inherited a large family estate.'

'Her family own a run down farmhouse and a few stony acres in the wilds of Yorkshire, and it certainly doesn't belong to April.'

'So her father isn't dead?'

'That bit is true. I was at his funeral, but April's mother and sister are very much alive. April Siward is certainly no heiress! But you still haven't told me what all this has to do with Charlie.'

'Charlie and April are lovers. They've been living together for years.'

The liquid eyes grow sad.

'How awful for Charlie. He was always such a sensible person.'

'Not where April Siward is concerned, I'm afraid. Are you quite sure about the children?'

'It's a coincidence you should be asking about April's children,' she says. 'I was talking to Ophelia on the phone when you knocked at the door.'

'Ophelia?'

My voice is sharper than I intend and Pearl Bonnet gives me a watery blink.

'Ophelia is April's stepdaughter.'

'And she lives in Yorkshire, in a place called Grymewyck?'

'She did, but she's in London now at university.'

'And would Ophelia's real mother be called Maisie?

Pearl Bonnet blinks several blinks in rapid succession.

'I can't imagine how you know that. Toby never talked about it to anyone.'

'Where is Maisie now?'

'Dead. The silly girl stole some sleeping tablets from the

midwife's bag and died of an overdose the night Ophelia was born.'

'And Ophelia was never told?'

'I really shouldn't have told you. I suppose it's the sherry talking. I can't think why you're so interested.'

I am interested nevertheless, and say so. I insist on knowing everything Pearl Bonnet can tell me about Ophelia's mother because one day very soon I intend to explain all this to Ophelia.

'Ophelia's mother was a barmaid in a Cairo nightclub. She wanted to be an actress and she latched on to poor Toby because she thought he could get her a job entertaining the troops.'

'And then she got pregnant?'

'I'm sure she did it on purpose. She probably thought Toby would marry her. As if he would!'

'Why didn't Toby have the baby adopted?'

'He was about to, but then his mother turned up and insisted on taking Ophelia back to England. She wanted to bring her up as her own daughter.'

'But it didn't work out?'

'Oh, the arrangement didn't last. Toby's mother is not maternal. She soon got bored with looking after a baby.'

'What happened to Ophelia?'

'Toby and April were married by then. As soon as they arrived back in England, Toby's mother sent Ophelia to live with them. There was nothing Toby could do about it. Poor Toby.'

A tear for poor Toby trickles down Pearl Bonnet's nose and she wipes it away with the back of her hand, and then the telephone rings and she goes off to answer it.

The house is stuffy and smells of stale sherry. I very much want to get out into the fresh air, but Pearl Bonnet is still on the phone and I have no choice but to wait until she has finished. I get up to stretch my legs and go to look at the only picture in the room.

It is a framed photograph of Princess Margaret shaking hands with a woman dressed as Elizabeth the First. On closer inspection I see that Queen Elizabeth has been cut out from another picture and stuck down in a bizarre collage to make it look as if the two women are shaking hands. The frame has been broken in several places and badly mended with Sellotape.

'You'll think me very rude,' says Pearl, returning with her coat on. 'But I have to go out.'

She sees me looking at the picture and laughs.

'That was a photograph of me taken years ago with Princess Margaret, but Toby's mother didn't like it. When she came to live with us she insisted I put her in the photograph instead of me.'

'Toby's mother lives here with you?'

'She thinks she's Elizabeth the First. I'm just off to collect her. That call was from the police.'

'Has she been arrested?'

'She's at Buckingham Palace. She goes there every day to watch the changing of the guard. She never misses.'

Lying at Will

April is unruffled as she opens the door, bare-footed and wearing Charlie's dressing gown. She leans back in Charlie's armchair, takes a swig of Charlie's whisky and helps herself to a cigarette from Charlie's silver cigarette box.

'There have been some dramatic changes here,' I say. 'I hardly recognised it.'

The flat is even more ludicrously decorated than I remember, and is now so crammed with bizarre ornaments that it looks more like a fairground stall than a home.

'A woman's touch,' she says lightly.

April crosses her legs and lights the cigarette, and I sit down facing her.

'Charlie's not here,' she says, blowing her smoke in my face. 'He's gone to France. Something to do with vineyards.'

'I've come to see you.'

She smiles and when I do not return the smile she tosses her head.

'You do look strict,' she says. 'Have I been a bad girl?'

I am here without Charlie's knowledge and know I must be careful so I say nothing.

'I must have been a very bad girl. If you've got something horrid to say, at least let me sit next to you while you say it.'

Quick as a cat, April crosses the room and sits beside me.

'How exotic you are, Asa. With your black hair and dark skin you could be a prince from the Arabian Nights.'

'I don't think many Arabian princes wore spectacles.'

April looks at me sideways through her mascara-coated lashes.

'I find men in spectacles irresistible.'

'I was sorry to hear about your father.'

Her composure falters, but only for a second.

'I'm an orphan now. I'm alone in the world.'

She puts her hand on mine and parts her knees until Charlie's dressing gown falls open. I disengage my hand, stand up and go to the other side of the room.

'Charlie tells me he's giving you money to buy a flat.'

'He's lending me the money until my father's estate is sorted out.'

She is composed and cool, but she is on her guard. Only shock tactics on my part now will shake April into telling the truth.

'Charlie's bank has asked me to guarantee the loan,' I say. 'It's just a formality.'

It is a lie to match her own and her eyes widen in surprise. Charlie would be furious if he knew what I was doing.

'My bank manager needs to see your father's Will. Perhaps your solicitor could forward a copy?'

April doesn't bat an eyelid.

'There's a copy in my father's bureau at home. I'll go for it myself.'

She is so utterly composed I wonder for a moment if she might even be telling the truth, but I feel this to be unlikely.

April is a liar. I know this, but I know too that it is sometimes possible for fact and fiction to merge in a person's mind to become one and the same thing. I have long suspected this to be the case with April. Either way, there is no backing down now.

'I have a better idea,' I say. 'I'll drive you there. It will save time.'

♂

April is in high spirits when I collect her from Charlie's flat and sings cheerfully as she climbs into the car beside me.

'We're off to see the wizard, the wonderful wizard of Oz.'

She has a voice that carries, and enough luggage for a year. We could be emigrating or setting out together for an illicit holiday, which is almost certainly what Charlie's neighbours will be thinking.

I am trying not to think about Charlie. This plan of mine could go very wrong. It might be that April really is an heiress who has problems getting to sleep. I suspect not, but I only have the sherry-addled Pearl Bonnet's word to the contrary. In any case, it is too late to pull out now.

'Where to?' I ask.

'It's a surprise.'

'I'm in your hands.'

I know very well where we are going and I also know very well how to get there, but April is not to know this and she has the map. She gets us on to the wrong road within minutes of leaving the flat.

'Women are terrible map readers,' she says. 'It's something to do with the synods in our brains.'

'Give me a clue.'

She tells me we should be heading north and I am able to turn the car around and take the short cut I always use to get to the A1 and Grymewyck.

April is still in holiday mood as she directs me down the familiar road into Grymewyck village, and when she tells me to turn into the farmyard I know exactly where we are. This is the home of the beautiful princess who many years ago gave me a ham sandwich.

The princess of course had been April herself. If I had half a brain I would have worked that out for myself.

'What do you think?' cries April. 'Isn't it magnificent?'

'Fit for a princess.'

April gets out of the car and gazes at the little farmhouse as if it was indeed the most palatial of all palaces.

Cold air hits us as we step into the kitchen, which is smaller than I remember. The stone flags are green with damp and littered with mouse droppings, but April seems not to notice. I follow her into the sitting room, which is darker, lower, and even colder than the kitchen.

'My family have lived here for centuries,' she says. 'This house is as old as the hills.'

'And now it belongs to you?'

'I have come home.'

There is still the pending matter of her father's Will, which is the reason for our visit. The dilapidated cupboard by the window must be the bureau April spoke of. I am also interested in a pair of women's shoes propped neatly against the fender, and the cat that is curled up asleep in front of the empty grate.

The Viking Finger

♀

Daniel says it is morbid the way I mooch around thinking about lost people. First Maisie and now Gloria.

He disapproves of Gloria even though he has never even met her because Gloria is an unmarried mother. Daniel thinks a baby needs two parents, which of course he would.

When I tell him Gloria's baby has a father after all and it turns out to be my little brother who was under age at the time, Daniel says that is not what he meant. He thinks a child needs a grown-up father not an irresponsible teenager, and he says he is most disappointed in Jack.

Until recently Daniel has shown no interest in finding Maisie because he takes a dim view of a mother who abandons her baby daughter at birth, but lately he seems to be coming round to the idea. Perhaps he has decided that a mother like Maisie, with all her shortcomings, is better than my having no mother at all.

'We could try Somerset House,' says Daniel. 'If you were born in London, there's bound to be a record of it.'

I am pleased that Daniel is offering to help find Maisie, because Daniel is methodical and with his help I might get somewhere.

'I was born in Egypt.'

'There'll still be a record of it somewhere. When did Maisie and your father get married?'

'I don't know.'

'What was your mother's maiden name?'

'I've no idea.'

Daniel scratches his head.

'You need to talk to your father,' he says. 'He's the only person who can give you the information you need.'

♀

May has been looking after my grandmother in The Barn since my grandfather died, and she has had a telephone installed there, in case my grandmother has a fall and she needs to call the doctor. My grandmother has forbidden May to use the telephone because of the expense, but at least I can ring her.

I ring her now to tell her about Pearl's little bombshell. May won't be surprised to hear about Gloria's baby. No better than she ought to be, that is what May used to say about Gloria. But I am not looking forward to telling her who the father is.

'What's happened?' shouts May. 'Is anything wrong?'

May always shouts when I telephone because London is so far away, but before I can tell her about Gloria and the baby, May has something to tell me.

April is on her way to Grymewyck and she is planning to

stay in the empty farmhouse.

'But why? April hasn't been home for years except for the funeral.'

'She says she wants peace and quiet and is not to be disturbed on any account. I do wonder what she's up to.'

'Nothing good, that's for sure.'

After her behaviour at my grandfather's funeral it is more than likely April is on her way to lay claim to The Barn, or even the farmhouse. Nothing would surprise me so far as April is concerned, but I don't say this to May because I don't want to alarm her.

'She's coming with a man,' says May. 'Perhaps April's got herself a boy friend.'

I feel it is more likely April has got herself a solicitor, and I wonder what I can do to stop her, if anything.

'I wish you were here,' says May. 'April can be very unreasonable.'

'I'll come,' I say suddenly. 'I'll be there this afternoon.'

'What about your studies?'

'It's Saturday. Anyway, the summer break starts next week.'

'You're a good girl, Ophelia. Why was it you rang?'

'I'll tell you when I see you.'

I hang up, light headed at the prospect of a train journey on my own without Daniel. In holiday mood I go to tell him I am leaving for Grymewyck after lunch.

'I'll come too,' says Daniel straight away. 'I'll drive you.'

'It's hardly worth your while, not for one day.'

'By a lucky coincidence my department is advising on a student excavation in Yorkshire. I'll tell them I'm making a site visit.'

♀

April's lips start to twitch when Daniel and I walk into the farmhouse. Her jaw goes into spasm and she has to slap her hand over her mouth to hide the involuntary grin. My stepmother is not pleased to see us.

'Darlings!' she cries. 'How lovely to see you!'

The man is in my grandmother's rocking chair, looking as if he owned the place. When he sees us he gets to his feet and casually throws another log on the fire.

He introduces himself as Asa Cohen and I dislike him immediately.

Everything about Asa Cohen is dark. He has dark eyes and dark hair that hangs over his forehead so you can't see his face properly. When he steps forward to shake hands he stands in front of the lamp and throws a long dark shadow across the room.

'You're just in time for tea,' he says. 'Shall I be mother?'

Asa Cohen has made the tea in my grandmother's best teapot, the one she only uses at christenings and funerals.

'Milk?'

I glare at him, take the jug from his hand and pour the milk myself.

He resettles himself in my grandmother's rocking chair and invites us to sit down. I tell him I prefer to stand. He shrugs and asks Daniel how far we have driven, but April interrupts before Daniel can reply. At least this way we won't have to talk to him.

I drink my tea as quickly as I can and tell Daniel it is time to leave, but Daniel is telling Asa Cohen about burial mounds and takes no notice. April is silent until she hears the word Viking and then she leaps to her feet.

'Look at this!'

April crooks the little finger of her left hand and waves it in front of Daniel's face.

'Are you hurt?' he asks.

She turns from Daniel impatiently and thrusts the crooked digit at Asa, almost poking him in the eye.

'Tell them what it is, Asa.'

'April has a condition called Dupuytrens Contracture. It's not serious.'

He is trying not to smile.

'Its other name is Viking Finger!' cries April. 'It's true, isn't it, Asa? You only get this Dupe – Du – whatever it's called – if you're descended from the Vikings.'

'That's only a theory,' he says. 'Viking Finger is most common in people with Scandinavian ancestry, hence the nickname.'

'We shall have to start calling you by your Viking name,' says Daniel.

My stepmother almost swoons.

'Do I really have a Viking name?'

'Your name would be Eggtid. That's what the Vikings called the month of April.'

'Eggtid,' sighs April. 'What a lovely name. You know, I even feel like an Eggtid.'

'What would May be?'

It seems April prefers not to talk about May because my question sends her jaw into spasm again and she has to slap herself to make it stop.

'What about you, Daniel?' says April quickly. 'Who are you?'

'Dan is the Viking word for Dane, so I suppose I would be The Dane.'

April is in heaven.

'Daniel the Dane. That's how I shall always think of you.'

Thankfully, talking of Vikings reminds Daniel we should be going because he is meeting some students at the excavation. Tonight we will be sleeping in a tent on a Viking burial ground. That was Daniel's idea.

April seems relieved when we get up to leave but at the door she strokes Daniel's cheek.

'We Vikings must stick together,' she whispers.

I turn away embarrassed and find myself looking into the amused dark eyes of Asa Cohen.

♀

'Well that was interesting,' says Daniel outside. 'Didn't you think that was interesting, Ophelia?'

'What the hell is going on?'

When Daniel is talking about Vikings he doesn't notice much about living people.

'What's that man doing here?' I ask. 'I think he's a solicitor.'

'He sounded more like a doctor to me.'

'Do you think they're sleeping together?'

'I imagine so.'

I tell Daniel I will not be going to the student excavation because I have yet to see May and my grandmother, and in any case I have decided to stay on at The Barn. Daniel is disappointed.

'I thought you liked camping.'

'I'm not sleeping on top of dead Vikings.'

'Then we'll find a hotel.'

'April's crazy. She could do anything.'

Daniel sighs and hands me my duffel bag from the boot of the car.

'She's just lost her father,' he says. 'April is grieving.'

♀

I sleep well and wake up in my own little bed in The Barn. Daniel has gone and I am able to breathe freely at last. It is not that I don't like Daniel because I do, it is just that I get this tight feeling in my chest whenever he comes near me.

Usually I don't bother to unpack when I visit May but I unpack now. I put my clothes neatly away in drawers and only then do I realise why I am doing it. I will not be going back to live with Daniel.

That decision came all on its own. I didn't even have to think about it.

My old school uniform is still here in one of the drawers, and so is the snake brooch. Seeing the brooch again reminds me of Gloria and makes me sad.

I pin it to the lapel of my duffel coat and promise myself to wear the brooch always as a reminder of Gloria, even though I don't particularly like it. Snakes aren't really my thing.

I haven't stopped counting things though, even now Daniel's gone, but the counting isn't nearly as bad as it was. I count the window panes in my bedroom and the panels on the door but that is all, and then May calls from the kitchen.

'You're talking to yourself. It's the first sign of madness.'

May has got the roast in the oven. I can smell it through the floorboards.

'Are you coming down today or not?' shouts May. 'These beans aren't going to slice themselves.'

I pull on my tee shirt and go downstairs. Slicing the beans was always my special job and I am good at it.

'That's grand,' says May when I have finished. 'Now, be a love and fetch us a bit of mint.'

'Not dressed like that, you don't,' says my grandmother. 'Cover yourself up before you go out.'

The Dark-Eyed Boy

April Siward is a lying bitch. That is my conclusion, although it is hardly a professional diagnosis. Mythomania has a better ring to it. Pearl Bonnet was right about April in every particular. The sherry spoke nothing but the truth.

I slept badly and the reason is Ophelia. Ophelia and this bed. The horsehair poking through the mattress was uncomfortable but it was as nothing compared to the painful thumping of my heart and the sneezing that bothered me all night. Ophelia was tossing and turning in my dreams and her hair tickled the insides of my nostrils.

She is still unhappy. I knew that the moment she walked through the door in her duffel coat and Doc Marten boots. Ophelia is no happier now than when she was a little girl, and that boyfriend is doing her no good at all.

Dan the Dane, for Christ's sake. Thinking about him is doing me no good either.

I go downstairs to find April stomping around the farmhouse kitchen in a bilious purple dressing gown and wellington boots.

'Breakfast?' I suggest. 'Or shall we look at your father's Will first?'

Her face is blank, so blank I know April has forgotten the reason we are here.

I leave April and go to find the Will myself, which is not there of course because the Will as April described it does not exist. Apart from stamps and stationery and a few farm bills, the desk is empty. Curious, I go to look round the rest of the house.

According to Pearl Bonnet, April Siward has a mother and a sister who are both alive and well and living here in the farmhouse. There are women's dresses in the wardrobe, jewellery in the jewellery box, and knickers and petticoats in the chest of drawers, but of the women themselves there is no sign.

In a dressing table drawer I find a box of family photographs and newspaper cuttings. The cardboard box is falling apart and covered in childish scribbles, but it is the contents that interest me, not the box. I am looking for clues.

April's wedding photograph is here, of course. I check that April, Toby, Charlie and Pearl Bonnet are still smiling and put it back.

There is an old newspaper cutting in the box, brittle and yellowed with age:

The Times, January 20th 1946
The marriage took place at Saint Stephen's Church, Cairo, on January 14th 1946 between Second Lieutenant Toby Gunn, son of Lady Effie Gunn of Kensington, and April, only daughter of Mr

and Mrs Harald Siward, of Grymewyck Hall, Yorkshire. The bride was attended by Miss Pearl Bonnet. Major Charles Manners was best man. A reception was held at Shepheard's Hotel.

The cutting is almost twenty years old and it seems April Siward was a liar even then. Little wonder Charlie believes her to be an only child and an heiress. He has seen it in print. I handle it as carefully as I can but even so the cutting crumbles and falls apart in my hands before I can put it back in the box.

Also in the box is a small black and white photograph of myself as a little boy. I am standing outside the hay barn with the hay makers and I can remember clearly the day the photograph was taken.

It is the photograph April took on the day I was made to eat a ham sandwich. I had forgotten to smile for the camera and she had been angry, and no wonder. What a sullen, squinting little thing I look!

I am about to replace the photograph when I change my mind and slip it in my pocket.

There is still no sign of the mother and sister though. I can only think they are away from home, a holiday after the funeral perhaps.

In any case there is nothing more to be done in Grymewyck. It is time for me to take April back to London.

♂

'London?' says April, surprised. 'I'm not going back to London.'

'That was the plan.'

My plan, but not hers it seems. I now realise April had not the slightest intention of returning with me to London, which is why she has brought so many clothes. She was using me as her removals man.

'I have returned to my roots,' she says. 'This farmhouse is

where I belong, and this is where I intend to stay.'

'I don't know what Charlie's going to say.'

'Charlie will forgive me. Charlie always forgives me.'

I have no choice but to leave without her. But before I go I intend to take a walk up to The Barn. I have a yen to see it again, for old time's sake.

Jenny Rodwell

A Danger to Others

I cut the mint for May and straighten up to see Asa Cohen at the garden gate. I have nothing on under my tee shirt and blush to think how long he has been watching, but his eyes are on the knife I am holding, not on me. He puts up his hands in pretend surrender.

'I thought you'd gone looking for Vikings.'

'I changed my mind.'

'Are you alone here?'

I was right. April and this man are after The Barn and he has come to see if the coast is clear. The nerve of him.

'Of course I'm not alone. Daniel's here, and Percy Hammer, and May and my grandmother, and… the place is

154

really quite crowded.'

'It sounds it.'

'When are you leaving?'

'I'm on my way, but I wanted to get some shots of the hills first.'

He has a camera round his neck, so this might just be true. On the other hand it might be a blind to put me off my guard. My grip on the knife handle tightens and I glare at him, trying to make myself look as fierce as possible.

'Goodbye, Ophelia,' he says, 'I'll see you again.'

It sounds more like a threat than a farewell.

I am about to get into my car when April, still in the purple dressing gown, emerges from an outbuilding holding a stick.

'I'm off,' I say. 'Have you any message for Charlie?'

She gives me a scornful look.

'I have an estate to run.'

My hand is on the ignition key when the man Percy Hammer appears and proceeds to herd his cows out through the gate I have just opened for myself. He is in no hurry and I can do nothing except wait.

The man leers at me and I look away, and as I do so I catch a flash of purple in my wing mirror. A second later April dashes past brandishing the stick, her dressing gown billowing behind her like a warrior's cloak.

'Get your animals off my land,' she shouts.

She runs at one of the cows and the cow bellows and breaks into a trot. The other cows follow suit and the whole herd disappears through the open gate and vanishes down the lane.

Percy Hammer looks first at the disappearing cows and

then at April, who is running towards him, waving her stick. There is a struggle, a flurry of purple, and Percy Hammer reels backwards, his forehead covered in blood.

April returns to the house and Percy Hammer staggers off up the lane after his cows. The expression on April's face as she passes me on her way back to the house is spine chilling, or at any rate it sends a chill down my spine, because April is laughing.

♀

'I told you to cover yourself up,' says my grandmother. 'Who was that man? He probably saw everything you've got.'

This is not a comfortable thought.

'Go and put some clothes on before Percy gets here,' says May. 'He won't know where to put his eyes.'

Percy always eats at The Barn on Sundays. He has done for years, ever since his mother died.

'I wonder where he's got to?' says May, worried. 'It's not like Percy to be late.'

Percy arrives as we are about to start without him, still in his overalls. He leans against the door gasping for breath, and he is holding to his forehead a very bloodstained handkerchief.

The roast goes back in the oven to keep warm, May goes to find witch hazel and I go to buy sticking plasters for Percy's head wound.

In front of me in the shop an old woman is taking an age to buy cigarettes and I shuffle my feet impatiently. The woman has lank straight hair and laddered stockings, and it is only when she turns to go that I recognise her as Gloria's mother.

'Oh, her?' sniffs May, when I tell her who I have seen. 'That one's never been right since her daughter left, and they say she drinks like a fish. She's been brought home in a police car more than once.'

May has not forgiven Gloria's mother for bleaching my hair, I can tell that by the tone of her voice.

♀

After lunch my grandmother sends me down to the farmhouse to check that April and her man friend turned everything off when they left. She does this because April once left a lighted cigarette on her dressing table and nearly burned the place down. My grandmother has not forgotten.

As I approach the farmhouse the door opens and out comes April.

'Why are you here?' she says. 'Go away.'

My stepmother is wearing a bright purple dressing gown and holding in her hand a paintbrush dripping with red paint. There are spatters of red on her face and in her hair.

'What on earth are you doing?' I ask.

'I am making my house fit for heroes.'

'It isn't your house.'

'It is my destiny and you are trespassing.'

'I'm not trespassing, and neither was Percy. You could have killed him.'

'The native must learn his proper place.'

♀

I decide to confide my worries about April to Percy, who is supposed to be cutting thistles in the top field, but when I get there he is nowhere to be seen. I go to the stream and lie down on Our Rock to wait and before long I fall asleep.

The dream I have is not about April but about Gloria's mother. It is a weird sort of dream because in it Gloria's mother is making up my eyes. She tells me to keep still or my mascara will run, but then she starts to cry and her tears drop all over my face.

I wake up with a jerk and a big black dog is licking my face and shaking water all over me. There is a man looking down at me from the cliff above. He whistles and the dog disappears.

By the time I get to my feet both the man and the dog have disappeared.

I am certain the man was Asa Cohen.

Mirror Mirror

An auburn-haired vision of loveliness in a baggy tee shirt floats across my windscreen. It obscures my view of the road ahead and when the vision bends over I very nearly crash the car.

I am jolted out of my trance by the brake lights of the vehicle in front and slam my foot down just in time to avoid driving into the back of an articulated lorry. The car behind is forced to swerve and overtake me on my passenger side and the driver honks his horn as he bumps past me along the grass verge.

'Idiot!' he shouts.

'Idiot, yourself.'

I could have killed us both and the narrowly averted accident jolts me out of my trance. At the first opportunity I pull off the road and stop the car. I have no idea where I am or how fast I have been driving and I am shaking all over. As my windscreen clears of the auburn-haired vision, so does my head.

April Siward could have killed Percy Hammer and she had walked away laughing. A patient behaving in the same way would be considered a danger to self and others and would almost certainly be restrained. The realisation brings me to my senses.

At the next junction I turn my car around and head back north because I have left April in Grymewyck with Ophelia. With any luck I will be at Uncle Ben's house in time for supper.

♂

I confide my concerns for Ophelia to my uncle and regret it immediately because he lays down his magnifying glass and fixes me with an unfocused stare, his milky eyes shining as they have not shone for a long time.

'Ophelia has a stepmother,' I explain. 'She is evil and mad, and I think she means to harm Ophelia.'

My uncle's little sitting room is stuffed with books and magazines on subjects loosely related to the human mind, many of them published before the turn of the twentieth century. Open on my uncle's lap is an American phrenology magazine, circa 1936, and the article he is reading is titled Tell Tale Bumps.

'Does this stepmother have insight?' he asks.

I look at him in astonishment because this is an expression I hear frequently in the course of my clinical work. My uncle is asking if April is aware there is a problem.

'You've been reading those books again, uncle.'

'I try to keep up with your career. Tell me, does the

stepmother have an unhealthy relationship with her father?'

'Her father is dead. And so by the way is Freud.'

'I don't suppose she's ever told you about her dreams?' asks my uncle, hopefully.

He runs through a long list of disorders and symptoms in alphabetical order, most of which I have never heard of.

'You forgot the four humours,' I say when he has finished. 'Not to mention demonic possession.'

'Are they relevant?'

'Come to think of it, demonic possession could well be relevant.'

'You surely don't think she's a venefica?'

He is doing this deliberately. My uncle likes to catch me out.

'It's in Malleus Maleficarum,' he tells me. 'You'll find it under the hall table.'

I look it up and discover venefica means witch.

♂

Uncle Ben is reading Grimm's Fairy Tales. He clearly wants me to know this because he is holding the book upright so that I will notice the title, which I do. I doubt my uncle is really reading though because his is an early edition and the print is impossibly small.

Uncle Ben coughs and I ignore him. He coughs again and I look up and comment on the size of the typeface but not on the title of the book.

'I'm surprised you can read it at all,' I say. 'I'm not sure my eyesight would be up to it.'

'You should try. It's educational.'

He puts down his magnifying glass and goes out to the kitchen leaving Grimms Fairy Tales open on the table in front of me. To make absolutely sure I don't miss whatever it is he wants me to see he turns the book around so it is the right way up for me to read.

Mirror, mirror on the wall. Who is the fairest of them all?

Got it! The jealous stepmother, of course. My uncle has a theory. Simply telling me about it would have been far too straightforward for Uncle Ben.

He thinks April is jealous of Ophelia. What woman wouldn't be? Uncle Ben has discovered the so-called Snow White syndrome and Walt Disney has much to answer for.

More worrying is the illustration of Snow White biting into a poisoned apple. The image disturbs me because I can well imagine April Siward as a poisoner.

When I hear Uncle Ben coming in with the tea I go back to the newspaper I am reading. It wouldn't do for him to know I have been rattled by a fairy tale.

Uncle Ben immerses himself in another book. This one is on Greek mythology and I can guess what is what is coming next.

My uncle has discovered the Electra complex. I doubt that penis envy is one of April's problems but I hear him out because Uncle Ben is at least doing something. Unlike me.

Apart from making regular trips to Grymewyck and hanging around the Stag's Head I am doing very little.

I go to the Stags Head hoping for information about April, and I am longing for a glimpse of Ophelia, but Percy Hammer and his friends continue to ignore me and generally I drink alone.

♂

It is uncle Ben's idea that I should try to help April in a professional capacity.

'She wouldn't agree to it,' I tell him. 'In any case, I know her too well.'

As a rule I can slip into professional mode as easily as I slip into my white coat, but not where April Siward is concerned.

'A doctor must recognise his personal moral position and refrain from allowing it to interfere with his professional judgement,' quotes my uncle.

'The Hippocratic Oath doesn't apply in this case, Uncle. This person is not my patient.'

'Then you should try to help in a personal capacity,' he says. 'For Ophelia's sake.'

'I mentioned no names,' I say, surprised. 'How on earth did you know who I was talking about?'

But my uncle has gone back to his reading and is peering at a magazine through his magnifying glass. It would seem his hearing is getting to be as defective as his eyesight.

Eggtid The Eager

♀

'Ulf the Unwashed, Thorstein Cod-Biter and Hagred Big Feet,' says Daniel. 'Klod Baby Eater and Olaf the Paunch.'

'What heavenly names,' sighs April.

'Ophelia would have been Ophelia the Cruel,' says Daniel. 'She deserves the name because she is being so cruel to me.'

We are on a damp hump in the middle of a field and I am sitting as far away from Daniel as I can get without sliding off the edge. Daniel is stroking the grass between April's knees and April is enchanted. She moves even closer to Daniel so their fair heads are almost touching.

I have been tricked into coming here, to Daniel's archaeological site. He told me he needed to talk to me about something important but he didn't say April was coming too.

The purpose of the trip is clearly to make me jealous.

'But what about *me*, Dan?' cries April. 'What is *my* nickname?'

'You would be Eggtid the Eager because you are so clever and so interested in everything.'

'I'm cold,' I say. 'I want to go home.'

'Under this very mound lies a Viking warrior,' says Daniel. 'Soon the whole world will know what he looks like.'

April rests her head against his shoulder.

'What about the women?'

'Viking women were clever and handsome,' says Daniel. 'They were just like you, Eggtid.'

April is a woman bewitched.

'They wore brilliant colours and beautiful jewellery, and they dyed their hair vivid shades of orange,' continues Daniel.

'What did they do, these Viking women?'

'When the men were away fighting the women were left in charge. Viking women were powerful.'

April is gazing into the distance as if expecting a fleet of longboats to appear on the horizon at any moment.

'I wonder what happened to them. I wonder where the Vikings went.'

'They are still with us,' says Daniel softly. 'They never left.'

He takes April's hand and looks into her eyes.

'The Vikings stayed and married into the indigenous population, which is why you've got a Viking finger. Let me see it.'

They contemplate April's finger in silent awe. Daniel strokes the disfigured digit tenderly and April lays her hand on his lap with the Viking finger pointing upwards.

'I want to show you something,' he says. 'Coming, Ophelia?'

Daniel gets to his feet and pulls April after him. I follow them into the churchyard where Daniel stops in front of a hideous hump-backed stone.

'This is a Viking tombstone,' he says. 'It is inscribed with the runic alphabet.'

'I've never seen anything so beautiful,' says April.

'It would once have been painted in brilliant colours. The Vikings loved colour.'

'So do I!' cries April.

'The Vikings worshipped lots of gods, even our Christian god.'

'How clever of you to know that,' says April. 'But how do you know the Vikings lived here?'

'This village is called Thinge,' says Daniel. 'Thinge was the Viking name for council or parliament, so it stands to reason that the Vikings settled here.'

April jumps up and down and claps her hands like a small child.

'The Thinge must have been just like Grymewyck Parish Council.'

I have had enough.

'I'm off,' I say. 'I'll see you back at the car.'

I leave them sitting side by side on the Viking tombstone with Daniel drawing letters in the mud with a stick. He is teaching Eggtid the Eager how to write her name in the runic alphabet.

♀

Stupidly, I tell my grandmother about April and the red paint. My grandmother frets and eventually sends me down to the farmhouse to assess the damage.

I find my stepmother standing on an upside down bucket outside the farmhouse door. The purple dressing gown has been fastened at the throat with a plastic hair slide and April is wearing in her hair my grandmother's pearls. I am particularly struck by the hair itself, which is a virulent shade of orange.

My stepmother is gazing into the distance, shielding her eyes with her hands against the late afternoon sun. Clearly she is expecting someone.

'It's unlike my father to stay away so long.'

April is waiting for my grandfather, and she looks so sad and lonely on her upturned bucket that I almost feel sorry for her.

'Your father is dead.'

She looks bewildered.

'Did he die in battle?'

'He died peacefully in his own bed two weeks ago.'

'Then I know what I have to do.'

April gives me her hand and I help her down, but then she disappears into the farmhouse and bolts the door from the inside. I look through the letterbox and see the red glow of the kitchen walls reflected in the hall mirror.

♀

I find Percy in the cowshed swilling down the stalls but he spits on the clean floor when I tell him about April's strange behaviour, and then April herself arrives. When he sees the hair Percy whistles.

'Bugger me!'

She beckons and walks slowly towards him. Percy has his back to the wall but when April's red finger nail is within inches of his face she slips on the wet floor and goes down with a loud plop.

Percy laughs so much that tears run down his face and he is unable to speak. I help April to her feet and she turns on Percy.

'You ungrateful native. Get off my land and never come back.'

'Oh, bugger off, April,' says Percy, wiping his eyes and taking his cap from its hook. 'The sooner you bugger off back to London the better it will be for everyone.'

♀

My breathing problem returns the moment I hear Daniel's voice on the telephone.

'You're wheezing,' he says. 'Have you got a cold?'

'It's an allergy.'

Daniel is full of himself. His head of department has asked him to stay on for the rest of the summer to supervise the student excavation.

'It's a career move,' he says. 'I've taken a double room at Thinge Inn. When shall I collect you?'

I explain again that I have decided to stay on at The Barn and I also tell him about April, who is still squatting in my grandmother's house.

'It's hardly squatting, not when she's one of the family,' he says. 'How is Eggtid?'

'She's dyed her hair and she's doing her best to integrate with the natives.'

Daniel laughs, 'That's my girl!'

'She's unhinged, Daniel. You shouldn't encourage her.'

'Are you jealous?'

'I'm worried.'

'Aren't you just a teeny, weeny bit jealous?'

Sadly not. I put the phone down on Daniel and go outside for oxygen.

'You're going to lose that nice young man,' says May, who overhears the conversation. 'Don't say I didn't warn you.'

I tiptoe past April, who is asleep on the sofa with an empty sherry bottle beside her. The kitchen has been painted red, the hallway is partially red, and there are random streaks of red on the wall up the staircase. At that point April must have lost interest because the bedrooms have not been touched.

I have come to fetch the dark-eyed boy. He is not safe where he is, not with April in the house.

The Ophelia Box is where it always was, in the drawer of my grandmother's dressing table, but the dark-eyed boy is missing. I check the back of the drawer and I check the contents of the box again, but the photograph has definitely gone.

Before I realise what is happening, April is hurling herself across the room at me.

'What are you doing?'

The Ophelia Box is knocked out of my hands, scattering its contents across the floor.

'What have you done with the photograph?' I shout.

April kicks the box under the bed and as I bend to pick it up she kicks me so hard I lose my balance and roll over on the floor.

♀

Doctor Harvey arrives in a green Morris Minor and examines my ribcage, which is badly bruised but no more. In any case it is not my ribs I am worried about. I want to talk to Doctor Harvey about April.

'Grief affects people in different ways,' he tells me. 'Your mother needs her family around her. Fresh air and family will soon put her right.'

'I'm not really family. You see, April's not my mother and I don't actually like her very much. In fact, I don't really know her.'

Doctor Harvey beams, not listening.

'Spoil her,' he says. 'Let your mother know you care.'

'Couldn't you give her some medicine?' I ask. 'Don't you think she should see a specialist?'

He pats me on the back.

'You're her daughter,' he says. 'You're the best medicine your mother could possibly have.'

♀

I pick nasturtiums for April from May's garden, much to May's disgust.

'Doctor Harvey told me to spoil her.'

'He didn't tell you to spoil my garden.'

I take the nasturtiums down to the farmhouse and I also take a large tin of white emulsion to cover up the red. April tosses the flowers into the bin and looks at the white paint with distaste.

'I liked the red better.'

'Shall I make us a pot of tea?'

April sits limp and listless while I make the tea. With her pale face and orange hair she looks for all the world like a life-sized rag doll.

'Doctor Harvey says you need exercise and fresh air. We'll do some decorating and then we'll go out for a walk.'

I give April her tea and she pours it down the sink.

'Where have you hidden my red paint?'

I have no sooner prised the lid off the white emulsion when Daniel's car pulls up in the farmyard. He bursts into the kitchen and stops short when he sees April's hair.

'Love it, Eggtid! It's your colour.'

Daniel is on his way to Thinge and wants me to go with him. I tell him definitely not.

'I'll come,' cries April. 'The doctor says I need fresh air.'

'Get your cloak, Eggtid,' says Daniel. 'The chariot awaits.'

♀

I have barely painted the first wall of the kitchen when my brother Jack lopes in.

'Watcha, Sis.'

This is the first time I have seen Jack since my grandfather's funeral, and even then he hadn't stayed long enough to speak to me. I am surprised to see him now, and not pleasantly so.

He lights a cigarette and leans against the dresser. Jack always preferred leaning to standing. I used to think this was because his backbone wasn't strong enough to support his body.

'You've just missed April. Your mother popped out to visit a Viking burial ground.'

Jack grins.

'Our Siward ancestors, no doubt. Is she still going on about that rubbish?'

'More than ever. What brings you here?'

'I was passing. I'm on way to visit an old school friend in Scotland. His family is loaded.'

'I'm surprised you dare show your face in Grymewyck. Is fatherhood suiting you?'

He smiles a crooked smile, exactly like my father used to do.

'Wild oats, Sis. How are you off for cash at the moment. I'm a bit short of the readies.'

I should have known he was here for a reason.

'Can't you ask your rich school friend for a loan?'

'C'mon, Sis. A tenner would do.'

'I don't have that much.'

'How much have you got?'

Before I can stop him Jack has emptied the contents of my bag onto the table but I slap my hands over the purse before he can reach it.

'Where's Gloria?' I say.

'A hospital in West London. Saint Mary's something or other. She's a village girl, Sis. Honestly, I wouldn't bother your head about her.'

He helps himself to what cash I have and turns to leave.

'I hope you'll go to The Barn before you go,' I say. 'May's been worried about you.'

'No time,' he says. 'Tell them I'll drop in on my way back to London.'

♀

Daniel's flat is buzzing with bluebottles and a cloud of fruit flies has settled on the kitchen ceiling, probably because I forgot to empty the rubbish before we left. As I am not planning on staying, the flies do not worry me. Nor do I bother to empty the rubbish.

I slipped out of Grymewyck on the milk train early this morning before anyone was up. No one saw me leave and with any luck I will be back before anyone realises I have gone. I am in London to find Gloria.

My destination is a hospital called Saint Mary's something or other in West London and when I find it the nurses will be wearing blue and white gingham dresses with red belts. One of those nurses will be Gloria.

I sit on the unmade bed with the telephone directory and ring the three Saint Mary's in West London. The third one is a teaching hospital and yes, the student nurses wear blue and white gingham dresses with red belts. Bingo!

I take a bus to the hospital and soon find myself in a long corridor of doorways and signs. X-ray. Administration. Chapel. Pharmacy. One of the doors swings open and twenty or so nurses in blue and white gingham dresses with red belts fill the corridor. Gloria is not among them.

The nurses shake their heads when I ask about her and tell me there is no Gloria in their class. As they move off a man pushing a trolley of linen stops to speak to me.

'I know your friend Gloria,' he says. 'She left a couple of weeks ago.'

'Where did she go?'

'Left to get a job. Said she was broke.'

'Do you have her address?'

The porter shakes his head.

'She was always cagey about that. The hospital didn't know about the little boy, see. Gloria thought she'd get the push if anyone found out.'

'What's her son's name?'

'Zachary. Gloria calls him Zac.'

Walking home from Grymewyck station I see April darting bare-foot across the square and heading for the village hall. I go after her, follow her inside and sit down beside her. It is the monthly meeting of Grymewyck Parish Council.

'April, what are you doing here?'

'Shh! The leader is about to speak.'

The chairman of the parish council welcomes everyone but he is looking at April in particular, which is not surprising because she is wearing her dressing gown pinned all over with Christmas tree decorations. With the orange hair the effect is dramatic.

'Come with me this instant. We're going home.'

April refuses to budge and the vicar gets to his feet.

'That man's a disgrace,' says April in a loud voice. 'How dare he come to the Thinge in that old tunic?'

The vicar is asking for parish money towards the upkeep

of the old graveyard but all heads are turned towards April.

'I have enough to do helping God to look after the living without tending the graves of the dead as well,' says the vicar.

'Which god is he talking about?' says April. 'Do you think he means Thor?'

'The old graveyard is badly overgrown and residents have complained,' continues the vicar. 'This is especially distressing for members of the older families, some of whom are with us this evening and whose loved ones are buried there.'

April gets up to speak.

'I take it you will not be cutting down the World Ash or the Great Elm?'

The councillors lower their eyes and the vicar assures April that neither the World Ash nor the Great Elm will be harmed in any way. I pull her back onto her chair.

'There is to be a working party,' says the vicar. 'All help is welcome. We are looking for volunteers to maintain the gravestones.'

April jumps up again, knocking over her chair in her eagerness to volunteer.

'Me! Me!' she cries. 'I'll paint them in colours such as you have never seen before.'

♀

I escort April back to the farmhouse and make my way to The Barn, where the vicar is waiting for me with May.

'I gather you and April were at the parish council meeting,' says May.

'And very pleased to see you we were too,' says the vicar. 'It's an open forum, you know. Everyone is welcome.'

'I'm sorry about my stepmother. She's not well.'

'She is a troubled soul,' says the vicar. 'Perhaps I could help?'

'April's not religious. She wouldn't listen.'

'There was something about the way she spoke that indicated an inner spirituality.'

'April's a heathen,' says May. 'She always was and she always will be.'

'Then I shall make it my duty to bring her back into the fold,' says the vicar. 'I shall encourage her to help clear the old graveyard, only I'm afraid I couldn't allow her to paint the headstones.'

May sniffs.

'Leave it with me,' I tell him. 'I'll have a word with her.'

'There's one other thing,' says the vicar. 'I noticed your mother has difficulty remembering words. This is common after bereavement. It's the shock, but it will wear off. You mustn't think it's permanent.'

'April's not my mother.'

'And she doesn't usually have a problem with words,' says May.

'Your mother referred to the Parish Council as the Thinge.'

'Thinge is the Norse word for council,' I tell him. 'April thinks she's a Viking.'

The vicar smiles and pats me on the back.

'There you are then. There's always a rational explanation if one only takes the trouble to look for it.'

♀

Percy comes next day to say April has been seen heading for the old graveyard. I pull on my coat and rush to the graveyard immediately, where I find April with a bucket of red paint.

'The man in the black dress did not exaggerate,' says April. 'Our sacred field has been shockingly neglected.'

I try to take the bucket from her but she whips it out of my reach.

'Look at the state of those runes,' she says. 'Raidho, Isa, Perthro. You can hardly read them.'

'R.I.P. It stands for Rest In Peace.'

April puts down the bucket and flings her arms around a large tree trunk where she clings tightly and refuses to let go. I consider going for Percy but he probably wouldn't come.

'Yggdrasil is the World Ash that gave birth to the first man,' says April.

I manage to prise her off the World Ash and she dashes across the graveyard at speed and prostrates herself at the foot of another big tree. April is wearing only her dressing gown and it starting to rain.

'This is the Great Elm.'

'You shouldn't be lying on the damp grass. You'll catch a chill.'

'I am praying to the Valkyries for the safe journey of my father's soul to Valhalla.'

'Get up.'

Blood spatters from the gory tapestry of the blood-soaked massacre as lengths of bloodstained thread.'

'Get up, April. It's time to go home.'

'That's from my father's favourite poem. The rain drops reminded me of it.'

'You can tell me the rest of it when we get home.'

'I can't remember what comes next.'

April gets up and takes my hand. She allows me to lead her like a small child towards the gate, where we meet Percy.

'Need any help?' he says.

'We're going home to read some poetry.'

Percy snorts and April remembers the rest of her poem, which she addresses to Percy.

'The weft is made from human innards. With splintered breastbone it weaves its bleeding entrails.'

A Second Opinion

'There's a woman on the phone for you,' says Uncle Ben, 'It sounds urgent.'

The woman is Sue.

'Thank God I've found you at last,' says Sue. 'Why didn't you tell me you were going away?'

'Has something happened?'

'April's left Charlie.'

In case I am about to tell a lie I push the door closed with my foot so uncle Ben won't hear. It will be bad enough lying to Sue.

'You should be delighted,' I say.

'Charlie will be devastated when he gets back. He couldn't get hold of April on the phone, and he couldn't get you either so he asked me to go round to see if she was all right.'

'What makes you think she's done a runner?'

'She left with a man in a car and they took a lot of her stuff. One of the neighbours told me.'

I return to the sitting room and Uncle Ben looks up from the book he is pretending to read.

'Problem?'

'A misunderstanding.'

I should have told Sue the truth but it was too complicated to explain over the phone and she might have got the wrong end of the stick. Besides, I want to tell Charlie myself what happened. It will be better coming from me.

♂

April opens the farmhouse door to me. She looks ghoulish, like death warmed up, but I am not here to pass judgement on her appearance. I am here to find out if April has insight.

Who am I kidding? That was my uncle's potty idea. I am here because I want to see Ophelia.

'All alone, April?'

'Have you come to pay your respects?'

'I was hoping to see your daughter.'

She looks at me slyly.

'I don't have a daughter.'

April is not showing much insight at the moment because I have to push my hands deeper and deeper into my pockets to stop myself from wringing her neck.

'Then I'd like to see Ophelia.'

'She left for London early this morning,' she says. 'I saw her go.'

With Ophelia gone I have no reason to stay. I will return to London, where I will at least be breathing the same air that she is breathing. Moreover, Charlie will be back from France any day now and I have some serious explaining to do.

For the second time in two days I pack my bags and prepare to head south.

'Off again?' grumbles my uncle when I go to say goodbye. 'Young people these days don't seem to know whether they're coming or going.'

I head for the A1 but can't resist taking the detour through Grymewyck where I stop at the Stag's Head and settle myself in a window seat so as to have an uninterrupted view of the farmhouse.

Grymewyck without Ophelia is a gloomy-looking place and I am about to get up and leave when Ophelia herself walks past the window followed by April and Percy Hammer. April is still in the purple dressing gown and Percy Hammer is carrying a bucket of red paint.

Percy disappears in the direction of the farmyard and Ophelia follows April into the farmhouse. There is not a moment to lose.

April smiles when she sees me.

'People say I'm mad,' she says. 'You don't think I'm mad, do you?'

'I think you're troubled. Where's Ophelia?'

April slips the dressing gown from her shoulders and lets it fall to the floor. I avert my eyes and count to twenty, and when I look again it is Ophelia not April who is standing before me in the doorway. She gives me a withering look and slams the door in my face.

Making Ripples

♀

Daniel comes to visit us at The Barn, and he brings flowers for May and some Viking toe bones for me. Percy is here too because he promised my grandmother a game of dominoes.

Daniel is playing footsie with me under the table and I am fighting for breath and counting the flower patterns on the peg bag. There are eight different flowers on the bag and another five on the tablecloth.

May and my grandmother like flower patterns. I have noticed this before and I think it must be to do with the war. Perhaps women who lived through the war needed flowers to cheer them up when it was over.

Thinking about the war makes me think of the dark-eyed boy and I wonder again what has become of the photograph.

'Do you remember the little Jew boy who was here during the war?'

May says this out of the blue for no apparent reason and nobody answers because nobody is listening, except me.

'What little Jew boy is that?'

'The evacuee that stayed with Doctor Brown. It was the dominoes reminded me. The boy liked to play with them.'

'What did this boy look like?'

May considers.

'Foreign. I think he came from abroad.'

'Who is Doctor Brown?'.

'He used to be the doctor here in Grymewyck before Doctor Harvey, but he's retired now,' says May. 'They gave him one of those nice bungalows in Thinge but he doesn't like it. None of them do.'

Daniel perks up at the mention of Thinge and so do I.

♀

The next time Daniel goes to his excavation I go with him, and this time I forbid him to bring April.

'What did you tell April about trees?' I ask, curious.

'I don't know anything about trees.'

'The World Ash and the Great Elm?'

'Ah. Those particular trees play a central role in Viking religion.'

When we reach the site, Daniel introduces me to a young woman in a bikini who is happily sifting soil from one pile to another. I leave Daniel talking to the young woman and slip away without them noticing.

♀

Doctor Brown's bungalow is on a new estate on the edge of the village and Doctor Brown himself is sitting on a bench outside the front door, reading. He is using a large magnifying glass and holding a newspaper so close to his nose that he doesn't see me even when I am standing right in front of him.

'Doctor Brown?'

He looks up, blinking at the sunlight, and his eyes are as pale and opaque as pearls. His skin is so thin with age that the blue of the sky is reflected in the old man's face.

I take the seat beside him but jump up immediately when the bungalow door opens and Asa Cohen comes out.

'Go inside, Asa.' says the old man. 'You're frightening my visitor.'

A dog runs out of the house and rubs its nose against my ankles. It is the dog I saw on Our Rock, and when Asa Cohen whistles the dog follows him inside.

'You mustn't mind my nephew,' says Doctor Brown. 'He's staying with me for a few days.'

I ask the doctor if he remembers a Jewish evacuee who lived with him during the war and the old man pulls a photograph from his pocket and hands it to me. It is the missing photograph of the dark-eyed boy.

'Is this your evacuee?' he asks.

'That's my photograph. Where did you get it?'

'One of the haymakers is my wife. She used to help out the farm, and she died not long after that photograph was taken. Asa found it and he thought I'd like to see it.'

'And the boy?'

The old man smiles and I know the answer before he speaks.

'You mean Asa? It's a pity he was screwing his face up like that. It quite spoils the photograph.'

♀

I leave Doctor Brown's bungalow and take the road to Grymewyck. It is a three mile walk, but I don't care. I want to be alone with my disappointment, and I can't face Daniel, not at the moment.

The dark-eyed boy, my childhood friend, is none other than Asa Cohen, and the discovery is worse than disappointing. It is frightening. Why has he returned to Grymewyck now? And what is his connection with my family?

It is starting to get dark when I reach the village, and as I walk past the farmhouse April calls to me from a bedroom window.

'Do you think my father will need this?'

She holds up my grandfather's overalls.

'Your father's dead. He died two weeks ago.'

April withdraws and shuts the window. I sigh and let myself into the farmhouse, wondering what my stepmother is up to now.

I find her laying out my grandfather's belongings in neat piles on the bed. She is calm and even seems pleased to see me. It is as good a time as any to find out what I want to know.

'Tell me about your friend Asa Cohen.'

'He's not a friend.'

'Did you know he lived here in Grymewyck when he was a child?'

'He never mentioned it.'

'Who is he?'

April looks up from the pyjamas she is folding.

'He controls people's minds,' she says. 'A lot of Jews go in for it.'

'You mean he's a hypnotist?'

'He has a treatment centre where he hypnotises people, and then he straps them to an electric chair and sends currents through their brains to change their personalities. That's what he wanted to do to me.'

Is Asa Cohen a psychiatrist then? April's psychiatrist, even? It could be that he is here in a professional capacity to keep an eye on her. That would make sense.

The Grymewyck connection might be a coincidence. After all, hundreds of London children were sent to Yorkshire during the war to get away from the bombs.

April springs up and grasps my hand.

'I'm frightened of him,' she says. 'Don't leave me alone here.'

Her grip tightens, her fingers tremble. She widens her eyes to demonstrate her fear, and I am not taken in at all.

'You'll be fine. There's nothing to be frightened of.'

'I'm lonely here. I wish I'd never come back to Grymewyck. I wish I'd stayed in London.'

For whatever reason, April wants me to stay with her at the farmhouse tonight. I have no idea why, but here is my chance to get rid of her.

'I will stay with you tonight, but on one condition. You must promise go back to London tomorrow morning.'

♀

I sleep in May's old room, which has not been occupied for years, not since May moved into The Barn to look after me and Jack when April left. The mattress is lumpy and damp, but I tell myself it is only for one night. It is a price worth paying to get rid of April.

I have no idea what time it is when someone calls my name. I lie very still waiting to hear it again, but nothing happens. Thinking it must have been a dream, or possibly an owl, I turn over and try to sleep.

'Ophelia!'

The voice is low but distinct, and it comes from outside the window. I get out of bed and go to look.

Outside, the farmyard is bathed in pale moonlight, the pond a perfect ellipse of metallic grey. Everything is silent, still and familiar, but in the middle of the pond I spot an unfamiliar dark shape. I am straining to see what it is when a movement closer to the house distracts me.

Across the farmyard a figure steps out from the shadows and creeps past the gate towards the back door of the house, the back door that I did not lock. My first thought is to go downstairs and bolt the door, but first I go to April's room.

'April, are you awake?'

There is no reply. I call again, and again there is no reply. April is sleeping soundly.

I feel my way down the stairs and into the kitchen, where I stand very still and listen. In the darkness I hear the beating of my own heart, and then I hear something else. It is the sound of another person breathing.

Groping in the dark I find the dresser and slide my fingers along the wooden surface until they touch something smooth and cold. It is the tin of emulsion.

I lift the heavy tin with both hands and throw it as hard as I can in the direction of the breathing. First a soft thud, then a growl of pain. A gurgle, a slosh, and straight away a dull metallic clunk as the tin hits the stone floor.

In seconds I am outside, running across the moonlit farmyard and screaming at the top of my voice. As I dash past the pond a flash of purple catches my eye and I skitter to a halt on the uneven cobble stones.

There is no mistaking the colour of April's dressing gown.

I run round the pond's edge like a mad thing, unable to reach her. In the semi-darkness I knock over one of Percy's milk churns, trip and fall headlong onto the cobbles.

I curse, pick myself up, take a deep breath, and then I wade into the freezing water. I do not believe in God but I know the words of the Lord's Prayer by heart and I say them now to stop myself from screaming.

'Our Father Who Art In Heaven, Hallowed Be Thy Name.'

She is floating face down, bobbing around, causing ripples. I am struggling to reach her. I lunge forward, grasp the hem of her dressing gown and tug.

The dressing gown comes away in my hand and reveals not April, but a heap of clothes. On top of the heap I can just make out the dark sinewy shape of my grandfather's walking stick.

There is another person in the farmyard. I can't see them, but as I stand shivering, waist deep in the icy water, I become aware that someone is watching me.

I keep absolutely still, not breathing. The fine mud on the bottom of the pond oozes between my toes, covers my feet and creeps up my ankles. I feel myself sinking into the slime.

There is petrol in the air. The moonlit night is heavy with the reeking fumes. I look down at the water, which is now an iridescent sea of gold and green and purple, and it is gurgling like a waterfall.

Pyromania

'Imaginary friendships are developmental phenomena that usually occur during childhood or adolescence. The relationships take place in the imagination and have no external physical reality.'

For some reason I find this idea extraordinarily sexy. I was listening at the window, of course, when Ophelia was talking to my uncle.

She was evidently attached to this photograph, so presumably Ophelia was attached to me. I study the five-year-old me in the photograph hoping to discover what he has that I haven't and conclude that the differences between us are not significant enough to account for Ophelia's evident change of heart.

The only possible explanation is my glasses. I take them off and am reminded there is no way I can see properly without them. In any case it is unlikely that a young woman like Ophelia will be put off by a pair of spectacles.

I kiss the photograph, now dog-eared from much handling, and then I curse it. I have stolen Ophelia's photograph. Whatever low opinion she had of me before, she now thinks I am a thief as well.

I slip the photograph into my pocket and wonder what to do next. It is a beautiful evening so perhaps I will drive into Grymewyck and drop in at the Stag's Head. The beer there is so much better than in my uncle's local.

♂

It is well past closing time when I walk out of the Stag's Head, a little drunk, into the moonlit village square. I am immediately seized with a desire to see Ophelia.

I make my unsteady way towards the lane that leads to The Barn, and as I pass the farmyard I hear someone calling her name. Ophelia!

The voice seemed to come from the other side of the farmyard wall and I go to investigate. Ophelia! There it is again.

A dark shape creeps along the edge of the yard, weaves in and out of the shadows, and then steps out into the moonlight. The creeping figure is April Siward.

She makes her way to the farmhouse door and disappears inside. Seconds later Ophelia herself hurtles out of the house and runs screaming across the yard.

There is a moment's silence followed by a sickening splash. Ophelia is in the pond, and I am already peeling off my jacket to go to her when a downstairs light comes on in the farmhouse and April reappears.

She is carrying a lighted blow lamp and holding it as if it was a loaded pistol. Her head and shoulders are draped in white. A shawl, perhaps.

I follow her silently across the cobbles, wondering what crazy, devious game she is playing now.

April makes her way to the edge of the pond, to where I can just make out the shape of a metal barrel. The barrel is on its side, discharging its contents into the water.

As the oily liquid spreads across the surface of the pond the smell of petrol hits my nostrils and I am sober in an instant.

April kneels and places the blow lamp on the ground beside the barrel, just inches away from the leaking fuel. Immediately the grass around the barrel catches light and crackles noisily.

She appears to be gathering handfuls of the leaking petrol and attempting to throw it into the water.

'You stupid bitch!'

She looks up, sees me and grins. Her clothes are darkly stained with petrol and I see clearly now the white, viscous substance that is dripping from her hair. Not a shawl then, but paint.

'Ophelia! Get out of the water!'

No reply. I shout again.

'Get out of the water!'

'Our Father, Who Art In Heaven, Hallowed Be Thy Name.'

It is Ophelia, faint but audible, and it is the first time in my life I have been pleased to hear the Lords Prayer.

I lunge at April and try to drag her away, but she is as slimy and slithery as an eel. I cannot hold her and she knows it. April throws back her head and laughs in my face.

A second later she slips out of my arms and slides into the pond through the burning grass. There, waist deep in the water, April Siward bursts into flames. At the same time the surface of the water around her catches fire and for a few seconds the pond burns blue like a Christmas pudding.

Ophelia rises from the water like Botticelli's Venus emerging from the waves. She is holding something. A stick perhaps. As April staggers towards her, Ophelia raises the stick and pushes her with such force that April collapses and falls backwards into the water.

The explosion that follows almost knocks me off my feet and I am quickly engulfed in black, suffocating smoke.

♂

Ophelia is saying her prayers and so am I. When the praying stops I call to her over my shoulder and when there is no reply from the back seat I begin to shout. I am ordering her not to die, and I am driving like a maniac

I am still shouting as I run into the hospital with Ophelia in my arms. A nurse comes, and then another, and then more nurses, and then a trolley. I watch helplessly as Ophelia is wheeled away, aware only that the place where she lay against me is wet and cold and very empty.

The front of my shirt is as black and soggy as an extinguished bonfire. I pick at a clump of charred hair that has caught on my shirt button and watch it disintegrate into a sooty paste on the end of my finger.

Burns Ward, Valhalla

♀

I am dead and buried, except that I can't really be dead because I am screaming. From the darkness a voice tells me to stop and the screaming stops.

Something scratches my face. I try to push it away but my arms will not move, and when I open my eyes it makes no difference at all because it is still dark.

'Keep still.'

It is Asa Cohen's voice.

'Where am I?

My throat is so dry the words come out as a whisper.

'You're in hospital.'

The treatment centre. I knew it. Asa Cohen has brought me to his treatment centre and now he is going to put me in his electric chair.

Flames are crackling close to my head but when I try to

move away from them the crackling becomes deafening.

'You've got a dressing on your face and the gauze rustles when you move.'

His voice is calm and matter of fact. I keep still and the noise stops but my face is sore and stretched, and my throat parched.

'I'm thirsty.'

'I'll give you some water, but don't try and move.'

'Is it drugged?'

'It's straight from the tap.'

He lifts my head and I hear his wrist watch ticking close to my ear. I gulp the water and ask for more.

'There was a fire,' he says. 'You've got minor burns on your forehead and eyelids but you're going to be fine. You had a narrow escape.'

'Why am I tied up?'

'Your arms are on a pulley. You've got a few blisters, but nothing serious.'

'Am I alone with you?'

'There's a policewoman sitting at the other side of the bed.'

'Thank goodness for that,' I say, much relieved. 'This isn't an ordinary hospital, is it?'

'Of course it is. You're in a room that is about twelve feet square with a window to your left and a door on your right.'

He is leaning over me. I know this even though I can't see him, but I remember the creeping figure in the farmyard and I am certain now it was him.

'You were there. I saw you.'

The policewoman coughs.

'I'm not allowed to discuss the accident,' he says. 'The police are waiting to talk to you as soon as you're well enough.'

'When did it happen?'

'Just after midnight. You've been in hospital about twelve hours.'

'And you've been with me all that time?'

'I wanted to be here when you woke up, but now I have to get back to London immediately. I've contacted your aunt and asked her to let Daniel know.'

He tells me he has left his address with one of the nurses who says she knows me, and I have no idea what he is talking about.

Asa Cohen goes at last and I am able to tell the policewoman that I have been drugged and kidnapped. I beg her not to let them put me on the electric chair and she pats my leg and tells me she is going to fetch the doctor.

♀

A woman comes, whispers in my ear.

'You're going to be fine. The burns aren't serious.'

I recognise that voice. I would know it anywhere.

'Gloria?'

'Shh! The police are outside. They're waiting to talk to you.'

'What happened?'

'No one will tell me and we're all forbidden to discuss it.'

'There was an accident.'

'I know, your boy friend told me that much. He's waiting to see you, by the way. Dishy, or what!'

'Where am I?'

'The City General. You're only twenty miles from Grymewyck.'

I hear approaching footsteps, voices outside the door.

'Shit,' says Gloria. 'I'm not supposed to be here.'

A quick squeeze of my toes, a click of the door, and I

know she has gone.

♀

My stepmother is dead. The police found April's body on the edge of the pond and the woman detective who is sitting by my bed wants me to tell her exactly how it happened.

I laugh out loud because I know they have made a mistake.

'It wasn't April,' I say. 'It was only a pile of clothes.'

'Please tell me exactly what you remember.'

A pencil is scratching away close to my right ear so I know every word I say is being written down. I finish speaking and the scratching stops.

'You say you were woken up by someone calling your name,' says the policewoman. 'Are you sure about that?'

I am not sure about anything any more. Everything is mixed up in my head and now that I have tried to put it into words it is even more mixed up.

'That's what I thought at the time.'

'You looked out of the window and there was something in the pond. You saw an intruder moving towards the farmhouse door. You went to your stepmother's room but she was asleep and then you went downstairs and someone was in the kitchen, breathing in the dark. You assumed it was the intruder and you threw a can of paint at them. Is this correct?'

I nod.

'Miss Gunn, I'm afraid it was your stepmother we found by the pond. She was badly burned and there was a quantity of white emulsion on the body.'

I imagine April lying there, burned and black, dripping with white paint. It is much worse imagining things in the dark.

'After you threw the paint, you ran outside and saw what you thought was your stepmother in the pond. You went to look but instead of the body you were expecting you found a pile of clothes and a walking stick.'

'They were floating on the water.'

'They were tied to a wooden sledge. Do you know anything about a sledge?'

'I've got a sledge. Percy made it for me. It must have been mine.'

'The police report doesn't mention a walking stick.'

'I'm sure it was my grandfather's walking stick on top of the clothes.'

'What happened after that?'

'I woke up here in hospital and Asa Cohen was with me.'

'You don't remember the fire?'

'No.'

'Did you put the sledge on the pond yourself?'

'Of course not.'

'Do you have any idea who the intruder was?'

I am about to tell her the intruder was probably Asa Cohen when I change my mind. Whatever I think of him now, Asa Cohen was once the dark-eyed boy and I won't give him away to a strange woman who I cannot see and do not like. Once upon a time Asa Cohen was my best friend.

'It could have been a shadow.'

'How well do you know Asa Cohen?'

'Hardly at all. I have no idea why he was there.'

'He says he happened to be in the area when he heard you screaming and he brought you here to the hospital. Could Asa Cohen have been the figure you saw in the farmyard?'

'I'm not sure about the figure any more. I might have imagined it.'

'Did you get on well with your stepmother?'

'I hardly knew her.'

'You hadn't had a quarrel?'

'No.'

'Was your stepmother unhappy about anything?'

'My stepmother was always unhappy. She was an unhappy person.'

♀

At last Daniel is allowed in to see me.

'You look like an Egyptian mummy,' he says. 'How are you?'

Daniel himself sounds dreadful. He kneels by my bed and lays his head on my lap, and he sobs until his tears soak through my hospital gown and I have to tell him to stop.

'I killed her,' he says.

'Don't be silly, Daniel. You weren't even there.'

'I have to talk to you. I have to tell someone'

Daniel talks and when he has finished I am still in the dark, in every sense of the word.

'I don't understand,' I say. 'My grandfather was buried already. We were at his funeral, remember?'

'Yes, but on the day of his parochial funeral I told April about real funerals. I told her about Viking cremations.'

'I still don't understand.'

'I told her how Viking warriors were sometimes cremated in their longboats and how Vikings go to Valhalla when they die. That's why their possessions were usually burned with them, in case they needed them in their next life.'

'Possessions such as clothes and a walking stick?'

'That sort of thing,' he says. 'I think April was sending your grandfather's things on to him in Valhalla.'

'And the sledge? Presumably she used my sledge because she couldn't get hold of a longboat?'

'The Vikings sometimes used sledges instead of longboats.'

'And of course April knew this because you had told her?'

'I had no idea she would take it so literally. Ophelia, if they send me to prison, will you wait for me? Can we get married when I come out?'

♀

From the balcony of Gloria's high-rise council flat I can see the sprawling rooftops of the City General Hospital from which I have just been discharged. I am free at last and I have come to stay with Gloria.

We are on Gloria's balcony and she is cutting my hair, or what is left of it. Curls are piling up around my feet.

'Short all over,' I tell her. 'Cut the back to match the front.'

I must have fallen backwards into the flames when the accident happened because only the hair at the front got burned.

'If you say so.'

She snips away, walking round me from time to time to see the effect of her handiwork from every angle, and then she stands back to look at the finished result.

'Elegant! It shows off your neck.'

I move to go to the mirror but Gloria pushes me back.

'Wait.'

I touch my hair, which feels like fur, and Gloria returns with a pair of long black earrings and clips them to my lobes.

'Now go and see what you think.'

A strange woman stares back at me from the mirror. Her neck is pale and thin and her eyes are enormous. When the woman tosses her head I feel the cold earrings brush against my own skin.

'How does it feel?'

'Draughty.'

'Do you like it?'
'I don't look like a chocolate box any more.'

Gloria steals sleeping pills for me from the hospital but none of them have any effect. When I do sleep I have horrible dreams and Gloria tells me I cry out during the night.

In one dream I see April by the pond, burned black but with grinning white teeth. In another dream a judge in an orange wig and purple robe sentences me to death for lying to the police about the intruder.

One night when I am screaming in my sleep Gloria runs in and finds me sitting up in bed trying to beat out flames on the blankets. Another time I wake up not able to breathe because the bedroom is full of smoke. And then, quite suddenly, my nightmares stop.

The nightmares are replaced by a single recurring dream that is an exact re-enactment of the night I waded into the pond. The dream ends when I discover it is not April under the purple dressing gown after all, but a pile of clothes.

This dream becomes so familiar it ceases to frighten me but it always wakes me up and afterwards I can never get back to sleep. Of the fire and April's death I have no recollection whatsoever.

I become obsessed by the idea that Asa Cohen is responsible for my loss of memory and Gloria tells me to pull myself together.

'He couldn't possibly have hypnotised you without you knowing it.'

'Then why did I tell the police there was no intruder? There was definitely an intruder. I know it was him. Why did I lie'?

Gloria looks at me closely.

'Perhaps there was another reason.'

♀

Each afternoon I collect Zac from his nursery and I always have a meal ready for Gloria when she gets home from work. Daniel visits often, and he visits Grymewyck too. May sends messages of support in the form of pies and we all love May's pies.

Lack of sleep makes me weepy and I often find myself crying for no reason. In three weeks time I am due back at university and the prospect is overwhelming. I consider staying in Grymewyck and getting a job, but even this seems daunting.

Daniel offers to drive me to Grymewyck.

'You'll have to face it some time,' he says. 'You don't have to see the pond.'

I tell him it is too soon and I also I tell him I won't be going back to live with him. Daniel is sad but not surprised.

'I've known for ages,' he says. 'It's as if you've got another lover, but I know you haven't because you hardly ever leave this flat.'

Daniel times his visits to coincide with Zac and me getting home from the nursery, and he likes to play with Zac while I get supper.

Sometimes Daniel and Gloria go out together in the evenings and I stay in with Zac. I enjoy this, which surprises me. Normally I don't like children but Zac is different.

For one thing I am not Zac's mother, so looking after him is only temporary. Also, Zac doesn't ask questions. More particularly, he doesn't ask questions about the accident because he is not interested, which is a relief to me.

Zac does like me to read to him though. I read Winnie the Pooh and Where the Wild Things Are and James and The

Giant Peach. Sometimes I read Noddy, and Zac listens for a while, but only to please me.

Gloria hasn't been out at all since Zac was born and she always comes back happy. Daniel is happy too but he tries not show it, probably because he feels guilty. I wish he wouldn't because I really don't mind at all.

♀

One day Daniel arrives with a mysterious message from May. She is coming to see me, and she is bringing Percy with her. I am the only one to appreciate the significance of such an excursion out of Grymewyck and I know this visit is important.

Percy and May arrive in my grandfather's car with Percy at the wheel. They sit hand in hand on Gloria's sofa and Percy tells me they are going to be married. They will live at the farmhouse with my grandmother, and May and my grandmother intend to move back into the house immediately.

'The Barn will be empty,' says May. 'It belongs to you and we hope that one day you'll come and live in it. It's what your grandfather would have wanted. I understand that now.'

Perjury and Perversion

I shuffle through the postcards that have piled up on Charlie's doormat and read Charlie's last messages to April.

Darling April, I miss you. Darling April, I miss you lots. Darling April, I love you. Darling April, I'll see you on Tuesday.

Today is Tuesday. What the hell am I going do? In the end I do what I always do in a crisis and ring Sue.

'Where are you?'

'In Charlie's flat. Can you come over?'

'I thought Charlie was in France.'

'He'll be back any time now. Just get yourself over here.'

'Say please.'

'Please.'

I help myself to a large glass of Charlie's whisky and light a cigarette from Charlie's silver cigarette box, and then I settle down on a pink, heart shaped sofa to wait.

Sue arrives at last and gasps as she enters the flat that was once her home.

''Struth,' she says. 'Is Charlie running a brothel?'

'Sit down, Sue. I've something to tell you.'

'I thought you didn't smoke.'

'Just sit down.'

'Is that sofa meant for conversation? Shouldn't I just take my clothes off and jump on you?'

'This is serious, Sue. Shut up and listen.'

I tell her what has happened and she turns as white as the marble angel on the pedestal behind her.

'Was it suicide?'

'It was an accident.' I say. 'No one else was involved.'

'What are we going to do?'

'We're going to wait here for Charlie and we're going to tell him what's happened. There's nothing else we can do.'

Sue pours herself a whisky and helps herself to a cigarette from Charlie's silver cigarette box.

'I thought you didn't smoke,' I say.

I am on the A1 yet again, only this time I am on my way to April's inquest. To perjure myself. Perjury… The wilful giving of false testimony under oath… I looked it up in one of uncle Ben's books, circa 1912. I looked up the penalty too. The punishment for perjury is up to seven years penal servitude.

Charlie is with me because he wants to meet April's children, the children he never knew she had. I am here because I have no choice. I have been summonsed to appear as a witness at April's inquest.

'Jack and Ophelia may not be there,' I warn Charlie.

'Ophelia might not be well enough to give evidence.'

'I expect Toby will be there though?'

Toby will certainly not be at the inquest because Toby is in prison but Charlie doesn't know this. I have not told him about my meeting with Pearl Bonnet or about April's nightly vigils outside Toby's bedroom window. There seems no point in causing my brother more pain than he is suffering already.

'I blame Toby for what happened,' says Charlie. 'To abandon a lovely wife and children as he did was unforgivable. Poor April.'

I have been patient with my brother during the past weeks and I try to be patient now.

'It was an accident, Charlie. No one is to blame.'

Apart from Ophelia herself, I am the only person who knows what really happened in the farmyard that night. Whether or not Ophelia has remembered what happened I am soon to find out.

'I can't imagine life without April,' says Charlie. 'It's going to be lonely.'

I have perverted the course of justice and interfered with evidence. If Ophelia's memory has returned I could well be spending tonight in a police cell and so could she. I imagine things don't get much more lonely than that.

Charlie is nervous and keeps looking at his watch.

'How much further?' he asks. 'You don't want to be late.'

Late is exactly what I want to be. It is my intention to be late because I need to hear Ophelia's evidence before I give my own. I reduce my speed to a snail's pace and this makes Charlie even twitchier.

'You'd better put your foot down,' he snaps. 'We'll miss the inquest altogether at this rate.'

When I pull in and stop on the side of the road Charlie is exasperated.

'What now?'

'There's a telephone kiosk. I'm going to ring the coroner's court and tell them to start without me.'

Lions and Unicorns

♀

The coroner's court has a low stage with red velvet curtains and in the centre of the stage is a wooden table and a bentwood chair. It is just like being at the theatre. Daniel, Percy and myself are in the front row waiting for the performance to start, and there are only two empty seats in the house.

Daniel and I have been called as witnesses. Percy is here to represent my grandmother and May, who couldn't face coming themselves. Percy is the man of the house now and he looks pleased with himself.

'I've taken them to my cousin in Scunthorpe until the fuss has died down,' he whispers. 'I'm joining them there tonight.'

I look at Daniel, the man I am not going to marry, and notice he has lost his rosy cheeks. Poor Daniel. He didn't bargain for this when he took me in. The West London

Viking has a lot to answer for.

The coroner is late but a young woman comes in and introduces herself as the usher. She is wearing a black suit with a very short skirt, and she gets up on the stage and drops a mock curtsey. The young woman then sits down in the coroner's chair and proceeds to put on her make-up.

'Just in case Ringo Starr drops by,' she says, and winks. 'The gentlemen on my left are from the press, by the way. Don't tell them a thing unless you get paid for it.'

'For Christ's sake!' whispers Daniel. 'This is sick.'

To steady myself I concentrate on the lion and the unicorn on the coat of arms above the coroner's chair.

'*Honi soit qui mal y pense,*' I read out loud to Daniel. 'What does it mean?'

'Shame be to he who thinks evil of it.'

'And what does that mean?'

'Ssh!'

The young woman bows and addresses the audience.

'The court will stand.'

I feel better when I see the coroner because she looks motherly and appears flustered. She takes her place at the table and apologises for being late. It seems one of the witnesses has not yet arrived but the inquest will start without him.

I hold the arms of my chair to steady myself and Daniel puts his hand over mine. It is a protective gesture and I am grateful for it.

A police doctor tells us April's death was almost certainly due to shock, not burning or drowning. She was almost certainly dead before she was pulled out of the water and I am pleased about that at least. Poor April.

The door swings open and Asa Cohen walks into the courtroom, followed by a broad-shouldered man with thick sandy hair. They pass in front of our table and take the two empty seats directly behind us. I try not to think about them.

The lion and the unicorn were fighting for the crown. The lion beat the unicorn all round the town.

I wish I could remember the next line. I am sure it is something about brown bread.

Daniel shakes my arm. The coroner is looking at me, smiling. It is my turn and Daniel gives my hand a little squeeze as I stand up.

The coroner reads out loud the statement I made to the police after the accident and asks if I have remembered anything since. It is most important to tell the court if anything has come back to me.

I look at my feet and mumble that I have not, and then I look up and speak clearly to everyone in the room.

'No,' I say, very loudly. 'I have remembered nothing more.'

The coroner asks about the intruder and I tell her there was probably no intruder. I think now I might have imagined it.

Daniel is accustomed to speaking in public and does better than me, but he is pale as he tells the court about my stepmother's fascination with Vikings. The coroner asks about Viking funeral rituals and Daniel explains about longboat cremations and Valhalla.

She questions Daniel about two books found in the farmhouse and Daniel looks uncomfortable. The coroner reads out the titles. The Viking Book of Poetry and The Vikings: Rituals and Religion. Daniel winces and says the books belong to him and, yes, he did lend them to Mrs Gunn.

Asa Cohen takes the oath next, cool and unperturbed. I refuse to look but am forced to listen as he tells the court how he heard my screams that night and went to investigate.

He describes finding April and myself in the pond and how he pulled us from the water. April was already dead but I was still breathing. He carried me to his car and drove me to hospital.

I want desperately to get out of the courtroom and into the fresh air but when I try to stand up Daniel pulls me back.

'It's nearly over,' he says. 'You're almost through.'

I take in snatches of the summing up, not all. The coroner pays tribute to Mr Cohen's great presence of mind. April is described as a vulnerable woman, her death a tragedy.

There is no evidence to suggest another person was involved and the police are not asking for a court hearing. The coroner returns an open verdict.

Daniel gets me out of the courtroom quickly before everyone else and Gloria is waiting for us in the lobby. She and Daniel are going to London for the weekend and I am to look after Zac.

It was my idea and I am looking forward to a peaceful two days in the flat. Gloria has never been to London and I could tell Daniel wanted to go.

♀

On the pavement outside, people are jostling and shoving. Someone holds a camera right in front of my face and I push it away. Across the road, Daniel and Gloria are chased by another photographer, then I see them get into Daniel's car and drive off.

I walk away quickly in the direction of the bus stop and when I look back the reporters have gone, but Asa Cohen and his friend are close behind. I start to run but a moment later Asa Cohen's hand is on my shoulder, bringing me to a halt.

'You're quite an athlete,' he says.

The sandy haired man comes up out of breath and

introduces himself as Charlie Manners. He wants me to have lunch with them.

'No, thank you. I have to meet a little boy from nursery school.'

'What time are you meeting him?'

'Half past three. What time is it now?'

'Half past twelve.'

Thankfully my bus is coming and I am about to get on it.

'I can hardly blame you,' says Charlie Manners sadly. 'You don't know me from Adam.'

I look at him again and realise that I do know him. Of course I know him. This is the man in my father's wedding photograph. Charles and Pearl. Pearl and Charles.

Once upon a time I was going to name my son after this man.

♀

Charlie does the talking. He talks about the wine list, the weather, and the film he saw at his local cinema last week. I realise he is doing this deliberately to put me at my ease and I am grateful.

When Charlie stops talking long enough to look at the menu, Asa Cohen speaks for the first time.

'You've had your hair cut,' he says. 'It suits you.'

I can't bear to look him in the eye but I can see his hands and I know Asa Cohen is as nervous as I am. He fidgets with his water glass, turning it round and round between his palms, and then he taps a little tune on the tablecloth with the tips of his fingers.

'You look like Jean Seberg,' says Charlie. 'Asa, don't you think Ophelia looks like Jean Seberg?'

I have never heard of Jean Seberg.

'I don't remember the name of the film,' says Charlie. 'But

Jean Seberg was in it and she had hair just like yours.'

'*A Bout de Souffle*,' says Asa. 'Jean Seberg had cropped hair and it became the fashion.'

I have never heard of the *A Bout de Souffle* either.

Charlie must have invited me here for a reason and I am curious to hear what that reason might be, but he orders the food and carries on chatting about films so perhaps there is no ulterior motive after all. When he forgets the names of actors and directors Asa Cohen prompts him and Charlie laughs.

'My brother was always the clever one,' he says. 'Is it any wonder I have an inferiority complex?'

'Your brother?'

Now I am really confused. The two men look nothing like each other, but they are both laughing so perhaps it is a joke.

'I have an ulterior motive for inviting you,' says Charlie at last. 'You see, I knew your mother very well, which is why I wanted to meet you.'

'April was my stepmother, not my mother, and I know who you are because I recognise you from the wedding photograph. You were the Best Man.

'The connection is more recent than that. You see, April and I have been living together as husband and wife for the last ten years.'

Charlie is watching me, anxious to see the effect of his words, but he is far more affected than I am. Nothing I hear about April can surprise me now, but Charlie is clearly upset.

'Did your stepmother never mention me?'

I shake my head.

'I hardly saw April when I was growing up, and I never knew where she was living because she never gave me her address.'

'April told me she had no children,' says Charlie. 'She was

quite explicit about that, and I have no idea why she lied.'

He is trying to make sense of April's behaviour and I cannot help.

'My stepmother was a strange woman. I don't know what else to say.'

I tell Charlie as much as I remember about April and my father, and I tell him what I know of Pearl Bonnet. I am aware of the pain I must be causing but each time I stop, Charlie prompts me to carry on. When I have finished he shakes his head, still baffled.

'Why were your father and brother not at the inquest today?'

'My father's in prison, and Jack's been away from Grymewyck for so long I'm not sure he thinks of us as family any more.'

Charlie is sorry to hear about my father but doesn't seem surprised, and then he wants to know about me.

I tell him I have finished my first year at university but am thinking of leaving and staying in Grymewyck, and I tell him I have recently split up with my boyfriend. I also tell Charlie about The Barn, which now belongs to me.

'Will you live in it?'

'I'm moving in after the weekend. To be honest, I'm not looking forward to it but I know I have to face Grymewyck sooner or later.'

'You are a very courageous young woman,' says Charlie.

This makes me want to cry because I don't feel in the least courageous. The truth is I am now regretting my decision to leave Gloria's and am very frightened indeed of going back to The Barn on my own.

I manage to hold back the tears but Asa Cohen is watching me and has seen my fear.

Charlie looks at his watch.

'I have a train to catch,' he says. 'Regretfully, I must leave you two to drink your coffee on your own.'

He gives me his card and tells me to let him know if there is anything he can do to help. Anything at all.

AQUAPHOBIA

Hypnotic Eyes

Not once do Ophelia's eyes meet mine, not even when I help her off with her coat and pour her a glass of water. She chooses to sit beside me, which delights me until I realise she is doing this to avoid having to look at me.

Ophelia has lost weight. She is thin, painfully so, and she has tried to disguise this by wearing a baggy shirt and a cotton scarf wrapped loosely around her throat.

I have a good view of her hands though, and I can tell she is nervous because she keeps twisting and untwisting her fingers and digging them into her palms. Ophelia has beautiful hands, long and slender, but her nails are bitten to the quick and her fingertips are raw and look painful.

She sees me looking and hides her hands under her napkin, ashamed of the chewed nails. *Onychophagia*. Nail biting. It is what people do when they are under stress. It is not serious and I would like to tell her that it doesn't matter.

Ophelia is still avoiding my eyes but she can't keep it up, not now Charlie has gone and left us alone together. Sooner or later she must look at me, even if it is only to say goodbye.

She thinks I am trying to hypnotise her, of course. She said as much in the hospital and I have come across it before.

Hypnophobics have a dread of being put in a trance against their will by someone who wants to harm them. In Ophelia's case, she believes that someone to be me.

I need her to raise her head and look me in the eye. I must know if she really remembers nothing about the accident as she said at the inquest, or if she is lying in order to protect herself. She can't stare into that empty coffee cup forever.

'Were you telling the truth at the inquest?'

'Of course.'

'You have no memory at all of the accident?'

She looks at me at last with those extraordinary eyes.

'Are you calling me a liar?'

The look is hostile, but at least I know she is telling the truth. So far, Ophelia has remembered nothing.

'Your missing memory will come back,' I say. 'You should be prepared for that.'

'I hope it doesn't. I'd like to forget all about the accident.'

'You will remember, whether you want to or not. You have no choice.'

'When will it happen?'

'Perhaps not for years, but it could happen during the next five minutes.'

This is cruel of me. I am deliberately frightening a vulnerable young woman in order to get my own way, but it can't be helped. I have one chance and I cannot afford to waste it.

'Returning to the scene of the accident is likely to trigger the memories.'

She does not want to go back to Grymewyck on Monday, she said so herself. I must play on that.

I suspect she is looking for an excuse not to go to Grymewyck at all, but she has no choice. The nurse is in London with the ex-boyfriend, and the aunt and grandmother are away. I heard her telling Charlie so.

'Is it dangerous for me to go back to Grymewyck?'

'It would be dangerous to go on your own.'

'I have no choice.'

'Then I should go with you.'

This is seriously unprofessional of me and I know I have gone too far. I am half expecting her to get up and leave, but she remains seated.

Ophelia appears to be considering the idea. I tell myself not to push, to let her make up her own mind.

'I like your brooch,' I say, changing the subject. 'It's unusual.'

She touches the brooch, which comes away from her collar and clatters on to the table. I pick it up quickly.

'The clasp's broken. I'll mend it before I pick you up on Monday. You'd better give me your friend's address.'

♂

Uncle Ben must have forgotten why I am back in Grymewyck because he doesn't ask about the inquest. I show him Ophelia's brooch, which he examines through his magnifying glass.

'Fascinating,' he says, turning it over in his fingers. 'Ugly, yet beautiful at the same time.'

He reaches for a book from the shelf beside him.

'Have you seen anything like it before?'

'I should think I have,' he says, 'Where did you get it?'

♂

Later, much later, Uncle Ben wants to know all about the inquest.

'How was Ophelia?' he asks.

I have given up wondering how he knows about Ophelia but the question makes me jump all the same because I thought my uncle was asleep. I stop pacing the room and sit down.

'She's suffering the after-effects of trauma,' I tell him. 'Ophelia doesn't remember a thing about the accident.'

It is difficult to know if my uncle is listening or if he has fallen asleep, but then he opens one eye.

'You should eat something, Asa. You look terrible. There's some cold meat in the fridge.'

♂

Night worry is the worst of all worries. I know this because my patients tell me so and my advice to them is always brisk but sympathetic.

'Get up and do something,' I say. 'Listen to the radio. Make a cup of tea. Read a book.'

I do none of these things but lie awake all night, agonising over what I have done. The miracle is I managed not to reach across the table and stroke her hair, although it was all I could do to stop myself.

Ophelia's hair is like fur, short and silky, and not in the least like Jean Seberg's hair. I really don't know where Charlie gets his ideas.

The seriousness of my deception at the inquest is something I am trying not to think about. Hiding the walking stick was of course a criminal offence. I tampered with the evidence and if I am found out the penalty will be severe.

The consequences of Ophelia remembering what she did with the stick will be infinitely worse. If she ever does remember, that is.

Right now my worst fear is that Ophelia will change her mind about Monday and I might never see her again. Inside me something hard and cold is gnawing at my empty gut and will not be laid to rest.

New Occupant, Same Dream

♀

The sun is shining and the road to Grymewyck is friendly and familiar, but I am not happy. Asa Cohen frightened me with all that stuff about memory triggers. I should never have agreed to him bringing me.

'I'll be fine when I get there,' I say. 'This is very kind of you, but you don't have to stay.'

When we reach the village square he stops the car and nods in the direction of the farmhouse. The curtains are drawn shut and the entrance to the farmyard has been cordoned off with rope.

'Shut your eyes.'

I close my eyes as he drives past the farmyard and then pond, and we are bumping along the lane that will take us to The Barn.

♀

My footsteps echo in the empty kitchen and my shoes stick to the bleached stone floor. I am home, and it doesn't feel like home at all.

There is an envelope on the table and I tear it open thinking it might be from May, but it is only a request for a meter reading from the electricity company. It is addressed to the new occupant, Miss Ophelia Gunn.

Asa Cohen is still here. I can see him through the window, leaning against his car with his hands in his pockets.

He hasn't driven away as he promised he would and I am pleased about that now because I have changed my mind about staying here. As soon as I stop shaking I will ask him to drive me back to Gloria's.

He comes in with carrier bags of food and puts them down on the dresser, and then he unpacks the bags and starts putting the stuff away in cupboards. I had not thought about food and this makes me laugh.

I laugh and then cry, and then I laugh again.

'Stop it,' he says.

'I want to go back to Gloria's.'

He pours brandy and gives it to me. May would never dream of buying brandy so he must have brought it with him. The brandy makes me splutter.

'Let's go. Please.'

'The worst is over,' he says. 'Leaving now will make it more difficult next time.'

'There won't be a next time.'

'Give it till sunset. If you still want to leave by this evening, I'll take you back to your friend's flat. You have my word.'

♀

Asa Cohen is in May's bedroom. I can hear his typewriter.

Clickety-click, clickety-click.

If he rolled back the corner of the sheepskin rug now he would be able to see me through the gap in the floorboards, and he would know I was still sitting at the kitchen table where he left me a couple of hours ago.

The thought galvanises me into action and I go into the garden to lie on the lawn where he can't see me.

It is late afternoon when he comes out, stooping to avoid the low lintel. He hands me a plate of sandwiches but I am not hungry. When he has gone I get up and tip the sandwiches into the flower bed, and then I go back to the lawn to wait for evening.

He is typing too fast for me to count the letters but there is a rhythm to the words so I count those instead. I count until my fingers grow stiff and I am too tired to count any more.

I tiptoe up the stairs to my own room, and I climb into bed and listen to the clickety-click of Asa Cohen's typewriter. My eyelids keep sliding shut, even though I am struggling to stay awake.

I don't want to fall asleep, not while I am alone in the house with Asa Cohen.

♀

My dream is the same one I have every night so I know exactly what happens and how the dream ends. April is bobbing around a few feet away from me, except I know by now that it is not really April at all. It is only a heap of old clothes.

As usual I am up to my armpits in cold water and as usual I am saying the Lord's Prayer. I gabble the words quickly to bring the dream to an end because I know I always wake up after I say Amen.

I say Amen and I don't wake up. I say it again. Amen. Something is wrong because I am still in the pond with the water lapping so hard against my ribs I can hardly breathe.

The downstairs light in the farmhouse comes on, the door opens and April comes out chasing a brightly-coloured bird that flutters towards me across the farmyard.

Asa Cohen comes and creeps up behind her, his hands raised to strike. I open my mouth to warn April because she hasn't seen him.

♀

I am woken by the lid of my grandmother's piano creaking open and Asa Cohen begins to play, very quietly. Outside it is not quite light. I close my eyes and count the notes, and immediately the room fills with petrol fumes.

 Green, gold and magenta crawl towards me across the pond and I dip the tip of my index finger into the oily colour. As I touch the water the pond gives a violent lurch and April is in the water with me.

Her head is a halo of pink and blue flame, and her shoulders are glistening and dripping like melted wax. She looks as pretty as a candle on a birthday cake.

'Ophelia! Get out of the water!'

A gentle sizzling, a whiff of burning hair, and I am alone.

In the darkness, someone is playing the piano.

♀

He stops playing when he sees me stumbling down the stairs and comes to help.

'I think I'm going to be sick.'

I reach the kitchen just in time and then drop slowly to my knees and press my hot face against the cool porcelain of the sink. He follows me back upstairs with a glass of water and offers to find me something clean to wear.

'Are you ready to go to your friend's house?'

'Later.'

What I want now more than anything is sleep. I close the door on Asa Cohen and crawl under the eiderdown so he can't hear me crying. I cry until I get hiccups and am too tired to cry any more, but I do not sleep.

The Quick Brown Fox

Utter bloody rubbish, that is what I am typing.

The quick brown fox jumps over the lazy dog.

Anything to keep me awake and out of her way.

Her amnesia is an act of self-preservation, an alternative to suicide. Freud again. How uncle Ben would be loving this.

The vomiting helped but she has not slept because she was crying all night. I heard her. Ophelia is exhausted and no wonder.

When it gets light I go in and find her calm but wide awake. She is staring at the ceiling, her eyes glassy from lack of sleep.

If Ophelia was my patient I would prescribe valium. The little worker of minor miracles. I take them myself, though not as often as I used to. I have some in my pocket. She will think I am trying to poison her but it's worth a try.

'How are you feeling?'

'Go away.'

'I have some tablets. They'll help you sleep.'

I shake two tablets into the palm of my hand. She pushes my hand away, as I knew she would. I shake out another two tablets.

'There are four pills here,' I say. 'Two for you and two for me. I'll take mine first.'

She is tempted, I can see. And she is desperate for sleep. Ophelia raises her head from the pillow and stares at the pills with red-rimmed eyes. She hesitates a moment, and then she chooses two of the tablets and pops them in my open mouth.

I slip the valium under my tongue and open my mouth wider for her to inspect inside. She peers down my throat, takes the other two pills from my hand and gulps them down.

It is the oldest trick in the book.

♂

Twelve hours later Ophelia wakes up smiling and my heart almost stops beating. It is too soon to be certain, but the smile gives me reason to hope.

'I had the dream again.'

'Do you want to tell me about it?'

'It was about the accident.'

'I know.'

I pull a chair up to the bed and sit down. She props herself up against the pillows and pulls the sheet up to her chin.

'April was there chasing a beautiful bird, and then you came and I thought you were going to hit her, but you didn't. You and April were dancing together in the moonlight, and then April came into the pond with me. The water was freezing, but the colours were amazing. Like a rainbow.'

She makes it sound like a Walt Disney film. I have been keeping a lonely vigil while Ophelia has been watching Fantasia.

'There was a gurgling sound, like a waterfall, and bees buzzing. Why are you smiling?'

'You're describing a holiday destination. Go on.'

She pulls a face.

'There was this horrible smell, first petrol, and then burning hair. That's probably what made me sick.'

She grows so pale at the memory I am afraid she is going be sick again and I press her to go on.

'There's nothing else to tell,' she says. 'After that everything went black.'

First relief, and then elation. My muscles relax and my body becomes as jelly. For the time being at least, Ophelia has no idea what really happened.

'I'm starving,' I say. 'Breakfast in ten minutes.'

♂

She bites into her egg sandwich and the fat runs down her chin.

'What was the meaning of my dream?'

Did she really just say that? Uncle Ben would be in heaven.

'Your dream was essentially correct, a replay of the night of the accident, but the petrol fumes were probably causing you to hallucinate. That's why everything looked so unreal and magical.'

She licks the fat off her chin with her tongue and regards me with her wide green eyes.

'Is that what happens to people who take drugs?'

'Things certainly weren't as pretty as you thought. April had a blow lamp. That was the bird you saw, and the buzzing was probably the noise of the flame.'

'But you were there because I saw you. You were dancing with April.'

'I was actually trying to stop her from setting fire to you.'

'Why didn't you say that at the inquest?'

'There was no point. It would have been upsetting for everyone, especially your family. An open verdict was the best possible outcome.'

Ophelia helps herself to another egg sandwich and considers this.

'Did she hate me that much?'

'Your stepmother was a fantasist. She sincerely believed she was the daughter of a Viking chief, and she knew that Viking chiefs were sometimes cremated with a living person, someone who would take care of them in their after life. I think April was sending you to Valhalla to look after your grandfather.'

Over the rim of her coffee cup Ophelia's eyes widen, and then she puts down the cup and looks at me very directly.

'What did you do with my grandfather's walking stick?'

And here is where I have to be careful.

'You must be mistaken,' I say. 'I saw no walking stick. The police saw no walking stick. There was no walking stick.'

'I saw the walking stick. I may have been hallucinating but I know without any shadow of doubt that my grandfather's walking stick was there on the pile of clothes. I saw it and I felt it.'

'Then where is it now?'

'That's what I'm asking you.'

'I expect it's exactly where your grandfather left it before he died. We could go and see if it's still there.'

She can't face the farmhouse, not yet. I am banking on that.

'You go.' she says. 'I can't face it.'

'Fine. Tell me where he kept his walking stick.'

Ophelia thinks about this for a few seconds, then she remembers.

'He used to hang it on the back of the cowshed door.'

I drive to the farmyard, which is only a few hundred yards down the lane. Ophelia is watching from the The Barn porch and will be thinking I am a lazy bastard but that can't be helped.

The walking stick is under the back seat of my car, where it has been since I hid it there on the night of the accident. As soon as I am out of sight of The Barn I pull up and retrieve the stick, then I count to a hundred, turn the car around in the village square and return to Ophelia.

'Where was it?' she asks.

'Exactly where you said it was. On the cowshed door.'

I hold the stick in both hands and present it as if it was a precious object. It is time to settle the issue of the missing walking stick once and for all.

Ophelia ignores the stick and takes my arm instead. She raises it to her lips and my heart races. I close my eyes and wait for the kiss.

She sinks her teeth into the flexed muscle and the silent popping of punctured flesh is followed by a pain so excruciating it takes my breath away and almost knocks me off my feet.

I drop the stick and open my eyes. From behind the upper edge of my flexor carpi radialis, Ophelia is glaring at me with angry eyes.

'For Christ's sake! Let go.'

She shakes her head, causing another spasm of searing

pain to shoot up my arm and into my neck and shoulders. Her mouth is clamped firmly on to my lower arm and there is not a glimmer of pity in those beautiful eyes.

'Ophelia, I'm going to ask you a question but please don't nod or shake your head. Blink once for no and twice for yes. Do you understand?'

She blinks twice.

'Are you angry with me?'

She blinks twice but bites harder, closing her eyes and forcing her teeth further together until the muscles in her own jaw seem in danger of going into spasm. A tear oozes out from between the closed lashes.

'Do you want me to go away?'

Two more blinks release the tear and it rolls slowly down her cheek, followed by another, and then another. I speak slowly and clearly.

'I will leave as soon as you take your teeth out of my arm.'

Unrequited love is a medically unrecognised condition, the symptoms of which can be physiological or mental, or both. My physiological symptom is a swollen forearm and the teeth marks therein.

I examine the arm, which is now almost twice its normal size, and kiss the swelling. The pain is excruciating but it is what I deserve. I was lying and Ophelia knew it.

My mental symptoms are manifold, but the self-hate is the worst. I look at myself in my uncle's dressing table mirror and see a weak, dishonest creature. It is little wonder Ophelia can't stand the sight of me.

The arm becomes infected and my temperature rises to a hundred and three. Uncle Ben gives me penicillin and orders me to bed but the fever has given me courage, or possibly it has affected my judgement.

In any case, I get up and go to find Ophelia, driving like a lunatic with my one good arm. My new job starts the day after tomorrow and this is my last chance.

The Other Side of The Pond

♀

Asa Cohen was lying, of course. That is why I bit him. I was really upset. Even so, I shouldn't have lost my temper like that.

I was about to tell him that my grandfather always left his walking stick leaning against the side of the fireplace when he wasn't using it, which is the truth. But something stopped me.

He was too eager for me to forget about the walking stick, so I lied, just to test him. My grandfather would never hang his stick on the back of the cowshed door. There isn't even a hook on the cowshed door.

I am sorry I bit him, but I was really angry. Afterwards I went upstairs for bandages and witch hazel but by the time I got down he had disappeared. He had left a note on the kitchen table though.

I am sorry if I upset you. Please do not worry about my arm. It is only a scratch.

The message is written on the back of the photograph. Asa Cohen has gone, but he has left me with the dark-eyed boy.

It is peaceful here in The Barn but there are echoes. Down the lane the farmhouse is still in darkness, so they must all still be in Scunthorpe. Someone must be coming every day to do the milking, but I haven't seen a living soul.

I can't bear to go down to the farm, not yet, and certainly not on my own. And I don't want to go to the village either because going to the village means passing the pond.

Gloria has no telephone otherwise I could ring Daniel to fetch me. It is probably a good thing I can't get hold of them because I haven't changed my clothes or cleaned my teeth since Asa Cohen left, and that was three days ago.

I don't even get undressed when I go to bed. Gloria would be horrified.

Sometimes I sit at the piano where Asa Cohen sat and I try to remember the piece he played, but it has gone completely. There are no dreams now, just a real desire to get out of Grymewyck.

I am missing London, but London is on the other side of the pond.

When I telephone the university and leave a message for my tutor he rings back almost immediately. He is curious about the accident, which he read about in the papers.

I tell my tutor I am ready to come back when term starts but that I have nowhere to live and am nervous about being on my own. He suggests a room in a residential block where I will be with other students and promises to see what he can do.

'You'll be safer down here,' he says. 'There are no Vikings

in Bloomsbury.'

♀

The walking stick is still on the floor where Asa dropped it. I have avoided touching it or even looking at it but now I pick it up and examine it, and then I sniff it. The smell of petrol is still strong and there are smears of white paint on the handle.

I take the stick into the porch and chop it into little pieces, and then I go back inside and light a fire with it.

♀

When the letter arrives from the university I open it without enthusiasm. It is my timetable and reading list for the coming term. I sit at the kitchen table and burst into tears because London seems so very far away.

A shadow falls across the kitchen table and I look up to see Asa Cohen in the doorway with his left arm in a sling.

'Why the tears?' he asks.

'I'm frightened.'

'Of me?'

'Of being here.'

'You'll be off to London in a couple of weeks.'

'How do you know?'

'I know that's what you should do.'

He sits down at the table opposite me.

'What are you reading?'

'My timetable for next year.'

'Your timetable is getting wet.'

He pulls the paper away from where I have been crying over it, wincing as he rests his arm on the table.

'I want to forget all about this summer,' I tell him. 'From now on I want to be a normal person and lead a normal life.'

'What sort of things do normal people do?'

It is an odd sort of question and one I have to think about.
'Normal people go for walks.'
'What else?'
'They clean their teeth.'
'And?'
'They make cups of tea.'
'Get your coat.'

Outside, I breathe deeply and fill my lungs with fresh air. This is the first time I have been out of the house since he left and Asa waits to see which way I will go. I hesitate for a moment and then turn towards the farm.

We walk down the lane in silence and he opens the farmyard gate. Together we cross the cobbles and stand for a few minutes on the edge of the pond staring at our reflections in the water.

The water is cloudy with mud and cow dung. There are a few streaks of petrol on the surface, but nothing else.

Asa picks up a pebble and gives it to me. I throw the pebble into the water where it sinks with a harmless little plop.

♀

Back at The Barn we stand side by side in front of the bathroom basin.

'You're not allowed to look,' I say.
'I'm not looking at you.'

I squeeze the toothpaste on to my brush and proceed to clean my teeth.

'Fascinating,' he says. 'You brush your bottom teeth first.'
'How do you know that?'
'I can see you in the mirror.'

Downstairs I put the kettle on and he spoons the tea into the pot. He struggles to open the caddy with one hand but he doesn't complain. He hasn't mentioned his arm, not once. The kitchen is a mess because I have done no washing up for three days and he doesn't mention this either.

'Milk?' I ask.

'Please.'

'Sugar?'

'I'd rather give you a hug.'

Asa hugs me with his good arm and I put my head on his chest. The echoes have gone now and the house is so quiet I can hear his heart beating. We stay like that until the kettle whistles and I have to go and take it off.

I carry the tea out to the lawn where Asa has taken his shoes and socks off and is stretched out on his back fast asleep. He must be really tired, and I can tell his arm is hurting because the blood is seeping through the bandage.

'Asa?'

It feels funny saying his name because I have never said it before. Anyway, I say it now and it doesn't wake him so I shake him by the shoulder.

'Ouch!'

He still doesn't open his eyes so I leave the mug of tea by his side and go indoors to find something normal to do. In the end I pull May's washing machine over to the sink and go round the house collecting all my dirty clothes, including the ones I have been wearing for the last three days.

Asa is still asleep when I go to peg out the washing so I spread one of the wet tea towels over his face to protect it from the sun. I don't want him to have a sore nose as well as a sore arm.

As a surprise for Asa I decide to make lunch, but there isn't much in the larder. Just a pack of sausages and a tin of baked beans. I poke around looking for something to go with them and realise I am humming Asa's tune. It has come back to me, probably because I stopped trying to remember it.

I am still humming the tune when Asa comes in from the garden.

'Ophelia's Song,' he says. 'It reminds me of you.'

'I hope you aren't going to be like Hamlet.'

'Not a chance. I'm much too normal for that.'

'I wish I could be sure.'

'I'll prove it. In fact, I can start right now by turning those sausages.'

Asa takes the fork from my hand and turns the sausages over. They are a bit black underneath and some of them have stuck to the frying pan, so it is a good thing he noticed.

'What's that you're wearing?'

'My school gym slip. Everything else is in the wash.'

♀

After lunch we sit side by side on the sofa and Asa looks at my course reading list.

'What are you thinking?'

He doesn't look up when he says this.

'That I know nothing about you.'

'What would you like to know?'

'About your work, for a start.'

His face is the face of the dark-eyed boy, but the grown up Asa has thick dark eyebrows that come together when he frowns and go up when he is surprised. His eyebrows go up now.

'Most people find my work boring.'

'I still want to know.'

'Well, the new job is in a hospital on the outskirts of London. The work is mainly clinical but I'll be doing some research and a bit of teaching. That's about it.'

'No electric shocks?'

'Occasionally.'

'What about hypnotism?'

He laughs.

'Not in a million years.'

Suddenly Asa stands up and suggests going for a walk.

'My clothes are still wet. I can't go out like this.'

His eyebrows come together as he contemplates my gym slip.

'I don't suppose we'll meet anyone.'

♀

We lie side by side in the bracken. Asa is propped up on his good elbow and he is picking pieces of gorse from my hair.

His face is so close to mine I can see the pores in his skin, and I can see now that his nose is ever so slightly not quite straight. He has extraordinary eyes though. Dark grey. I cannot believe that I once liked blue eyes.

His hair is nice too. For one thing it is not blond, which is a big relief. Asa's hair is black and quite long, and a little bit greasy, and I like it when it flops over his forehead and he has to shake it back out of his eyes.

I close my own eyes because the light is dazzling me and the colours of the sky and hills are brighter today than I have ever seen them. They are making me a bit giddy.

'Why are you screwing up your face?'

I tell him about the colours and the brightness and how I am feeling light headed, and he laughs.

'I hope that's as much fun as it sounds.'

'Could it be the tablets?'

'The Benzo? I doubt it. It's more likely to be the LSD I dropped in your coffee earlier.'

My eyes snap open immediately and I sit up, banging his nose hard with my forehead as I do so. He pulls back in surprise and rubs his nose, testing for blood.

'I was joking.'

'You shouldn't make jokes like that.'

'Obviously not.'

Asa doesn't know what I mean about feeling light headed, and I can't explain because I don't properly understand myself. He takes my hand.

'May I?' he says.

I nod because he is being very polite, which I really like. Imagine Daniel asking permission to hold my hand! Daniel would have half suffocated me by now.

'You're trembling,' he says. 'And so am I.'

'Are you cold?'

'It's what happens when I go walking with young women in school gym slips.'

He jumps up and pulls me to my feet.

'Come on,' he says. 'I'll race you to the top of that hill.'

Jenny Rodwell

A Fragile Song

I have treated it in others but have never experienced the symptoms myself, not until now that is. Hypersexuality is a more than usual or frequent desire for sex, and the treatment is usually anti-depressants. What rubbish psychiatrists do talk.

Exercise is the thing. A brisk, bracing walk to take my mind off the erection that has been pestering me since the throbbing in my arm began to subside, although my arm is still quite painful.

Ophelia is nineteen. I have to remember that. Self control is the thing, and I must try not to drone on and on like a medical textbook because that is what I do when I am nervous, and that gym slip is not helping one little bit.

She beats me to the top of the hill, but only because I have a bad arm and because she knows the way. Ophelia bounds up the hill like a gazelle, showing her school knickers as she leaps from rock to rock.

She laughs when I arrive beside her, out of breath. I groan and rest my bandaged arm on her shoulder.

'Is it still hurting?'

'Only a little.'

My arm is actually throbbing painfully, but it is nothing compared to the throbbing in that other part of my anatomy, the part of which Ophelia is so blissfully unaware. I am not sure how much longer I can keep this up.

'Ophelia, we only have a few more hours together before I go back to London.'

'Which way is London?' she asks.

I point with my good arm.

'According to the sun, London is that way. Vienna would be over there.'

'Vienna?'

'That's where I was born.'

She looks in the direction I am pointing and screws up her face. Clearly she has no idea where Vienna is. I swing my arm around in the opposite direction.

'Scandinavia must be over there.'

'Who comes from Scandinavia?'

'You do. The Grymewyck Vikings came from there.'

'I don't want to think about Vikings. Can't we talk about something else?'

It is a start.

'What would you like to talk about?'

When she does not reply I bury my face in her stubbly hair and kiss the top of her head. I try again.

'If you had a wish, what would it be? What would you like more than anything else in the world?'

'That's easy,' she says. 'I'd just like to be normal.'

'Then can we go home and make love like two very

normal people?'

'What is normal love?' says Ophelia.

Playing for time, I remove my glasses and clean them on the bottom of my tee shirt.

'Well, the physical union of a male and female is known as coitus...'

'I know that, but what else?'

I replace my glasses and wonder what it is she wants to know.

'The average length of sexual intercourse is eleven minutes.'

She regards me with her wide green eyes.

'I didn't know that.'

'Trust me. I've had a medical training.'

♂

Walking home, I snap. I grab Ophelia with my good arm and kiss her so hard I feel the shape of her teeth through both our lips. When I finally let her go she stands back and runs her finger along my lower lip.

'You're bleeding,' she says.

'Come to London with me tonight.'

As she sucks my blood from the end of her finger I feel so faint I have to lean against a tree trunk to steady myself.

'My clothes aren't dry.'

'Pack them wet.'

'Where would I stay?'

'With me.'

'Come live with me and be my love? That's what Daniel said.'

I have not the faintest idea what she is talking about, but it sounds good to me.

'Something like that.'

'And you will give me roses and a thousand fragrant posies?'

'I'll give you anything you want.'

'I want a room of my own where I can write. I'm going to be a writer.'

'Sounds great.'

And then she tells me.

'I've found the room,' she says. 'It's a student residence and meals and heating are included.'

♂

I imagine Ophelia's room. It has a bed with sailcloth cushions and a crumpled cover, posters of half-naked men on the walls, and shelves full of modern novels. There are hanging plants in macramé holders.

Ficus Benjamina. Weeping figs, weeping because Ophelia is too busy to water them.

There are men in Ophelia's room, only they are not men but boys. Boys like Daniel Brandon, playing cheap guitars and listening to ghastly music.

'Asa?'

She is shaking my good arm. Ophelia is still here but not for much longer, not unless I can get a serious grip of what is happening inside my head. I have never considered myself a jealous person but the green-eyed monster has a firm hold of me now.

'Asa?'

With a huge effort I pull myself together.

'I was just thinking how much I'm looking forward to you coming to London,' I say.

'Really?'

'I could take your books and stuff down in my car, if you like so they'll be in your room waiting for you.'

The cloud lifts, the green eyes sparkle.

'Would you really? I was wondering how I was going to take it all on the train.'

'We're going to have a lot of fun together, you and I.'

I bend and kiss the tip of her nose.

'I'm a very normal sort of guy,' I say. 'You can be as normal as you like when you're with me.'

♂

I offer to drive her to the shops to stock up on food to see her through the next few days. Normal enough, considering there is not a bite to eat in the house and Ophelia hasn't even noticed.

I lend her my duffel coat to cover up the school gym slip, and I hold the car door open for her to get in. So far, so good.

While Ophelia buys food I go in search of champagne and a special present. I have something in mind, but first I need to find a florist and a greengrocer who sells fresh herbs.

♂

Back at The Barn I go down on one knee and present Ophelia with a bouquet. She looks alarmed, but no matter.

'There's rosemary,' I say. 'That's for remembrance. Pray you love, remember. And there are pansies for your thoughts.'

And there I have to stop because that is all I remember from Ophelia's speech. I am not strong on Shakespeare.

'There's rue for you, and here's some for me,' she prompts.

'Neither the florist nor the greengrocer had ever heard of rue. I'm not even sure if it grows in this country any more.'

'Thank goodness for that. Rue means regret. I'm pleased you couldn't find any rue.'

The Roman writer Pliny had some interesting things to say about rue. Once upon a time it was used to bring on menstruation, and it was also used to induce abortions. I share this information with Ophelia who backs away horrified.

'You're nicer when you're being romantic,' she says.

If I stop talking, even for a minute, the green-eyed monster will reveal itself by saying something stupid and I cannot afford for that to happen, so I pursue the subject, like the fool I am.

'I have a theory that Shakespeare's Ophelia was pregnant, which is why she drowned herself. Perhaps that's the significance of the rue in the play.'

My theory seems to have a negative effect on Ophelia's mood because she stares at her bouquet as if she was holding a bunch of stinging nettles.

'No more talk of Ophelia!' she says. 'Would you like me to sing to you?'

'I should like that very much.'

'What shall I sing?'

'Anything you like. Sing the first thing that comes into your head.'

Ophelia sings.

'Tomorrow is Saint Valentine's day, all in the morning betime, and I a maid at the window…'

It is Ophelia's Song, the song Shakespeare's heroine sings as she descends into madness. The singing stops abruptly.

'Don't stop,' I say. 'You have a lovely voice.'

'I didn't mean to sing that. It just came out. Do you think the real Ophelia is controlling what I do?'

She has only had a couple of sips but the champagne has clearly gone straight to her head.

'I didn't mean to upset you,' I say. 'Was it something I said?'

'You said the real Ophelia got pregnant and went mad.'

'You're the real Ophelia. Shakespeare's Ophelia is just

fiction.'

Fact or fiction, the notion of pregnancy obviously bothers her, and I wish I had never mentioned it.

'Does being pregnant make women go mad?' she asks.

'Pregnancy doesn't usually cause insanity.'

'But it can?'

'Well there's postpartum depression...'

'Do you want babies?'

The question takes me by surprise but she is in earnest and I must be careful how I reply. At the same time it crosses my mind that Ophelia is not as fully recovered from her trauma as she thinks she is.

'I hadn't given it much thought. Why?'

'Because I don't want babies.'

'Lots of women don't want children. There's nothing wrong with that.'

She is staring into her glass, talking to herself. Either that or Ophelia is counting the bubbles in her champagne.

♂

While Ophelia counts bubbles I search my pockets for the brooch. I have been looking forward to telling her what uncle Ben discovered about her brooch and now seems a good time. Anything to lift her mood.

'Close your eyes and hold out your hand.' I say.

She obeys and I press the brooch into her palm.

'Now you can look.'

'It's only my old brooch.'

'That is where you are wrong. This is a rare Viking brooch from the eighth century. Originally it would have been one of a pair.'

To my disappointment Ophelia looks at the brooch without interest and turns away.

'I've had enough of Vikings,' she says. 'I don't want it.'

'But it's extremely valuable.'

'Then I'll give it to Gloria.'

'I wouldn't do that, not if I were you.'

'Why not?'

'Because your ex-boyfriend might recognise it for what it is and Grymewyck would immediately be overrun by amateur archaeologists.'

'Daniel's probably seen it already because Gloria's got the other brooch. It is one of a pair. We found them in the pond when we were little.'

She slips the brooch into my pocket and goes back to counting the bubbles in her champagne.

♂

Ophelia is still fragile and I hate leaving her here alone. She does not yet know about Maisie, and this bothers me. I need to tell her soon, but this is neither the time nor the place. It will have to be broken to her gently, and when I can be around to keep an eye on her.

'Come to London with me,' I say suddenly. 'You could stay at Charlie's if you're worried about staying with me.'

She shakes her head.

'We'll see each other soon.'

'Not for two whole weeks,' I say.

Ophelia considers this.

'What if I go mad before then?'

'Are you going mad?'

'You won't tell anyone?'

'It will be our secret. What are your symptoms?'

I put down my bag and prepare to listen. Rule number one. The patient needs to feel you have all the time in the world. Saying goodbye was never going to be easy.

'You won't laugh?'

'Madness is my business. Of course I won't laugh.'

'I count things.'

'Everyone counts things.'

'I count everything.'

'That doesn't make you mad.'

'I hope I'm not going mad.'

'I hope so too, but if you are I'm probably the best person to deal with it.'

When I am ready to leave, Ophelia buries her face in my chest and locks her arms behind my back. Beneath her silky auburn stubble my fingers find the occipital bone at the base of her skull and stroke it. I am playing for time while I muster enough will power to walk out of the door.

We are standing thus when a young man enters, lopes across the room and props himself up against the mantelpiece as if his backbone wasn't strong enough to hold him up.

One of The Family

♀

Jack is surprised to see Asa and he is even more surprised when he sees my gym slip. He averts his eyes from my bare legs and addresses Asa.

'I want a word with my sister.'

'Well, there she is,' says Asa.

He offers Jack champagne, but Jack is in his usual hurry.

'Can't stay. Things to do.'

'You'll stay a little while, surely?' says Asa. 'You haven't seen your sister since before the accident.'

'I've come to talk to her about The Barn.'

Asa laughs and hands me his jacket.

'Cover yourself up,' he says. 'Your brother doesn't know where to put his eyes.'

I put on Asa's jacket and Jack feels able to speak to me directly.

'It's not fair you should inherit, Sis. It's not as if you're a blood relative.'

Asa's eyebrows come together in an expression I haven't seen before, and it is scary.

'A cash adjustment would make it fairer,' continues Jack. 'I'm a bit short of the readies at the moment.'

Now I am the one who is embarrassed. So far my family can't have made a particularly good impression on Asa.

'How much?' asks Asa.

He is clearly angry, but Jack appears not to notice the change of tone because he gives Asa one of his lopsided little smiles.

'How much can you spare?'

Asa takes all the notes out of his wallet and hands them to Jack without counting them. My brother is about to sit down when he sees Asa holding the door open for him.

Jack leaves the house with one long lope and he doesn't look back, not even to say goodbye.

♀

Asa promised to write and he does, but when his letter arrives it is more drawings than words. The best one is a cartoon of the patients queuing outside his door at the hospital and everyone in the queue is me.

He says he is looking forward to seeing me on Sunday evening, which is tomorrow. I am so excited I can hardly wait.

Pearl has sent me a letter too:

Dear Ophelia,

I have some good news. Your father is home at last. Your granny lives with us now and Jack is here too. We are a proper little family. Come and see us when you are in London.

Love, Pearl

It is so long since I saw my father I can hardly remember what he looks like. Even so, I am surprised at my lack of reaction to Pearl's letter.

I am pleased my father is out of prison, of course, and that he and Pearl are happy, but I feel no desire to see them. I read the letter again and still feel nothing. As I push it aside there is a knock at the door.

Daniel comes in carrying Zac on his shoulders. He is out of breath and out of sorts.

'How's the dig going?' I ask. 'Did you find your Vikings?'

'There were no Vikings.'

'What were all those mounds?'

'Rubble tips from when the railway line was built. The locals must have known.'

Daniel tells me he is not going back to London because he wants to stay with Gloria and Zac. He would like to sell his flat but is worried about me having nowhere to live. When I tell him about my room he looks relieved.

'Where will you and Gloria live?' I ask. 'Her flat is very small.'

'We'll look for somewhere in Grymewyck. Gloria wants to be near her parents.'

Zac has picked up a fork and is stabbing at the tabletop. Daniel takes the fork away and Zac screams. I can see now how very like my brother Zac has become. He is a Siward and I am not. Zac belongs here and I do not. And then I have this really brilliant idea.

'Live here!' I say. 'You can all come and live at The Barn.'

I go to the farmhouse to say goodbye and am surprised when Percy opens the door to me in his vest and slippers. When May appears and thrusts her hand in front of my face to show me a wedding ring, I am even more surprised.

'When did that happen?'

'Yesterday,' says Percy. 'Just the two of us. No fuss.'

I kiss them both, which embarrasses Percy and makes May giggle.

'Fetch the sherry, dear,' says Percy to May. 'We'll have that drink now.'

My grandmother shakes her head when I tell her Gloria will be moving into The Barn, but Percy nods his approval.

'I saw the little lad this morning,' says Percy. 'They were on their way up to visit you.'

'What do you think of Zac?'

Percy is busy pouring four very small glasses of sherry but he looks up and winks.

'I don't think,' he says. 'I know.'

Of course he knows. Percy would have seen the resemblance immediately. Zac is Jack's son, and now that Percy is married to May, Percy is Zac's uncle.

Zac is family.

Unlucky Thirteen

Ophelia's narrow divan is fitted with a grey cover made of something nasty that snags my socks when I take my shoes off to lie down. My feet stick out over the end of the foam mattress, and the artexed ceiling and plastic lampshade do more to calm my jealous heart than all the valium I have swallowed this past week.

I stretch my arms behind my head and feel dizzy with hope. Ophelia's room is as bare and clinical as my new consulting room at the hospital. There is nothing to fear from this room.

I have bought Ophelia a dozen red roses and they will be the first thing she sees when she walks through that door tomorrow afternoon.

I stack her boxes in a corner and arrange the roses in the

Jenny Rodwell

electric kettle, using the furred element coil to separate the
stems. On the little card the florist gave me I write my address
and phone number and invite Ophelia to supper. I put the
card among the roses and stand back to admire the effect.

In less than twenty four hours we will be together.

Meanwhile, the senior consultant at the hospital has
invited me to dinner. I don't want to go because he will almost
certainly have invited an unmarried woman as well, and the
woman will almost certainly be looking for a husband.

This happens to me all the time.

♂

On this occasion the unmarried woman turns out to be
the senior consultant's own daughter, so I know I must be
extra careful. The daughter is about the same age as me and
seems nice. She is strikingly good-looking and beautifully
dressed in clothes chosen not to attract attention. It is the
consultant's wife who is the problem.

'How are the canapés?' says the consultant's wife. 'My
daughter made them. She's the most wonderful cook.'

The daughter smiles and tells me she enjoys cooking.

'Do you play tennis?' says the consultant's wife. 'My
daughter belongs to our local club. You must get her to
introduce you.'

The daughter tells me she would be delighted but that her
tennis is not very good.

At the end of the evening the consultant's wife tells me
her daughter will run me to the station because it looks as if it
might rain.

'Sorry about that,' says the consultant's daughter as soon
as we are out of the house. 'I hope you weren't too
embarrassed.'

There is something about the consultant's daughter that I

like very much. She is to be trusted.

'Tell me something,' I say. 'If you were in a relationship with a man several years older than yourself, would you find that restricting?'

'That would depend on the man. How much older?'

'Thirteen years.'

'That's nothing. Go for it.'

'I intend to. What about you?'

'I've been in a relationship with a man thirty years older than me since I was eighteen.'

'And you don't feel you've missed out on things? I'd hate the person in question to feel any resentment towards me.'

'The man's married, otherwise it would work very well,' she says. 'Can I trust you?'

'I'm not likely to meet the man concerned.'

'You probably already have. He's one of my father's colleagues at the hospital. My parents don't know anything about it.'

♂

The table looks good. Nothing too pretentious because I don't want Ophelia to be intimidated. There are candles, but I have put them in bottles to keep things informal.

Champagne cocktails to start with, followed by smoked salmon with brown bread and butter, followed by stuffed chicken breast with fondant potatoes and grilled asparagus, followed by summer pudding and whipped cream.

I made the summer pudding last night, and it is perfection. Summer pudding is my speciality. The secret is not to use strawberries. One of the Anna Cohens told me that.

I just have time to pop upstairs and clean my teeth again. Five more minutes and Ophelia will be here.

Pearls, Death & Resurrection

♀

I throw the window open and take a deep breath. It is a warm Sunday afternoon, I am in Bloomsbury and I have a place of my own at last. Nothing could be more perfect.

The room is filled with the scent of Asa's roses. I bury my face in the flowers and then I unplug the kettle and waltz around the room with it, leaving a trail of water across the carpet behind me.

A late arrival moves into the room next to mine. She knocks on my door and introduces herself in a Welsh accent.

This is her second year in the block and she tells me her fiancé stays with her most weekends and no one minds.

'Do you have a fiancé?' the Welsh girl asks.

I repeat the question. It sounds like something May or my grandmother might ask. It has never crossed my mind to have a fiancé.

'I'd offer you a coffee, except my kettle is full of roses.'

The Welsh girl lends me a vase and as I transfer the roses from the kettle to the vase I count them. There are thirteen, my unlucky number. I drop the thirteenth rose into the waste paper bin but the Welsh girl retrieves it and sticks it in the top button hole of her blouse.

'No one ever sent me roses in my life,' she says.

My new friend sits on my bed, takes a sip of her coffee and immediately spits it back into her mug.

'Ugh!'

'What is it?'

'Something slimy. It must have been lurking in your kettle.'

She fishes the slimy thing from her coffee and holds it up for me see.

'Soggy cardboard,' she says. 'How disgusting.'

Ten o'clock and still no Asa. I don't suppose he'll come now. That must be why he left the roses, because he didn't want to come himself.

Probably that is why there were thirteen instead of twelve.

The dining room is closed but I still have some fruit cake and a sandwich left over from the train, except that I am not hungry any more. Perhaps I will feel better in the morning.

Three weeks and still no Asa. The Welsh girl says I should telephone him, but I don't think so. He would have left his number if he'd wanted me to do that.

'He'll be in the directory,' says the Welsh girl. 'There can't be that many men in London called Asa Cohen.'

The Welsh girl is missing the point. As far as I am concerned there is only one Asa Cohen in the whole world and he doesn't want to see me.

I am pleased now I brought the dark-eyed boy with me. He is a great comfort and I sleep with him under my pillow.

♀

Daniel and Gloria come to London to clear Daniel's flat and I go over to collect my things. Afterwards they drive me and my belongings back to my room in their hired van.

An envelope has been slipped under my door and I snatch it up thinking it might be from Asa, but I am disappointed. The note is from Pearl Bonnet and it is an invitation to my father's fiftieth birthday party. Daniel is shocked when I screw it up and toss it into the waste paper bin.

'You should go,' he says. 'He is your father after all.'

Gloria is snapping off the brittle heads of the dead roses one by one and dropping them in the bin.

'Don't do that!'

'But they're dead.'

'I like dead roses.'

'He's keen, whoever he is,' says Gloria. 'Twelve red roses means true love.'

'There were thirteen when they arrived.'

'That just means he can't count.'

When it is time for Daniel and Gloria to leave I go down to see them off, and as we pass the Welsh girl's door a young man comes out. This is the first time I have seen her fiancé, who has a beard and looks nice.

I smile at the man and he follows us down the stairs. Outside he stops to roll a cigarette and as Gloria and Daniel drive away the fiancé asks me for a light.

'I've left my matches upstairs again,' he says. 'I do it every time.'

I tell him I don't smoke and we go indoors together, the young man for his matches and me to unpack the boxes I have brought from Daniel's flat.

♀

I knock at the door of Pearl's little house and wait. It is not because of what Daniel said that I decided to come, but because I want to ask my father about Maisie.

April is dead now and I am an adult, so there is no reason why my father shouldn't tell me where my real mother lives.

And it could be that Daniel was right. It could be that on the other side of this door a real father is having a real family birthday party and that he is looking forward to seeing me.

That is what I am hoping, anyway.

♀

I have bought my father a birthday card and a box of Black Magic chocolates, nicely wrapped in tissue paper. He might have preferred a gift box of Senior Service, but that didn't seem quite right.

Perhaps I will like my father, and perhaps he will like me, and perhaps one day I will introduce Asa to my father and they will like each other. That would be really nice.

'Take care of her, son. Ophelia means the world to me.'

'Have no fears about that, sir. Your daughter is as precious to me as she is to you.'

♀

An elderly man in a gangster-style suit opens the door. He is short and bald with a face the colour of tomato ketchup, and he holds my hand to his lips for so long it makes me uncomfortable. The man looks up and smiles a lopsided smile and I know this man is my father.

I follow him into Pearl's sitting room where he points to the sofa and indicates with another lopsided smile that I should sit down. At the other end of the sofa my brother Jack is slumped horizontally with his eyes closed and his legs propped up on the fender.

No one speaks, and there is no sign of a party.

Soon, Pearl arrives, supporting on her arm a tiny ancient woman who snatches the chocolates from my hands and rips off the wrapper. Pearl leads the old woman to a high-backed chair in the centre of the room, drops a curtsy, and leaves the room backwards.

My father puts his mouth to the old woman's ear and shouts.

'We have a surprise for you, mother. Do you know who this young lady is?'

The grandmother who sent me back when I was a baby shows as little interest in me now as she did then. She opens the Black Magic and crams a handful of the chocolates into her mouth, papers and all, and my father shouts louder.

'This is Ophelia!'

She stares for a moment, spits out the chocolates and screams a scream so piercing that Jack opens his eyes. Pearl rushes in and scoops up my grandmother as if she was a baby, and as she is carried out the old woman twists her head round to get a proper look at me.

'It's Maisie!' she screams. 'Maisie's come back from the dead.'

My father smiles his lopsided smile.

'Your grandmother's getting eccentric. Now, shall we get down to business?'

Jack opens his eyes and this time he keeps them open.

'Your brother and I have started a little business and we would like you join us. It's a family concern. We will soon be making money. We will make a lot of money and very soon.'

I am not paying proper attention because I am wondering what my grandmother meant about Maisie coming back from the dead.

'What happened to Maisie?' I ask.

'You're a lady of property now,' says my father. 'Jack and I are offering you the opportunity to invest your money in our venture.'

'Is Maisie dead?'

'Maisie?' says my father, cross at being interrupted. 'Maisie died the day you were born.'

♀

My little room is as cold as a morgue when I get back and I can't go to bed because Maisie is on the divan, laid out in a hospital gown. I have always imagined my mother in an evening dress so the white gown comes as a bit of a shock.

Maisie is the spitting image of me, with short cropped hair exactly like mine. I suppose it is only natural she would look like me because she is my mother after all, but that comes as a shock too.

She is younger than I imagined, about my own age. But if Maisie died when I was born, this would make sense. I hope my mother didn't die in childbirth. That would be terrible because it would be my fault.

The dark-eyed boy is watching all this from the mantelpiece and I am curious to know what he thinks.

'What shall I do?' I ask. 'I don't mind Maisie having the bed, it's just that I haven't got anywhere to sleep.'

I already know what the dark-eyed boy is going to say and he is right. He thinks I should go and find Asa.

♀

Asa's house has a black painted door with a stained glass window and a brass doorbell, which is just as I imagined it. The downstairs light is on and Asa is in there, pacing up and down the room and waving his arms around as if he was conducting an orchestra.

My finger is on the bell and I am about to press it when I see he is not alone. Sitting by the window behind a giant cheese plant is a woman. Through the leaves of the cheese plant I can just make out the back of a smartly bobbed head, and the bobbed head is tilted to one side, intent on catching every word he is saying.

Love Bites

There is a bench in the square where Ophelia lives and at the weekends this is where I come to sit. I can see her window through the bushes and I have an uninterrupted view of the doorway, although I haven't seen Ophelia herself yet.

On the afternoon of the third Saturday my view is obscured by a parked van. When the van pulls away I see Ophelia on the pavement with a man, and when they turn and go inside together my worst fears are realised.

I am too agitated to take the bus so I walk home, and when I get there I find Sue Manners waiting outside my house.

'You look as if you'd seen a ghost,' she says. 'Are you ill?'

She follows me inside and takes off her coat.

'Can I get you something?' she says. 'Shall I make us some

coffee?'

She goes into the kitchen and starts to tidy up. My nerves are already jangly and her interference irritates me.

'Leave it, Sue. I'll do that.'

'This place is a tip and the fridge is full of rotting food. There's a summer pudding in there that's green with mould.'

'Leave it. I like mouldy pudding.'

Sue returns, picks up a fistful of dirty mugs and marches back into the kitchen without speaking.

'I'm not myself,' I say. 'Would you think it very rude if I asked you to leave?'

'Very.'

I tell Sue about Ophelia because I have to tell someone. Sue sits very still and listens while I explain that if I can't have Ophelia I would rather not be alive at all.

When I have finished Sue locks the front door, pockets my keys and refuses to leave.

'You're in no state to be on your own,' she says. 'I'm staying with you.'

I beg her to go, and then I argue, and then I shout, but there is nothing I can do. At midnight Sue curls up on my sofa and bids me goodnight. Furious, I stomp upstairs to bed.

Night time is our special time, Ophelia's and mine. It is our only time together. We like to hold hands and talk, and Sue is spoiling things. Her presence in the house is inhibiting the conversation.

It is late when I wake and go downstairs to find Sue making toast and coffee.

'Breakfast?'

'I have to go out. I'm already late.'

I need to get back to my bench. Sunday is a busy day in the gardens and I don't want to find someone else sitting on my bench.

'There wasn't a thing to eat,' says Sue. 'I had to go out to buy bread and milk.'

'You didn't have to do anything of the sort. This isn't your house.'

'There's a woman asleep on next door's step. This area is going downhill.'

'Then don't distress yourself by staying in it any longer, but before you go would you kindly return my keys?'

'Charlie's mother has invited us to lunch.'

'I have other plans. Where are my keys?'

'I'm not telling you.'

Sue stands in front of me, all five foot two of her, her feet apart and her lower jaw pushed so far forward she looks like a pug puppy. She barely comes up to my armpits and as I look down at the top of her head I do something I haven't done for a long time. I laugh.

Charlie notices the teeth marks on my arm when I roll up my sleeves to do the washing up.

'So you finally met a woman who could say no to you?'

I am in no mood for Charlie's jokes and ignore him.

'She's got a good set of molars, whoever she is,' says Charlie. 'Shouldn't you have a dressing on that?'

'It's formed a sanguineous crust,' I tell him. 'It's better left uncovered.'

'Impressive' says Sue, examining my arm. 'Are we allowed to know the lady's name?'

Considering our conversation of last night I feel Sue is being unusually dim but then I realise she has her reasons. Charlie's face breaks into a slow grin of understanding.

'Is this Ophelia we're talking about?'

Sue avoids looking in my direction.

'Isn't that the name of April's daughter?' she says.

'How is Ophelia, Asa?'

'I haven't seen her for a while.'

'I'll look her up,' says Charlie. 'I wonder what she's doing tonight?'

'Hurry up, you two,' says Sue, taking off her apron. 'Mrs Manners is waiting for her coffee.'

Souffle de Heart

♀

Maisie has gone by the time I get back from Asa's house but my room is still cold so probably she is not far away. I don't mind getting into the bed Maisie was lying on. It is quite nice, actually. Comforting.

I have a sore throat, which is my own fault for sleeping out in the rain. The Welsh girl gives me codeine, which makes everything seem floaty and far away, and then she asks if there is anything else she can do.

'The roses,' I croak. 'Get rid of the roses.'

The woman I saw in Asa's house stayed with him all night and she went out to buy food for their breakfast this morning. She gave me a filthy look when she saw me on the neighbour's doorstep, as if I was a stray dog or something.

It would have been better if Asa had told me about his girlfriend. It wasn't very nice finding out the way I did, especially when I had nowhere to sleep because of Maisie being in my bed.

The Welsh girl wakes me up with hot lemon and gives me a note from a man she met on the stairs earlier who was looking for me. It is from Charlie Manners.

> *A Bout de Souffle* is on at my local cinema tonight. Please come. You can compare hairstyles with Jean Seburg.

My throat is hurting like anything and I ache all over but I go anyway, and Jean Seburg's hair is nothing like mine. Even Charlie has to admit that.

I like the film, though. It starts in Paris and I have always wanted to go to Paris.

Afterwards Charlie invites me back for a drink and I accept. I feel very normal with Charlie, which is nice, but then he stops suddenly in front of big metal door in a high brick wall. It looks like a prison and I wonder what he is up to.

'This is my favourite secret place,' he says. 'Would you like to see it?'

'Not really.'

'Don't worry. We're not going in.'

He links his hands to give me a step up and over the top of the wall I see a tiny crowded graveyard with rows of graves lying edge to edge under very tall trees. In the dappled light I can just make out the writing on the graves, which is foreign and written in thin slanting letters.

'An old Jewish cemetery,' says Charlie, lowering me down. 'Very few people know it's there. We discovered it by accident when Asa threw my wallet over the wall and I made him climb over and fetch it.'

I don't really want to hear about Asa, but Charlie is not talking about the Asa I know. He is talking about the dark-eyed boy, who is much nicer than the grown up Asa. I am pleased to know the dark-eyed boy could be mischievous because in the photograph he looks serious and a bit sad.

'How old was he?'

'I can't remember,' says Charlie. 'He seems to like his new job.'

But it is the dark-eyed boy I want to hear about, not Asa Cohen.

'What was he like when he was little?'

'Much the same as he is now.'

Sadly, I have reason to know this isn't true.

'You're fond of your brother, aren't you?'

Charlie laughs.

'I love him.'

'And Asa's girlfriend? Do you love her too?'

'I believe I do.'

♀

Asa is waiting outside Charlie's flat and his girlfriend is with him. They are leaning against the bannister and when he sees me he almost falls backwards over the rail, but he collects himself quickly enough and straightens up.

He introduces his girlfriend, whose name is Sue. She is quite a lot older than Asa, but she is definitely the woman who stayed at his house last night while I was sleeping on next door's step.

Luckily she doesn't recognise me. That would be really embarrassing.

'Have you two been out on the town?' she says.

'*A Bout de Souffle*,' says Charlie.

'Good?'

This is addressed to me and I tell her coldly that I enjoyed the film very much indeed and then I turn my back on her and follow Charlie into the flat.

Inside I stop short because in front of me is the biggest

fish tank I have ever seen except at the zoo. It takes up nearly the whole of one wall and the water is fluorescent pink. Hundreds of fish are darting around in the coloured water looking for a place to hide but there is nowhere for them to go.

Charlie puts his arm out just in time to stop me from tripping over a real tiger skin rug with a real tiger's head attached to it. The tiger looks up at me and bares its teeth.

'Careful,' says Charlie. 'He doesn't like visitors.'

Asa comes and stands behind me.

'Would you like to see the rest of the flat?'

I don't answer and I can't turn round because my nose is running and I have lost my handkerchief.

'A drink?' says Charlie and ushers us into a room that is even more horrible than the hall.

'Ophelia wants to see the flat,' says Sue. 'I'll give her the guided tour.'

'Let's have the drink first,' says Asa. 'She looks as though she needs it.'

'I'm not feeling well,' I say. 'I think I'll just go home.'

Asa puts his hand on my forehead and tells me I am running a temperature, and then he gives me his handkerchief.

'Remind us, Charlie,' says Sue. 'What was the name of your interior designer?'

'Chiaroscuro.'

Asa sits down beside Sue on a hideous heart-shaped sofa and they laugh until the sofa shakes and tears run down Sue's face, and that is when I turn and run from the flat. On my way out I kick the tiger's head as hard as I can and I don't stop running until I reach the end of the street.

It is not the fish tank or the tiger or the heart-shaped sofa I am running away from. I am running because Asa had his arm around Sue's shoulders.

♀

Asa pulls up alongside me and winds down the car window.

'Hop in,' he says. 'I'll run you home.'

'I'll walk. I need fresh air.'

He gets out of the car and stands in front of me.

'You're not well. Get in.'

He insists and I get in, and I say not a word until we reach my street and neither does he, and then he turns off the engine. We stare ahead looking at our reflections in the darkened windscreen and it is Asa who speaks first.

'I've missed you.'

'Won't she be wondering where you are?'

'Who?'

'Your girlfriend.'

Asa frowns and then he laughs.

'You're talking about my surrogate sister,' he says. 'Sue is Charlie's ex-wife and she wants them to get back together.'

♀

Asa doesn't laugh when I tell him about the dead roses and how I spent the night on his neighbour's doorstep. But when I tell him how I sleep with the photograph of the dark-eyed boy under my pillow every night he bangs his head on the steering wheel really hard.

'My sweet Ophelia. Are you still dreaming of your dark-eyed boy?'

I don't tell him about Maisie because I don't feel like talking about her now, not even to Asa. If I told him that Maisie could be in my room at this very moment, asleep on my bed even as we speak, he would probably think I was mad.

Dark Eyes, White Room

If I allow her out of the car now she could disappear forever into that little white room. I might never see her again, and the prospect of that doesn't bear thinking about.

I would rather sit here forever, with Ophelia's clammy forehead on my chest and her hot breath coming through my shirt. She snuggles closer and my arms tighten around her.

Ophelia doesn't suggest going inside. She seems comfortable and content enough where she is so we sit in silence until the temperature in the car drops and Ophelia sneezes. She has a cold and no wonder. It will be a miracle if she doesn't get pneumonia, sleeping out in the rain like that.

When her breathing becomes slow and regular I know she is asleep. I move my arm carefully to look at my watch, trying not to wake her but waking her anyway.

'What time is it?'

'After midnight. Shall I come back another time?'

Much to my relief she shakes her head.

'It might be safe to go up to my room now.'

♂

I follow her up the stairs expecting her to change her mind at every step. On the landing she stops outside her room, reluctant to go inside.

'Wait here,' she says. 'I'll see if the coast is clear.'

My green-eyed monster is on the alert but Ophelia opens the door, peeps inside, and turns to me with a sleepy smile.

'She's not here at the moment,' she says. 'You can come in.'

Clearly it is not a lover Ophelia is expecting to see. She is expecting someone though, and she is obviously not going to tell me who it is.

Her room is cold, abnormally so. Ophelia shivers and so do I. She turns to me for guidance and I cannot help because I have no idea what she wants me to do.

The dark-eyed boy is on the mantelpiece, dog-eared and crumpled from being under Ophelia's pillow, but I don't feel sorry for him in any way. I have come to regard the dark-eyed boy as a rival because he gets to sleep with Ophelia every night.

'Shall I tuck you up in bed and come back when you're feeling better?'

This is not what I want and it seems it is not what Ophelia wants either because she reaches for my hand and hangs on to it tightly. Her own hand is excessively hot.

I pick up the photograph of my five-year-old self and appeal to him.

'You've known her longer than I have. Tell me what I

should do.'

Ophelia laughs.

'What does he say?'

'The dark-eyed boy says I should stay. He thinks we should get into that narrow bed and try to get some sleep, and he thinks that tomorrow we should talk.'

She gets into bed fully dressed and looks the other way as I strip down to my underpants and climb into bed beside her. Ophelia is as hot as a radiator. I kiss her chastely on the back of her neck and put my arm around her.

The arm is necessary to prevent one or both of us from falling out of bed. The aching frustration is something I am learning to live with. For me this is going to be a sleepless night.

♂

Somewhere in Bloomsbury a clock strikes two. I am still awake, and so it seems is she, because when I roll out of bed in the darkness and start to get dressed, Ophelia hears me.

'What are you doing?'

'There's something wrong with this room.'

I turn on the light and stand by the bed jangling my car keys.

'Where are you going?'

'Home.'

'What are you waiting for?'

'You.'

Millais Blues

♀

Asa's house is quite untidy with lots of bookshelves and paintings on the walls, and a giant cheese plant in the bay window. I knew about the cheese plant already but it is even bigger than it looked from the street.

Hanging above the mantelpiece are two framed drawings of Asa in the nude. In one of them he is curled up asleep on a crumpled bed, and in the other he is awake and lying on his back with his hands behind his head. The signature on both drawings is T. Sainsbury.

'Charcoal and chalk,' says Asa. 'Do you like them?'

'Who's the artist?'

'Tamsin Sainsbury. She has an exhibition coming up. We could go if you like.'

How relaxed Asa looks in the drawings, and how well he must have known Tamsin Sainsbury to let her draw him with no clothes on. It makes me feel funny just thinking about it.

'Shall I take them down?' he says. 'You don't have to look at my Jewish anatomy if you don't want to.'

'I like your Jewish anatomy.'

Asa laughs.

'You haven't seen it yet. Do you play backgammon?'

I tell him I do and he opens up the board and lays it out on the coffee table.

'I'll make us some hot chocolate,' he says. 'You take your coat off and set out the pieces.'

My cold is feeling much better and we play backgammon until it starts to get light and I am almost asleep. Asa stands up and stretches.

'Time for bed,' he says. 'Are you sleeping with me or do you want the spare room?'

His directness startles me and I feel my panic coming back.

'I should warn you that I desperately want to make love to you,' he says. 'If you choose to sleep in my bed I will not be responsible for my actions.'

♀

I choose to sleep in the spare room, and I sleep in one of Asa's hospital shirts that I find in the dirty linen basket. Going to bed in his house with no clothes on would seem a bit weird.

In the morning I meet Asa on the landing with no clothes on. His hair is wet, so he must have had a shower. He doesn't bat an eyelid but I blush deeply.

'Breakfast in ten minutes,' he says 'Boiled eggs?'

'With toast soldiers?'

'Is that my shirt you're wearing?'

This makes me blush even more.

'Erythnophobia,' he says. 'Fascinating.'

'What's that?'

'Fear of blushing. How did you sleep?'

'Well.'

He laughs. 'So much for the aphrodisiac properties of hot chocolate.'

'I wish I could be like you.'

'Being me isn't a bundle of fun at the moment.'

'I mean I wish I could walk around with no clothes on.'

'So do I. I'd like to see where your blushes start.'

He takes me by the wrist and leads me into his bedroom.

'I'm not going to hurt you,' he says. 'I want to show you something.'

He stands behind me in front of the wardrobe mirror and tells me he would like his shirt back. The shirt is warm and smells of him and I don't want to take it off, certainly not while he is watching me. I hug it closer to me.

'It's my shirt,' he says. 'I'd like it back.'

'I'll go and get dressed.'

'I want it now. Close your eyes if that helps.'

He undoes the buttons and I let him take his shirt but I keep my eyes tightly shut.

'What are you doing now?' I ask.

'I'm looking at your reflection. You have a very beautiful body.'

'Am I blushing?'

'All over.'

'Can I have the shirt back now?'

'No shirt and no soldiers unless you open your eyes and keep them open while I count to ten.'

In the mirror my eyes meet his.

'You're not counting,' I say.

'I'm counting to myself.'

'I feel vulnerable.'

'Tell me one thing, why are you shy of me?'

'It's not just you. It's everyone.'

'Didn't Daniel ever get to see you with no clothes on?'

'For Daniel, the sexy part was having babies. He wasn't interested in my body so I never worried about him seeing it.'

Asa whistles. 'More fool Daniel.'

'Anyway, I was always too scared of getting pregnant to think about anything else.'

Asa presses my stomach with his thumbs as if I was a teddy bear.

'That won't happen,' he says. 'You have my word.'

He ends the conversation by getting dressed.

'It's a lovely day,' he says. 'We could go for a walk after breakfast.'

Asa is sitting on the edge of his bed pulling on his shoes and I watch his hands as he ties the laces. He has large hands, strong and capable, and he has long fingers like a pianist.

I don't want to go for a walk, not really.

'Say it,' he says without looking up.

'I don't want to go for a walk.'

'Tell me what you do want.'

I want to hide my hot face from his eyes, which are now looking directly into mine and waiting for an answer.

'Say it, Ophelia. I need to know it's what you want too.'

I wake up when Asa leans over me to look at his watch, which is on the floor beside the bed. I am dying for a pee.

'What time is it?'

'Lunch time. Are you hungry?'

'I didn't get my soldiers.'

My arms are flung backwards on the pillow and I am lying on my back with one leg bent underneath the other. I straighten up immediately when I realise how exposed I am and try to cover myself with the sheet, but Asa is lying on the sheet and refuses to budge.

'Were you looking at me while I was asleep?'

'Every inch of you. Where are you going?'

'To the bathroom.'

I swing my legs out of bed but when I try to stand my legs give way under me and I remember nothing more.

♀

Asa helps me to the bathroom and has to hold me steady while I pee, which is really embarrassing. My legs are so wobbly I can't walk and he carries me back to the bedroom where he lays me out on the bed like a corpse.

'What happened?'

'You fainted. It's not serious.'

'I've never fainted before. What caused it?'

'Too much sex. We've been shagging all morning.'

'I've never heard it called that.'

'It's the medical term for sexual intercourse.'

'You're lying.'

'Come on,' he says. 'Let's go out and get something to eat.'

♀

We have lunch in a pub overlooking the Thames and afterwards we walk along the Embankment, Asa holding my hand in his pocket.

'Feeling better?'

'Do you have that effect on all your girlfriends?'

'You're the first one to faint.'

'Will it always be like that?'

'Not if you eat something first. Your blood sugar levels must have been low.'

We go into the Tate Gallery and wander around looking at

nothing in particular and Asa points out his favourite paintings. It is fun learning what he likes and he knows more about the paintings than I do.

I see the drowned Ophelia as soon as we enter the Victorian galleries. She is floating there right in front of my eyes, and without being able to stop myself I walk slowly towards the painting and peer into the dead woman's face.

'Your namesake,' says Asa.

'Her eyes aren't green at all. They're blue!'

'So they are.'

I call to a couple standing nearby, 'She's not me. She's got blue eyes!'

The couple smile and move away quickly. I shout to everyone in the gallery.

'Ophelia's got blue eyes!'

People turn to look and hurry off into the next room. The attendant comes and tells me not to touch the painting and Asa looks alarmed. He leads me out of the gallery and downstairs to the restaurant where he fetches tea and cakes and tells me to put plenty of sugar in my tea.

I stir the tea slowly and think about the painting. It is the same picture as the one on the Ophelia Box, but the drowned Ophelia in the painting looks nothing like me. She doesn't even look like the Ophelia on the chocolate box because the colours on the box were different.

'Which cake would you like?' says Asa. 'Chocolate sponge or raspberry slice.'

I take the chocolate sponge and he watches me eat it.

'Chocolate cake is one of the few things I remember from Vienna,' he says. 'The smell still comes back to me sometimes.'

'You should have said so before. I've finished it now.'

I eat the raspberry slice and Asa watches.

'So you like Millais?' he says.

'Millais?'

'The artist who painted Ophelia.'

'I didn't know he was called Millais.'

'Tell me why the painting had such an effect on you,' he says. 'Or would you like some more cake first?'

I tell Asa about the chocolates my father gave to my mother on the day I was born, and about the picture on the lid of the box. And I tell him how Maisie went away to be an actress before she had a chance to eat the chocolates.

'And that's why you're called Ophelia,' says Asa. 'It's a lovely story.'

'Except that it's not true.'

I am thinking back to my father's birthday and I want Asa to know the truth.

'I found out something. Maisie died when I was born, and I think having me might have killed her.'

Asa wipes a crumb from the corner of my mouth with his finger.

'I found out something too,' he says. 'Your mother took some tablets, and that's why she died. It wasn't your fault.'

Suicide. I hadn't thought of that. It is not a nice idea, but it is better than Maisie dying because of me being born.

'We could probably find out more about your mother's family. It might help.'

'Did it help you, looking for Anna?'

'It helped with the guilt, but I'll always regret not finding her. I'll probably never know what happened to my sister, and that makes me sad.'

'But I don't feel guilty about Maisie, and I know what happened.'

'You probably have relatives on your mother's side though. Wouldn't you like to find them?'

I shake my head.

'The Maisie I was looking for wasn't a real person. And the dark-eyed boy and the Ophelia on the box weren't real either. They were just people I made up because I was lonely.'

'The dark-eyed boy turned out to be a real friend.'

'But not Ophelia. She was dangerous.'

I explain to Asa that I have grown up to be like the Ophelia on the chocolate box, which is why I have to take extra care not to drown or go mad.

'I hope I'm ready for this,' he says. 'Go on.'

'That's why I was worried about the counting,' I tell him. 'And that's why I can't swim and don't like water.'

'But you walked into a pond in the middle of the night. I was there.'

'I was certain I was going to drown though. That's why I said Our Father over and over.'

'But you didn't drown because I pulled you out. That's not what happened to the Ophelia in the painting.'

'That's what puzzles me. You weren't supposed to rescue me. I was meant to drown with my mouth open.'

'Perhaps I broke the curse.'

'It's funny about the eyes, though. The Ophelia on the box definitely had green eyes like mine. The colours on the lid must have been wrong.'

'Cheap printing,' says Asa in disgust. 'Colour reproduction can be terrible.'

He gets up and pulls me to my feet.

'Come on,' he says. 'I need to take another look at this painting before we go home. It's obviously something I should know about.'

The attendant is alarmed when we reappear in the gallery and comes and stands guard over the picture while we examine it. Asa turns to him.

'I would appreciate your opinion,' he says. 'Would you say my girlfriend looks at all like the woman in the painting?'

'There's no resemblance,' says the attendant. 'And if you don't mind my saying so, your young lady is a sight better looking than the one in the picture.'

'Thank you,' says Asa. 'I think so too.'

White Horse, Dark Thoughts

Sunday afternoon, and Ophelia is telling me she wants to go home. I had not expected this, not so soon.

'Don't go. Have another barley sugar.'

We are in bed, and the barley sugar was my idea because I need to raise her blood sugar level. I don't want her passing out on me again.

Ophelia sucks a barley sugar and tells me she has an essay to write on Shakespearian slang and she hasn't even started it.

'Write it here,' I say straight away. 'I'll help you.'

'My books and everything I need are in my room'

'We can fetch them.'

I grab her by the wrists. Anything to prevent her from leaving.

♂

I drive at a snail's pace in order to gain extra time with Ophelia, who stares gloomily out of her window, not speaking. I have my reasons for driving so slowly.

We pull up outside her block and Ophelia gathers her things and reaches for the door handle. I remind myself I will see her soon and brace myself to let her go. If I cannot curb this infernal possessiveness that has gripped me, I am in danger of losing her altogether.

'Thank you,' she says, in a small voice. 'It's been a lovely weekend.'

Her hand is on the handle but she has not moved.

'Get out now,' I say, still not looking. 'It will be easier if you go quickly.'

Still she does not move. I breath in deeply and dare to hope.

'What are you waiting for?' I say.

'I don't want to leave you.'

She has said it. At last she has said it and I exhale slowly, limp with relief.

'I'm not sure I was ever going to let you.'

I lean across and sniff her hair.

'Do I smell funny?'

'You smell of me. What are you going to do?'

'I have no choice.'

'There's always a choice. You have your room, and you can always pop back to my place for a shag or a game of backgammon whenever you feel like it.'

I am safe to say it now because Ophelia has already made up her mind.

'It's not enough though. That's what I meant about having no choice.'

I knew this is what she would do, and I have known since

yesterday morning, from the moment I took back my shirt. This is why I drove here at ten miles an hour. I was giving her time to get used to the idea.

'Shall we go in and collect some of your stuff?'

♂

I should let the matter rest but I can't. We are in bed, in the dark, our legs wound around each other like lengths of rope. Ophelia is half asleep but I need to know about the man I saw her with in Bloomsbury from the park bench. I cannot help myself.

'Tell me about your other boyfriends.'

'There's only been Daniel.'

'What about the other students? The men must have noticed you.'

'Not really.'

'Surely there must be someone? Think.'

'Once upon a time there was the Frog Man. When I was a little girl I imagined he would ride by on his white horse and take me away from Grymewyck.'

I smile to myself in the dark as Ophelia describes the day she met the Frog Man. One day I will tell her that I am her knight in shining armour, but not now. I put my arm around her knowing that I have all the time in the world.

'Do you still think about the Frog Man?'

'Sometimes. But recently I've begun to wonder about him.'

'What do you wonder?'

'Well, don't you think it's rather odd, a grown man taking such an interest in a six-year old girl?'

Sex, and Other Variables

♀

Asa's alarm goes off in my ear at six o'clock. He reaches over and turns it off, and then he disentangles himself from me and rolls out of bed. I slide over on to his side of the mattress, into the warm dent he has left behind, and watch him getting dressed.

'Are you in tonight?' he says.

'I think so.'

'I'll see you tonight then. Go back to sleep.'

He bends and kisses me and then he is gone, just like that.

Asa knows what he is doing tonight. He knows what he is doing for the rest of his life, and I have forgotten what I am doing this morning. A lecture, I think, at ten o'clock. Writers of the Great War. I am reasonably sure about this but my timetable is still pinned up in my college room.

Wrapped in Asa's Indian cotton bedspread I walk around the house opening cupboards and pulling out drawers. I don't feel guilty about doing this because I feel I have a right to know what's in them. I also have a right to know more about Asa.

I pick up his tee shirt from the bedroom chair and hold it to my face, and I do the same with one of his socks. There is a pair of gym shoes under the chair, which smell of rubber and sweat. I sniff them and then I go downstairs.

Asa has hundreds of records. Most of them are classical, but he has other stuff as well. He likes The Beatles and the Rolling Stones, which is good because I like them too. And he has lots and lots of jazz, which I don't know about.

There is art everywhere. Every bit of wall space is taken up with a painting or a drawing. Most of them are abstract, but quite nice. I look again at the drawings by Tamsin Sainsbury and they don't seem nearly so bad, not now I've seen Asa's Jewish anatomy for myself.

There is only one drawer I cannot open. The left hand drawer of his desk is locked and I cannot find the key so I go back upstairs. Light-headed with happiness, I get ready to go to college.

♀

On the rush hour tube a woman with red lips and a shiny handbag almost knocks me over as she elbows her way down the carriage. I feel sorry for her and turn up my coat collar to hide a smile. She doesn't know what it is like to be me, and she has no idea what it is like to be with him.

♀

Happiness is dyeing my Doc Marten's orange on Asa's kitchen table, which is what I am doing at the moment. I look up. He smiles at me and I am lost.

The boots are part of my outfit for the hospital Guy Fawkes party tonight. My happiness is utter and complete.

♀

At the hospital party I catch Asa's eye across the room and immediately forget where I am. I stop speaking in mid sentence and the woman I am talking to asks if I am unwell. Asa comes over, his eyes screwed up in sympathy.

He is well aware of the effect he has on me simply by being in the same room, and he knows he only has to look at me to make me lose track of whatever is going on around me. This can happen at any time and it can happen suddenly.

'Do other men have this effect on you?'

'Not so far. Are you cross?'

'I love it, but I don't think we can leave just yet. We've only just arrived. Let's stay for ten more minutes and then we'll slip out quietly by the back door.'

♀

I am finding the course work easy. Modern literature, 1910 to the present day, that is what we are doing at the moment and I love it.

Working at home is an impossibility though because Asa is too much of a distraction. When he is around I can think only of him, so when I have reading to catch up on or essays to write, I do this in my university bedroom.

My room becomes my private study, and it is where I go between lectures to read and write and think.

The only problem is my own writing. I am trying to write a short story about a young woman whose fiancé goes missing during the war. I have done some research in the university library but have very little spare time to write it up.

I snatch odd moments during the day, and whenever Asa is working late at the hospital I stay late in my university bedroom. This is my writing time and it is precious.

One night I put down my pen and realise it is too late to get home so I stay the night in my room.

I miss Asa to a degree that shocks me. My need for sex with him has crept up on me without my noticing and when I am deprived of it for whatever reason my concentration is affected and I become forgetful. I lose books and keys and my attention wanders in lectures.

'You could be suffering from low plasma glucose level,' says Asa gravely when I describe my symptoms to him.

'Is that serious?'

'It can be.'

'What can I do about it?'

'We should run a controlled test by eliminating the variable factor of the sex deprivation. It would help my research.'

'How would we do that?'

'By you coming home every night.'

♀

Work is going well and my tutor is delighted.

'Something's happened to you,' he says. 'I was worried at the beginning of term but now you're one of the best students in my group.'

My tutor suggests I enter for the college writing prize because he thinks I have a good chance of winning. When I tell Asa he is so proud he lifts me off my feet and swings me round the kitchen, but when I tell him my tutor visits me in my room and wants to take me to a poetry reading to hear some of his own poems Asa's eyebrows come together in a deep frown.

'Invite him over,' he says straight away. 'I'd like to meet your tutor.'

Asa asks friends to supper and suggests I invite my tutor.

Without discussing it with me he also invites the artist Tamsin Sainsbury, who has taken to telephoning Asa and turning up at the hospital when he is busy.

She is older than I expected, too thin and dressed all in black, but my tutor seems to like her. Tamsin Sainsbury asks my tutor all about his poems and says she would be honoured if he would allow her to read them.

My tutor and Tamsin Sainsbury ogle each other throughout the meal, and at the end of the evening they leave together in a taxi.

'You knew that was going to happen,' I say, when we are alone. 'You manipulated the whole thing.'

Asa hums as he clears the table but he knows I am cross. I hate it when Asa manipulates people to get his own way.

'Ophelia, they are two people in love. Let's just be happy for them?'

The Memory Spy

The letter from Grymewyck lands on the doormat and I let it lie there like an unexploded bomb, until Ophelia finds it and scoops it up with a whoop of delight. Daniel the Dane is to marry the nurse and the theme colours of the wedding are to be cream and lemon. It sounds crass.

'What shall I wear?' says Ophelia.

'You could dye your Doc Martens yellow. Do you really want to go?'

'I haven't been home for ages. Seriously, what shall I wear?'

Ophelia is jumping up and down with excitement so of course we will go.

'I'll buy you a new dress. I haven't bought you a present yet and it would give me a lot of pleasure.'

'A dress?'

While Ophelia gets used to the idea of owning a dress I push the wedding invitation behind the toaster out of sight. The prospect of a trip to Grymewyck is not something I relish and it is not something I want to think about before I have to.

In Ophelia's mind there is still a question mark over April's death, although mercifully she seems to be thinking about the accident less and less. I cannot forget because I know about trauma triggers, the untimely little reminders that can shatter lives. I have seen it happen.

The reminder when it comes will be seemingly insignificant but the consequences for Ophelia could be devastating and there will be nothing I can do to protect her.

Of one thing I am certain, returning to Grymewyck is a bad idea.

♂

Daniel the Dane greets us as we leave the church, smug in a new suit and tie.

'So pleased you could come,' he says. 'Gloria has something to tell you. She wants you both to be the first to know.'

Ophelia claps her hands and Daniel winks at me. The nurse is obviously pregnant.

He has put on weight since the inquest and his golden curls have disappeared. The rustic haircut is not an improvement.

'Still looking for Vikings?' I ask, and Ophelia gives me a warning look.

'Not any more. I help Percy on the farm now, and I look after Zac when Gloria's at work.'

'You've got rosy cheeks, Daniel' says Ophelia. 'Don't you think Daniel looks well, Asa?'

He looks more than well. Daniel is looking positively bucolic.

'Country life suits you,' I say, and he grins with pleasure.

I am immediately collared by Daniel's mother, who talks non-stop without pausing to draw breath. She is clearly curious to see what sort of man Ophelia finally washed up with. Meanwhile, I do not let Ophelia out of my sight, not for a single second.

The nurse's son runs up to Ophelia, chased by the aunt and Percy Hammer. The little boy hides behind her legs and throws a fistful of confetti at Percy Hammer, who pretends to box the child's ears.

'Say hello to Ophelia, Zac.' says the aunt.

But it seems the boy has forgotten who Ophelia is because he turns his back on her and runs away.

♂

Ophelia looks great in a dress and shoes, even though the buying of them was not an experience I want to repeat.

'It costs a fortune,' she had said. 'There's nothing to it. It's more like a tube than a dress.'

'In this case, less is more. It's a designer dress.'

'I could make one for a fraction of the price.'

'Let's just buy it and go home. What are you going to wear on your feet?'

Meanwhile, Daniel has left Ophelia by herself and she is looking lost. I can't go to her rescue because Daniel's mother is still talking and shows no signs of letting up.

In front of the church a photographer is organising the guests into groups and Ophelia is biting her nails. Unsure which group to join, she turns and disappears into the church alone.

'I think you're needed for the photographs,' I tell Daniel's mother. 'Don't let me detain you.'

I hurry into the church and find Ophelia alone in a pew.

'You're following me,' she says. 'You've been watching me since we arrived.'

'I like looking at you.'

'You're spying on me. Anyway, I'm not thinking about the accident, if that's what you're worried about.'

That is my worry, and with good reason.

'You feel like an outsider in your own family. Am I right?'

'I never was one of them, not really.'

'And now you've turned up with a foreigner, who isn't one of them either. Does my being here make things difficult for you?'

'I just want to go home.'

On the way out we say goodbye to Ophelia's grand-mother, who has a problem pronouncing my name, and then we leave.

♂

My relief is profound as we drive out of Grymewyck, but it is not only Grymewyck and Ophelia's family I fear now. I see memory triggers everywhere. Vikings, fires, ponds and accidents of any sort are all on my list of potential dangers and the list grows longer by the day.

When Ophelia first came to live with me she slept with her arms locked tightly around my neck. The strangler position I called it, because if I moved too suddenly she would tighten her grip until I could hardly breathe.

Now she sleeps with one arm flung across my stomach, but so lightly I hardly feel it. Now it is me who feels anxious and insecure. It is the price I pay for protecting her, but Ophelia doesn't know that. She thinks I am spying on her.

It was risky coming to Grymewyck today, but I did it for

her sake. Now she is rebelling against me as if I was an unreasonable parent.

♂

Ophelia is quiet as we drive along the lanes on the way to the main road. I assume she is sulking, but then she perks up.

'I fancy a shag,' she says.

I am so surprised I almost crash the car.

Secrets of The Desk

♀

No more manipulating. Asa has given me his word and he takes his promise so literally it turns into a war of attrition between us. Today is Saturday and we are shopping for food because Charlie and Sue are coming to lunch tomorrow.

Sue always manages to make me feel inadequate in matters domestic, so I want to do it right.

'Chicken or lamb?' I ask.

'Your choice.'

'They're your family. You know better than me what they like.'

'I'd hate to impose my will.'

I choose lamb and we move on.

'Which vegetables?'

'You know best.'

'Well… potatoes, obviously.'

'If you say so.'

'What else?'

'There are plenty to choose from.'

We pay for the potatoes and walk home without speaking. This is our first quarrel and it is not about vegetables.

♀

It is the middle of the night when Asa wakes me up to apologise.

'Forget about the vegetables,' I say. 'I'll open a tin of peas.'

'I'm not talking about vegetables. I want to make love.'

Asa seems to think he can get what he wants simply by wanting it. I turn my back on him and he sits up in bed, bolt upright, and turns the bedside light on.

'Ophelia, what's the matter? Don't you want to make love?'

'Of course I do, and I probably won't get back to sleep now you've started me start thinking about it, but I don't like being manipulated.'

'Then let me help you to get a good night's rest. It's the least I can do.'

Asa once told me he has a professional interest in erogenous zones and had been delighted to find such a zone on the inside of my left wrist. This fascinates him and he strokes my wrist in exactly the right place at times that are entirely convenient to himself. He is doing it now.

'I have erogenous zones too,' he whispers. 'Shall I tell you where they are?'

I tell him he is one big erogenous zone and that I want to go to sleep.

♀

Asa was up early this morning buying vegetables, so I think I made my point.

Meanwhile, Sue helps herself to more beans and cabbage and tells us that she and Charlie are getting married for the second time. Asa jumps up and runs around the room waving the carving knife, and then he hugs Sue so hard her face turns bright red.

'We'd very much like you two to be the witnesses,' says Charlie. 'Always supposing Asa hasn't crushed Sue to death in the meantime.'

'This is the last time, Charlie,' says Asa. 'A man can tire of going to the same wedding too often, even yours.'

♀

On the morning of the wedding I wake up with a temperature of a hundred and two.

'No wedding for you,' says Asa, who plies me with Aspro and hot drinks. 'You should stay in bed. Charlie and Sue will have to find other witnesses.'

I get up anyway because I have no intention of missing a restaurant lunch with Sue and Charlie, with champagne and all the trimmings.

'I thought you'd gone off weddings after the last experience,' says Asa. 'I thought you'd decided marriage was a bourgeois institution.'

'It is, but I want to wear my designer dress.'

♀

He was right. I should have stayed in bed. Usually I love champagne but today it tastes most peculiar.

I put down my glass not wanting Asa to see my shaking hand, but he sees it anyway and raises his eyebrows. His expression is telling me it is my own fault for not taking his advice in the first place. I toss my head and look out of the window.

This is a bad move because the window is wobbling like a

jelly and I have to blink really hard to make it keep still. It stops wobbling for a few seconds and the same thing happens again, only this time there is a face looking at me through the moving glass.

It is the face of an old woman, deathly pale, with bright orange hair and a big lace ruff. The woman waggles a finger at me and disappears.

'Are you all right, Ophelia?' says Asa. 'You look as if you'd seen a ghost.'

Sue, Charlie and Asa turn to the window and then to me and then they look at each other.

'I think you should take Ophelia home and put her to bed,' says Sue, and Asa gets to his feet.

Sometimes I wish Sue would mind her own business.

Asa goes for my coat and Charlie takes the glass from my hand, which annoys me so much I snatch it back again. Two more faces appear at the window and I raise my glass to them.

It is my father and Jack wearing striped blazers and straw boaters.

The waiter helps Asa get me to my feet and they take me outside where Asa tells me to breathe deeply. I take a deep breath and remember nothing more until I wake up in a taxi with my head on Asa's lap.

At home my temperature rises to a hundred and four and Elizabeth the First comes and sits beside me on my bed. She takes my pulse and I ask her if she regrets not getting married.

'People think I'm a virgin queen, but it's not true,' she says and winks at me. 'I have a son, a love child.'

'My father?'

'You should be very proud.'

Queen Elizabeth holds my hand and little by little I start to feel better. Gradually I come to realise I am at home in the darkened bedroom and it is Asa sitting on the bed and not Elizabeth the First. He tells me I have been delirious for two days.

'Were they real or did I imagine them?'

'I have no idea what you're talking about.'

'I could have sworn my family were there, outside the restaurant.'

Asa sighs.

'You're quite right,' he says. 'I was hoping you wouldn't remember.'

'So they were real?'

'Very real. In fact, they were quite chatty while you were out cold on the pavement.'

'Why were they in fancy dress?'

'They were advertising their stall on the Portobello Road. Apparently they do a brisk trade in vintage clothing and theatrical costumes.'

'Did you introduce yourself to my father?'

'He's invited me to buy shares in the family business.'

The bizarre troupe that is my family bothers Asa more than it bothers me and he watches me more closely than ever.

'Will you be seeing them again?' he says

'Not unless I bump into them in the Portobello Road.'

Later he brings the subject up again.

'Are you going to invite them over?'

'Would you like me to?'

'Not particularly,' he says. 'But if you do, I want to be here when they come.'

I wish he'd shut up about my family. If he didn't keep going on about them I would probably forget about them altogether.

♀

My 'flu is of the Hong Kong variety and it is doing the rounds of the university. I am still weak and Asa suggests I light a fire and stay at home in the warm to work on my entry for the college writing prize. The judges want a short story, three thousand words on any historical theme.

'Go for it,' he says. 'You'll probably win.'

This is a really lovely thing about Asa. He thinks I can do anything, and that makes me think so too. With Asa, everything seems possible.

'I have an idea for a story. It's about the Vikings.'

'Vikings are unlucky. You should write about something else.'

He means it too, which is weird because Asa isn't usually superstitious, so I am writing my Viking story without telling him.

I don't like having secrets from Asa, but then he has a secret of his own and it is in the left hand drawer of his desk. He keeps the key under his typewriter and he thinks I don't know where it is.

♀

Asa's secret turns out to be a drawer full of photographs. I can guess what they are even before I look at them. Pin ups. I have seen his Golden Dreams calendar so I know what to expect.

Poor Marilyn. I look up to where she is still stretched out on her red velvet, the calendar still in its place of honour above Asa's desk. She is a bit dog-eared and dusty now, and these days he never so much as glances up at her.

Anyway, I am expecting more naked women as I pick up the first of Asa's photographs and look at it. I am quite disappointed when it turns out to be a black and white picture of the hills behind Grymewyck.

I lift out the pile of photographs and flick through them. There are more black and white pictures of hills and trees, and a few of skyscrapers in New York, but no naked women. It seems Asa has no secret after all.

Then, towards the bottom of the pile I find a photograph of myself. It was taken outside The Barn and I am bending over in my tee shirt cutting mint.

The final photograph is a snapshot, and so small I almost miss it. It was obviously taken with an old-fashioned box camera and is so faded it is difficult to see the image.

I hold it under the light and can just make out a little girl standing against a stone wall. The picture is pale and grainy but I recognise it immediately and I remember exactly when it was taken. The girl is me.

I turn it over and taped to the back of the photo is a tangled ringlet of auburn hair. My hair! It is the hair I gave to the Frog Man.

I am still staring at the photograph when I hear footsteps coming up the stairs.

'Asa?'

I try to cram the photographs back into the drawer but in my haste I drop them and have to get down on my hands and knees to collect them. I look up and see first his feet and then his legs and then he speaks.

'This is the Frog Man and he's coming to get you.'

The shock is so absolute I scream, scramble to my feet and run downstairs.

'It was a joke,' Asa calls after me. 'I came home early to see how you were.'

Ringlet of Fire

Ophelia has calmed down now but she is still extremely upset. That was about the stupidest thing I ever did in my life.

I should have told her about the Frog Man ages ago. Better still, I should have got rid of that stupid photograph. As it is she obviously thinks I am some sort of pervert who pedals around the countryside looking for little girls with red hair.

'I know about your nasty secret.' she says.

'You do?'

'You've got a hair fetish.'

I readily admit to having a fetish for red hair. Too readily it seems because Ophelia is on her guard straight away. Her eyes indicate suspicion.

'A fetish is simply the attribution of mystical powers to inanimate objects…'

'Don't treat me like a child.'

She has never spoken to me like that before.

'You shouldn't have gone through my things? That drawer was locked.'

'Why was it locked? Why the secrecy?'

'If you must know, I had a crush on your mother. I took your hair so I could pretend it was Maisie's hair.'

'But you never met my mother.'

'No, but you described her to me and she sounded – well, she sounded sexy. I had fantasies about her.

'About Maisie!'

'Ophelia, I was seventeen. I had a few wet dreams about her, and that's all. It's what adolescent boys do. It's no different from you going to bed with a photograph of a boy you never met.'

'And that's the only reason you took my hair?'

'I wish to God I'd never touched your bloody hair.'

'Good, because I want it back.'

I fetch the photograph with the attached ringlet and give it to Ophelia, who throws it straight on the fire without looking at it. There is a gentle sizzling, a whiff of burning hair, and Ophelia staggers backwards and collapses in my arms.

I help her to a chair where she sits as still as a statue, and there is no response when I take her hand, which is as cold and heavy as wet clay. I unplug the telephone and sit beside her, and there we stay for the rest of the day without speaking or moving.

It is almost dark when I go to the piano and play Ophelia's Song, the first thing that comes into my head. Ophelia groans and stirs at last.

♀

A gentle sizzling, a whiff of burning hair. Sparks fly from April's hair, spinning away into the night. The stench of petrol is overpowering.

I raise my stick and push it hard into April's chest. She falls backwards and an explosion rocks the pond. Night turns into day, and then darkness… and from the darkness comes Asa's voice…

'It's all right. You're here with me.'

♀

Now I know what happened I can think of nothing else. It all comes back to me over and over again as clearly as if it had happened yesterday. How could I possibly have forgotten something like that?

'That's easy,' says Asa. 'You forgot because you didn't want to remember.'

'I killed her.'

'Bollocks. You heard what the coroner said.'

'I pushed her just the same. It was deliberate.'

'In self defence. She was trying to set fire to you, for Christ's sake.'

'I'm a murderess.'

'You're a drama queen, and it's time you snapped out of it. The world doesn't revolve around you, you know.'

Asa's shock tactics do no good.

When I close my eyes I feel the smooth handle of my grandfather's walking stick and realise the force behind that final, fatal shove.

'I thought you lied to protect yourself,' I say. 'It was me you were protecting all the time. You should have told me.'

'Possibly. Now shall I make us some cocoa before we go to bed?'

The Face in the Water

I am chopping onions for supper and they are making my eyes water. Ophelia is putting the finishing touches to her story, but she won't let me read it. I imagine it is about Vikings, but that doesn't matter any more.

The memory trigger is no longer a threat. I have nothing to fear now from the Vikings.

The point is, my strategy is working. Ophelia is so engrossed in her writing she has stopped thinking about the accident. It doesn't matter that I am watching her as closely as I did before.

I am watching her now. She looks up from her writing and says something that makes me cry for real.

'I want it to be like this for ever. Just the two of us, and just as we are now. Promise me nothing will ever change.'

Her Biro is leaking all over her fingers and all over the string vest she has helped herself to from my drawer. I am too choked to reply.

'Promise?' she says.

I bury my face in her hair and promise. She reaches up and clasps her hands behind my neck.

'Kiss me,' she says.

'You're getting bossy, and you've got ink all over my new vest.'

♂

The evening Sue brings the letter, Ophelia and I are lying on the sofa doing a crossword. I curse, roll over Ophelia onto the floor, and go to let her in.

It is an airmail letter with a Vienna postmark and it is addressed to me at Mrs Manners' house in Finchley.

I open the letter and read it.

> Dear Mr Cohen,
>
> It is my sad duty to inform you of the death of your sister, Anna Landau, who was killed in a traffic accident on January 10th.
>
> I apologise for the delay in contacting you but until this morning I had no idea Mrs Landau had a brother, or indeed any living relative except her son.
>
> Mrs Landau was a widow, her husband Yakob Landau having died in 1963. A neighbour and former employee of Mr Landau, a Miss Olga Valentine, gave me your name and address only yesterday.
>
> Mrs Landau leaves a three-year-old son, Asa Landau. The boy is currently being cared for by Miss Valentine.
>
> As the Landau family solicitor I would ask you to contact me as a matter of extreme urgency. There are important matters to discuss, not least the future of the child.
>
> There is also the question of the family house. I had assumed the house would pass to Mrs Landau's son. However, it is likely you have a claim on the property as the deeds are still in the names of your parents, whom I understand died during the war.

In the event of receiving no reply to this letter I will endeavour to continue my search for you through the usual channels.

Yours, etc,

Karl Spiegelman.

♂

I stride along in my bare feet, faster it seems to me than the wet wind that is whipping up my shirt and stinging the back of my neck.

I have no idea how long I have been walking or where I am, but I can smell water. Somewhere, close by, there is deep, stagnant, foul-smelling water.

In the darkness I trip, stumble and fall. My face smashes into concrete and I lie where I fall with blood running into my eyes and sharp rain beating down on my back. The pain in my feet is so excruciating I want to scream. Perhaps I do scream.

When I wake my feet are hurting as badly as before. I lift my head and a shaft of dim yellow light in the darkness ahead shows me I am sprawled face down on a canal tow path.

The thing I tripped on is the metal fixing of a sluice gate, and the yellow light is coming from the window of a lock keeper's cottage.

I pull myself up and slide along the top of the sluice, edging myself out of the light and into the shadow. There I sit, precariously balanced, and lower my throbbing feet into the cold water.

To take my mind off the pain I concentrate on the flickering reflection of the light from the cottage window. A familiar face emerges from the changing shape and looks up at me from the canal.

The flickering image, suspended just below the surface of the water, is the face of my sister Anna.

'Go away!'

As the wavy outline steadies itself the features pull

themselves slowly into focus. First the mouth, then the nose, and finally the eyes. I am seeing my sister clearly for the first time and her expression is one of triumph.

I kick my feet furiously, churning up the water like an angry child. The floating face wobbles, cracks, and finally breaks up. Anna sinks to the bottom of the lock in a hundred little pieces and I watch her go.

As the last fragment of my sister disappears the beam of a torch shines full in my face. A man's voice is telling me to stay exactly where I am because he is coming to get me.

Lost in Transition

By the time I am off the sofa, Asa has gone. The front door is swinging on its hinges and the letter from Vienna is blowing across the floor.

Sue runs after him while I retrieve the letter, which is typewritten and in German. The only words I recognise are Anna's name and the date. The letter was written two weeks ago.

When Sue comes back she tells me there is no sign of Asa but that his car is still there. He hasn't taken his jacket or wallet and he has nothing on his feet because his shoes are on the floor by the sofa where he kicked them off.

Midnight, and still no sign of Asa. Sue rings Charlie who

arrives distraught. I fetch the German-English dictionary and together we try to translate the letter, but the words are long and official and we soon give up.

At one o'clock in the morning Sue rings the caretaker of the block where she and Charlie now live. His wife comes from Munich, and he invites us over.

The caretaker's wife is waiting for us in her nightdress and hair curlers. She ushers us in, puts on her spectacles and reads Asa's letter to us in English.

♀

Charlie takes me home and we sit by the telephone until it starts to get light, when Sue rings to say Asa is safe and he is with her. The relief is huge.

'Let me speak to him.'

'He's asleep.'

'I'll come over.'

'Don't do that. Asa's had a shock. He needs rest.'

Muffled voices, arguing. Sue must have her hand over the receiver because I can't hear what they are saying. More arguing and then Asa is speaking.

'Ophelia?'

His voice is flat. He sounds exhausted.

'What happened? Are you OK?'

'I'm fine, just tired.'

'Why are you with Sue? Are you coming home?'

Silence.

'Asa?'

More silence.

'Shall I come over.'

'Not yet.'

'When then?'

'I need a little time. Try to understand.'

'You don't want to see me?'

'I'll explain everything very soon, but I need time. You must give me time.'

He says goodbye and rings off. I stand for a while staring at the silent receiver, not believing the conversation I have just had.

It had not sounded like Asa at all. He had spoken as if I was a stranger. Charlie stubs out a cigarette and rubs his eyes.

'He's not coming back,' I say. 'Asa wants to stay with Sue.'

'I'd better get home and see what's happening,' he says. 'You try and get some sleep. I'll be back later and as likely as not Asa will be with me. You mustn't worry.'

♀

When Charlie returns alone a couple of hours later I am still sitting by the phone where he left me.

'Where's Asa?'

'He's going to Vienna.'

'Well of course he's going to Vienna. I'll be going with him.'

'He wants to go on his own.'

Charlie doesn't look at me when he says this. His eyes are darting around the room as if searching for something, and then he sees what he is looking for. Charlie is here for Asa's shoes.

♀

Asa is not coming back. When the truth dawns it is like a body blow and it leaves me winded. There will be no place for me in this family once Anna's son arrives. I will simply be in the way.

If Asa was here now he would laugh and tell me to stop being paranoid. But Asa is not here and the black thoughts persist.

In my mind's eye I have a clear picture of Anna's son, who is wilful and scheming with treachery in his dark eyes.

Charlie follows me upstairs, sits on the edge of my bed and watches me flinging clothes and books into my rucksack at random. My packing is chaotic, ridiculous.

'Where are you going?'

'Home.'

'This is your home.'

'I'm going back to my room.'

'Don't leave, Ophelia. Asa needs you.'

I drag the rucksack on to the landing where Charlie stands in front of me and tries to stop me from going down the stairs.

'Asa's had a shock,' he says. 'Give him time.'

He gets clumsily down on one knee and throws his arms around my legs.

'Please don't leave,' he says. 'I am begging you to stay.'

A Sense of Remaining

The policeman who pulls me off the sluice wants to take me to hospital. I peel off what remains of my socks and tell him there is no need.

'I'm a doctor,' I say. 'I'll attend to my feet when I get home.'

'Not very clever, going out with no shoes,' says the policeman. 'You must have walked miles to get your feet into that state. A night on the town was it, sir?'

'I had some bad news. My sister was killed in a car crash.'

Driving home in the police car a baby's face appears before my eyes, dangling and glowing in the dark like a Chinese lantern. It has a big nose and cunning black eyes. The baby is my nephew, Asa Landau, who is waiting for me in Vienna.

I change my mind about going home and ask the policeman to take me to my brother's house instead.

'Good idea,' says the policeman. 'It's best to be with family at a time like this.'

The truth is… I cannot face Ophelia. Just the two of us for ever and ever, that is what she wants. I gave her my word, and that was only yesterday. What the hell am I going to do?

As we speed down the dual carriageway towards London I know what I must do. I will take Anna's child far away, where Ophelia need never see him. Perhaps I will stay with him in Vienna and speak to him in German. Uncle Ben would approve of that.

If Ophelia was here now she would laugh and tell me not to be silly. But Ophelia is not here, and after what happened last night she will probably never want to see me again.

Oh, God!

The policeman turns his head sharply to look at me, so I must have said that last bit out loud.

'Not far now, sir. We'll have you home in no time at all.'

Little by little my senses return, but not so the use of my feet, the soles of which are still red raw and bleeding. The nightmare of last night is coming back to me now, but the worst of that nightmare is not yet over. There is still Ophelia, and there is still my nephew.

Anna's son is now my responsibility and I need to go to Vienna immediately. But what then? If I lived on my own I would bring the boy back to London, but that would not work, not with Ophelia.

Ophelia has a dread of parenthood, understandably so because she had a rotten childhood herself. Such reactions are not uncommon.

'I'd make a terrible mother,' she had once said. 'I'd be even worse than April. Anyway I won't have time for children, I want to be a writer.'

I had given my promise. No children. Just the two of us… for ever and ever.

Sue would help with the boy, of course, if I did bring him to live in London. There is nothing she would like better, but being Sue she would take him over completely, treat him as if he were her own.

How would Ophelia feel about that? Come to think of it, how would I feel about that?

And what about my nephew? Would he adapt to a new country, a new language? At the moment he is being cared for by a family friend, someone he knows.

It might be best for everyone to leave him where he is, at least for the time being. I would pay for his upkeep of course, and he could visit us in the holidays. Eventually Ophelia might even get used to the idea.

Painfully, I pull myself up from the sofa.

'Where are you going?' says Sue.

'To Ophelia.'

My mind is made up. Anna's son will remain in Vienna, but explaining this to Sue will not be easy.

'You can't go yet,' she says. 'You can't walk.'

'Then you can drive me.'

But Sue is not listening because she is making plans for the arrival of my sister's son, and is already worrying about schools and English classes for the young Asa.

'Ophelia's not there,' says Charlie. 'She's gone back to her college room.'

I turn on him in pain and fury.

'Then why the hell didn't you try to stop her?'

Life in Green Velvet

♀

I throw my rucksack down on the floor, myself onto the bed, and I count the pieces of furniture in my room. One bed, one bedside table, one desk, one chair, and one chest of drawers. And there I stop because there is no other furniture to count.

For months this room has been my haven, a private place where I have been able to work and focus my thoughts, but it doesn't feel like that now. At the moment I am too agitated to work and too restless to do nothing at all so I decide to go out.

I walk for miles, trying not to think about Asa or the future, or about anything at all. I just walk and walk because as long as I keep moving I am able to blank out the awful thing that has happened for many minutes at a time.

It is almost dark when I find the jacket on a park bench somewhere near Battersea power station, so I must have walked for miles. I haven't really been paying attention.

At first I think the dark shape is a cat and bend down to stroke it. I pull my hand back immediately. It is cold and lifeless, not a cat all. Not fur but fabric.

I pick the jacket up and hold it to my cheek. It is made of velvet and has a smooth, slippery lining. The jacket is a bit damp but it feels comforting and soft, even though I can't see it properly.

I walk back to Bloomsbury with the jacket tucked under my duffel coat and my walk now has a purpose. I am going to try on my new jacket.

♀

In the electric light of my room I see the jacket is emerald green with a black silk lining, and has a high mandarin collar and a tailored waist. It could have been made for me, except that when I look at myself in the mirror, it is a different person who returns my look.

The woman in the mirror has a determined expression. Her chin is high, her jaw set. She is a woman who knows exactly what she is going to do.

At the bottom of my rucksack I find Gloria's black earrings and put them on. These are the earrings she gave me after she cut my hair when it got burned in the accident.

They dangle coldly against my neck as I go to put the kettle on. A quick cup of tea, and then I have an essay to finish, and then I will do some writing.

Nothing, not even Asa, is going to keep me from my writing.

The title of my essay is Poetry from Pain and it is about the poets of the Great War. My tutor has already objected to the title and says it is pretentious but I don't care. I like the sound of the words.

A knock at the door makes me jump. I have no idea what time it is.

'Come in. It's not locked.'

I am expecting the Welsh girl but it is Asa who comes in and closes the door behind him.

'Am I disturbing you?'

I sit up very straight. The velvet jacket is good for sitting up straight in so the rightful owner must have had good posture.

'I was in a trench talking to Wilfred Owen and Siegfried Sassoon. I thought you were in Vienna.'

'I'm on my way.'

'Alone?'

I am expecting him to say Sue is going with him, just to make sure her little nephew comes home safe and sound.

'Charlie's coming with me. He's waiting in a taxi outside.'

Asa moves slowly towards the bed and sits down, and I see he is limping.

'Come with us,' he says.

'You don't need me.'

My voice sounds different so perhaps I am starting to speak like the owner of the green velvet jacket. Or perhaps the tight mandarin collar is affecting my vocal chords, or maybe it is just the unlucky green. My grandmother would never have allowed this jacket in her house.

'Anna's son is not coming back with us.'

'What will happen to him?'

'I don't know yet. It's possible he can stay in Vienna with the woman who is looking after him.'

Asa holds his hands out to me but I don't take the outstretched hands. I would like to but the woman in the green velvet jacket is telling me not to.

'It's not that simple, Asa.'

'It is very simple.'

Useless to explain how I feel, and in any case the woman in the velvet jacket is urging me not to try. But it is not Asa's nephew that has come between us. It is the child in me. Deep down I know this quite well, just as I know there is nothing I can do about it.

'What I did was unforgivable,' he says. 'I went to pieces, and I'm sorry.'

Asa looks tired, defeated. I have never seen him like this before yet I can show no pity. I toss my head and the dangling black earrings bang against my neck.

He pulls himself up and walks slowly to the door, and then he turns.

'I almost forgot,' he says. 'Your tutor rang while I was at the house. He's had the result of the college writing competition. You won.'

Asa's face lights up with pleasure when he gives me the message, and then he is gone.

I go to the window and watch him limping across the pavement. Before he joins Charlie in the taxi Asa looks up at my window and waves.

♀

I resume my dialogue with Wilfred and Siegfried but the sparkle has gone from the conversation, and in any case I am distracted now because I am thinking about Asa.

The mandarin collar is chafing my neck and the heavy earrings make my lobes itch, so I take off the jacket and earrings. I feel more comfortable without them.

Angry now with the woman in the velvet jacket I throw the jacket on the floor and jump on it hard, but then I pick it up and put it on again. The jacket is not to blame, and the colour green is not to blame. I put the earrings back on and go to the mirror.

The woman in the mirror returns my gaze only now she looks less self-assured. She is biting her lip because she knows she has just done a very foolish thing.

Shabby Shoes

7 Mühlenstraße

I sit on the floor in the centre of the room with my eyes closed, and I think about shoes. My mother's are grey suede, like moles. My father's shoes are so black and shiny I can see my face in them.

One of my mother's suede shoes slides towards my father's shiny shoe and presses against it. It happened here in this very room and I remember it as if it had been yesterday.

My sister married a man called Yakob, so it could be that Anna married the man with the shabby shoes.

The lower half of the dining room is badly painted in canary yellow. The top half of the room, as high again, is a grim cavity of ornately carved plaster encrusted with soot and cobwebs. Perhaps Anna couldn't reach the top half of the room when she was decorating, or perhaps my sister never looked up.

The immensity of the room dwarfs the cheap furniture, which looks as forlorn and wretched as I feel. My sister's attempt to create a modern living space within the vastness of the original dining room is pathetic.

Charlie sits on the sagging plastic sofa and I pick up a record sleeve from the top of the gramophone. The Rolling Stones Album No. 2. I have the same record at home.

In Anna's room the bed is unmade, presumably as she left it on the morning of the car crash. The bottom half of the room is papered in shocking pink, the upper half has not been touched for decades. There is a tatty silk kimono hanging on the back of the door and the dressing table is littered with screwed up tissues.

On the bedside cabinet is a framed photograph of Anna and myself as children. My face is screwed up against the camera and my sister's arms are clasped tightly around my waist.

I pull a fistful of photographs from the cabinet drawer and spread them on the bed. There are photographs of Anna and myself with our parents and an old lady, presumably my grandmother, and photographs of Anna and her son. The child has dark hair and dark eyes, and he too is squinting at the camera.

My mother and father are strangers to me. I have no recollection of them at all.

I find a letter with my own name on the envelope but no address. It was written five years ago. Charlie comes and sits beside me and I read the letter out loud, translating it into English for Charlie's benefit.

Dear Asa,

My husband Yakob died a few hours ago. He has been ill for some time. I am not sorry.

The worse thing Yakob did was to stop me from finding you. He knew where you were all the time. I am still not sure why Yakob did what he did but it will be hard to forgive him. He said your friends came looking for me and he told them I went to America before the war. I almost did go to America but at the last minute the American government refused my visa application so it never happened.

Yakob and our father were sent to Dachau before you left for England. Yakob survived but our father died of typhus in 1944.

Not long after you left for England I went with my mother and grandmother to Holland but our grandmother was already old and hated being away from Vienna and she died during the war. Our mother was arrested and sent to Auschwitz and did not come back. I was at a friend's birthday party when they came for her and they hid me until the end of the war. I was lucky but it did not feel like that at the time.

It is strange that you probably know nothing of all this

After the war I came back to Vienna. I thought if I stayed here you would know where to look for me. I came to this house and found Yakob was still living here. He looked after me and two years later we got married. Yakob was thirty-four and I was eighteen.

I have tried so hard to find you. I wrote to many people but never had a reply, or that is what I thought. My worst fear is that I am too late and may have lost you again.

I have just thought of a funny thing. Perhaps you don't speak German any more and won't be able to read this letter.

Your loving sister,
Anna

Charlie puts his arm around my shoulders and together we go into the adjoining room, which has a small mattress on the floor covered with a union jack bedspread. There are Carnaby Street posters on the wall and the bare floor boards are littered with toys and clothes. It is the child Asa's bedroom.

I follow Charlie up the wide wooden staircase where we stumble over missing treads and broken banister rails. There are six or seven rooms on each of the five floors, all derelict and empty, and in the attic the floor is ankle-deep in broken roof tiles and fallen wet plaster.

♂

'The solicitor told me you would come,' says Olga Valentine. 'I have been expecting you.'

She speaks German without an Austrian accent and her voice is familiar. I feel I have heard it before but I also know this is impossible. I am just very tired.

Olga Valentine has bowed legs and brittle, peroxided hair. She greets me with a smile that reveals teeth darkly stained with cigarettes and red wine, but there is no sign of Anna's son.

In an airless drawing room, barely big enough for the two chairs we are sitting on, I thank her for taking care of the boy and Olga Valentine smiles again.

'For Anna I would have done anything.'

There is no trace of a child in this apartment. No toys. No noise. Nothing. The silence makes me uneasy.

'Where is Asa?'

She gestures vaguely with her hand.

'He is with a friend. He will be having fun.'

'Miss Valentine, when my sister died you gave my address to the solicitor.'

'Of course. You are her next of kin.'

'You had my address, and yet my sister did not?'

'Yakob trusted me. I was an old friend and had worked for the Cohen family for many years. I looked after you when you were little although you will not remember.'

Kuckuck! Kuckuck!

Of course! I have not heard the words for nearly thirty years but I hear them now. Anna and I are under the table and Olga Valentine is calling for us. My sister and I had been hiding from Olga Valentine.

'Why was Anna not allowed to contact me?'

'Yakob thought it would unsettle her. Anna was a sweet girl but she was feckless.'

'Did my sister have a job?'

'Anna looked after spastics and children who are not right in the head.'

She does not bother to hide her contempt. As Olga Valentine's face twists into a sneer I abandon all thoughts of leaving my nephew in the care of this woman.

'That is not the job of a feckless woman.'

My thoughts are now for my sister's son and of getting him away from Olga Valentine as quickly as possible. Other arrangements will have to be made. Meanwhile, I need to know where he is.

'I want my nephew. Please fetch him immediately.'

Miss Valentine is no longer smiling.

'I am to keep the boy. The solicitor said you did not want him.'

My young nephew is now the owner of one of the largest houses in Vienna and it occurs to me now that Olga Valentine is after money. But if so, why give my address to the solicitor at all? I am too tired to think of the answer.

'I am not leaving without my nephew. If necessary I will call the police.'

I have no idea why I say this but I do say it and the effect on Olga Valentine is instantaneous. She is up from her chair in a second.

'I will get him. Wait here.'

I am uncertain where to go from here but I sense I have

the advantage. For whatever reason, Olga Valentine is afraid of the police.

'Shall we sit down?'

She resumes her seat and waits.

'Before you fetch my nephew there are things I need to know. You have nothing to lose now by telling the truth.'

'I have nothing to hide.'

'Start with Yakob. Who was he?'

'He was your parents' lodger before the war, a medical student. At that time he and I were engaged to be married.'

If this is true, if Yakob had been engaged to Olga Valentine before marrying Anna, then this woman had every reason to dislike my sister.

'Yakob and your father were arrested and sent to the same camp but Yakob returned before the end of the war. Your family house was empty and he took up his old lodgings, only this time there was no landlord.'

'Yakob escaped?'

'He was released. He came back to Vienna to find me, but then Anna returned. When your sister was eighteen, Yakob married her. He did it because it gave him security of the house.'

How this woman must have hated Anna, and yet here she is looking after Anna's child.

'Did Anna know any of this?'

The woman shakes her head.

'Your sister never knew she owned the house, that you both owned the house. That is why Yakob did not want her to find you. He told her the house had been requisitioned during the war and that they were living there illegally. Anna thought she was a squatter in her own home.'

I have heard enough. It is too late to help my sister, but it is not too late to help her son, which is what I intend to do.

Olga Valentine leaves the room and returns dragging a small boy with un-brushed hair and large, startled eyes. He shrinks away when I kneel in front of him.

'Hello, Asa,' I say. 'My name is Asa too.'

The boy says nothing.

'They can't speak,' says Olga Valentine. 'They're not like normal people.'

I frown, not understanding. The woman touches her temple with her index finger and makes a screwing motion.

'The child is an idiot. He's not all there.'

I pick the boy up and he doesn't resist. Olga Valentine takes hold of his arm, unwilling to let him go.

'I have not yet been paid for looking after him.'

'You will be paid in full, and in return you will make sure that neither myself nor my nephew ever set eyes on you again.'

Olga Valentine turns on me so violently I step back thinking she is about to hit the boy, who is trembling in my arms. Instead, she spits at me.

'You Jews are all the same,' she says. 'Thankfully there are not so many of you in Vienna now.'

♂

Charlie whistles when he sees my grim face and then he sees Asa, who is trying to hide under my jacket. He grins at the boy.

'Hello,' says Charlie. 'Who have we here?'

I set the boy down and he immediately goes and sits in front of the blank hotel TV screen and waits for it to be turned on. Charlie obliges and as he does so I kneel down and clap my hands behind the child's head so loudly that Charlie jumps out of his skin. From the boy there is no response at all.

'For Christ's sake,' says Charlie. 'Was that really necessary?'

'The boy is deaf,' I tell him. 'He's probably been deaf since birth and it has never been diagnosed.'

'I find that hard to believe.'

'True nevertheless, and not uncommon. And all this time they have been treating my nephew as if he was mentally retarded.'

'Our nephew,' Charlie corrects me and I am able to smile at last.

'Will you do something for me?' I ask.

'Whatever it takes.'

♂

I get into the bed beside my nephew without waking him and reach over to turn out the light. In the adjoining room I hear Charlie pick up his bedside phone and ask the hotel receptionist to connect him to his home number. I cross my fingers and fall asleep with my fingers still crossed.

♂

'This is sudden,' says Mr Spiegelman, when I tell him I am taking my nephew to London. 'I thought you wanted the boy to remain here in Vienna.'

'I've changed my mind.'

'The child has his own passport so technically there's nothing to stop you from taking him with you.'

'And after that?'

'Any residency issues will be with the British Home Office, unless you intend to apply for guardianship, in which case I assume the Austrian authorities will be involved. As you are the child's only living relative, I can't imagine there will be insurmountable problems.'

'I intend to adopt my nephew.'

'That should not present any difficulty, except for the bureaucracy, which I understand is a nightmare. It will take time.'

'But it is possible?'

'I am not an expert. In Austria this would be a straightforward private adoption, but in England it may be different. It could be that you and Mrs Cohen will have to prove yourselves suitable parents. You must take advice when you get home. Are there other children in the family?'

'There is no Mrs Cohen.'

Mr Spiegelman seems surprised.

'I'm not sure how the *loco parentis* law stands in your country but, here in Austria, a single male would be regarded unfavourably.'

'Are you suggesting I find myself a wife, Mr Spiegelman?'

'Under the circumstances, you might find it a happier arrangement all round.'

No manipulating. No children. That is what I promised. Forgive me, Ophelia. I am about to betray you on both counts.

'I will see what can be done.'

Mr Spiegelman seems much relieved and asks what I intend to do with the house.

'It is a valuable property, even in its present condition,' the solicitor says. 'Should you decide to sell it, a house of that size will almost certainly be bought by developers and converted into flats.'

'I've already decided to sell. I intend to open a bank account in my nephew's name and the money will be his. Will there be problems about ownership?'

'Not problems, but you might have to come back to Vienna at some point and you may have to sign an affidavit.'

I am still confused about Yakob's behaviour regarding my parents' house and say so.

'The fact that your family still owns the house at all is a

mystery,' says the solicitor. 'Other houses owned by Jews were taken over during the war and made over to non-Jews. It was government policy. It happened to my own family house and those of our neighbours.'

'I'm sorry to hear that,' I say. 'Why did my family's house escape this policy?'

He shrugs.

'It is possible your house was overlooked or used by the Germans, who never bothered to change the ownership.'

I tell him this seems unlikely and the solicitor agrees.

'Maybe there was an understanding between Yakob Landau and the authorities, some sort of collusion perhaps. I gather Mr Landau returned home early from the concentration camp and lived openly in the house, which was unusual.'

'Do you think Olga Valentine had something to do with that?' I ask. 'She's German, not Austrian, and she claims she was engaged to Yakob before the war.'

'That too is a possibility, but the fact is we shall probably never know the truth.'

I sigh. I do not care. I am not interested in the house, or Olga Valentine, or Yakob with the shabby shoes. I am thinking of my nephew, who at this moment is at the zoo with Charlie Manners.

And I am thinking of Ophelia.

Re-Union Jack

♀

I give the green velvet jacket to the girl from Wales and she is over the moon. She dances out of my room wearing it and almost collides with Sue Manners, who has come with a message from Charlie.

It is late and I am surprised to see her, and for once Sue seems unsure of herself.

Charlie wants me to telephone him immediately and did not say why. Sue suggests I use the phone in her office, which is not far away, and we walk there together. She leaves me alone while I speak to Charlie and afterwards I invite her back for a coffee.

Sue kicks off her shoes and curls up on my bed.

'I wasn't sure whether I'd be welcome here,' she says. 'Charlie tells me I behave like Asa's older sister and that I interfere too much in his life. We had a bit of a row about it, actually.'

She doesn't ask about my conversation with Charlie so perhaps he has told her to mind her own business. Even so, I can see Sue is dying to know what is going on.

'Is everything all right in Vienna?' she asks.

Before I tell her that, there is something I need to know from her.

'Tell me about Asa's former girlfriends.'

I have never felt able to ask before but I have always been curious. Tonight it seems all right to ask because tonight I have no place in Asa's life. Tomorrow will be different.

'There were lots, but none of them lasted. Asa never seemed to want commitment. Usually the relationship just fizzled out or he simply walked away from it.'

'Do you think he's trying to walk away from me? Is that what this is all about?'

'I'm sure it isn't. Asa's changed since he came back from America. Before that he couldn't settle. Survivor guilt, he used to call it. He needed to look for his sister, and even though he didn't find her, he had at least tried.'

And now that he has found her it is all too late. Asa will never know his sister, but it is not too late for me to let him know his sister's son.

♀

I walk to Foyle's in Charing Cross Road and look for books on childhood deafness, and then I go to the children's department for the latest Snoopy and Peanuts books.

Charlie told me on the phone that there were Snoopy and Peanuts books in little Asa's bedroom. How clever of him to have noticed that.

After Foyles I go to Carnaby Street and buy a union jack

bedspread and then I go home. There is a lot to do before Asa and his nephew get back tonight.

The house feels cold and unlived in although it has only been empty a couple of days. I try to light a fire, but without success. The room quickly fills with smoke so I open the windows and go upstairs to make up the spare bed with the union jack cover.

In less than two hours Asa and his nephew will be here and I still have a cake to bake. I want a Viennese chocolate cake to be waiting for them when they arrive.

The smell of Viennese chocolate cake is one of Asa's few childhood memories and according to his cookery book the recipe is more than two-hundred years old. It is infinitely more complicated than the chocolate sponges May used to bake for our birthdays in Grymewyck.

I finish the cake just in time and place it at the centre of the table where it will be first thing they see when they walk in.

It is magnificent.

I take one last look before I let myself out of the house and walk quickly towards the station.

Jenny Rodwell

Extract from The Grymewyck Vikings

(from a collection of short stories by Ophelia Gunn. Published 1969)

Gunnhilda dies of exhaustion in a northern peat bog, dreaming of clear fiords and snow-capped mountains. Grymn drags his dead wife across the misty moors for three days, holding her by the ankles as she bumps along behind him through gorse and bracken and water-filled groughs, leaving a swathe of flattened landscape behind her.

His wife was a big woman and Grymn is tired. He blames himself entirely. He should never have allowed Gunnhilda to come with him on this expedition. She had done nothing but complain since stepping out of the longboat.

On the evening of the third day Grymn comes to a round pond in a beautiful green valley and makes a decision. He lets go of Gunnhilda's ankles and gently rolls his wife into the water with his foot. As he does so the two gilt brooches that fasten Gunnhilda's dress twinkle for one last time before disappearing into the murky depths.

Across the pond, Grymn's warriors have thrown down their shields and are bathing in the cool water. Grymn sighs but before the toes of Gunnhilda's leather boots have sunk below the surface, he has joined his marauding crew and is splashing about with them on the other side of the pond.

Grymn is sad and weary and he has nothing to return home for. He resolves to stay on the grassy banks of this little round pond forever.

Jenny Rodwell